"A FINE PIECE OF WORK...' ᴇ ᴿ IS ALMOST IMMEDIATELY DRAWN IN BY THE INTRIGUE AND RICH DETAIL."
—*Southern Pines Pilot* (NC)

"A MESMERIZING BLEND OF TANTALIZING SUSPENSE, HIGH-SPEED ACTION, AND GRIPPING HISTORICAL INTRIGUE....[Robinson's] masterful plotting, in-depth knowledge of this period in history, and obvious enthusiasm for her subject give her latest book a rare and welcome energy and freshness."
—*Booklist*

"A CLEVER STORY...MOST UNUSUAL...Robinson does a terrific job."
—*Deadly Pleasures*

"[A] VIVID MIX OF CONFLICTS AND INCIDENTS...[in] Lord Meren's fine series."
—*Kirkus Reviews*

"DELICIOUS...Robinson makes history live and breathe again. Good scholarship authenticates the historical setting; imagination provides the sense of danger and romance to make it come alive."
—*New York Times Book Review* on
Murder at the Feast Rejoicing

"As Robinson deftly juggles ancient Egyptian political intrigue and a riveting mystery, SHE PROVES AGAIN HER MASTERY OF THE HISTORICAL WHODUNNIT."
—*Publishers Weekly* (starred review) on
Murder at the Feast Rejoicing

Also by Lynda S. Robinson

Slayer of Gods
Eater of Souls
Murder at the Feast of Rejoicing
Murder at the God's Gate
Murder in the Place of Anubis

DRINKER OF BLOOD

LYNDA S. ROBINSON

Published by Warner Books

A Time Warner Company

Copyright © 1998 by Lynda S. Robinson
All rights reserved.

 Mysterious Press books are published by Warner Books, Inc.,
1271 Avenue of the Americas, New York, NY 10020.

Visit our Web site at www.twbookmark.com.
For information on Time Warner Trade Publishing's online publishing program,
visit www.ipublish.com.

 A Time Warner Company

The Mysterious Press name and logo are registered trademarks of Warner Books, Inc.

Printed in the United States of America.

Originally published in hardcover by Warner Books, Inc.

The Library of Congress has cataloged the hardcover edition as follows:

Robinson, Lynda Suzanne.
    Drinker of blood / Lynda S. Robinson.
      p.   cm.
    ISBN 0-89296-673-4
    I. Meren, Lord (Fictitious character)—Fiction.   2. Egypt—History—Eighteenth dynasty, ca. 1570–1320 B.C.—Fiction.   3. Nefertiti, Queen of Egypt, 14th cent. B.C.—Fiction.   I. Title.
PS3568.031227D75   1998
813'.54—dc21   98-16322
                                                                                      CIP

ISBN: 0-446-67751-5 (Pbk.)

Cover design and illustration by John Martinez

To my niece, Stephanie Woods, a young woman as talented and indomitable as the queen about whom this book is written.

Acknowledgments

An understanding of human behavior, its motivation and parameters, is of course essential to any writer. Although much of this understanding comes from experience, for me a great deal of the more specialized information comes from a friend and an expert, Dr. Susan Jennings. Her experience as a psychologist has been invaluable to me in navigating the twisting and meandering tributaries of motivation that lurk inside us all. Her advice was critical in creating the characters of Lord Meren, Kysen, and the villain in *Eater of Souls.* I wish to thank her for her insight and her generosity in sharing it.

Of great importance also is the understanding of non-human behavior. In this book, I am especially indebted to Debbie Battista, Mammal Supervisor with the San Antonio Zoo, for her expertise in the area of baboon behavior.

In the area of the Amarna period (Amunhotep III and Akhenaten), I must acknowledge the help of Mr. Barry Kemp, Reader in Egyptology at the University of Cambridge, England, and Field Director of the Egypt Exploration Society's excavations at Amarna (Horizon of the Aten). The foremost excavator at the site of Akhenaten's capital, Mr. Kemp has been kind enough to share his data and interpretations with me, and I am privileged to be able to call upon his expertise, which is unparalleled. Readers will find in Mr. Kemp's *Ancient Egypt: Anatomy of a Civilization* an extremely insightful reassessment of one of the world's great cultures.

Dr. Bill Petty of Museum Tours, Inc., has also been of immense help in visualizing the reality of Horizon of the Aten, a difficult site to reach and one seldom visited by tourists. Dr. Petty has generously shared his firsthand knowledge of the ceremonial and residential palaces and the impression this isolated place makes on the visitor.

Finally I wish to thank Dr. James P. Allen, Curator of Egyptian Art at the Metropolitan Museum of Art, New York, for his gracious hospitality at the museum and for his invaluable insight into the art and the cognitive world of ancient Egypt. In addition Dr. Allen was kind enough to review the manuscript for *Drinker of Blood*. Without his expertise and willingness to take time out of his busy schedule to help, this ancient mystery would have been far less authentic. As always, any mistakes are mine. Readers interested in the unique and often exquisite art of the Amarna period will find *The Royal Women of Amarna*, by Dorothea Arnold, with contributions by James P. Allen and L. Green, fascinating.

Historical Note

Drinker of Blood continues the story of Lord Meren's investigation of the murder of Queen Nefertiti, the wife of the heretic pharaoh Akhenaten. In the previous book, *Eater of Souls*, Meren discovered several suspects for the killing, but was distracted by the advent of a serial killer.

The events of these two novels are based in part on data from Egyptology that cover the reigns of several pharaohs—Amunhotep III (the Magnificent), Amunhotep IV/Akhenaten, Smenkhare (briefly), and Tutankhamun. However, these data are often open to different interpretations; even dates of reigns may vary from reference to reference, scholar to scholar. When opinions vary, I have had to choose an interpretation and stick with it, regardless of any new information that may come to light afterward.

The historical context of *Drinker of Blood* and the other Lord Meren novels begins with the family of Amunhotep III and Queen Tiye, early in the fourteenth century B.C. Amunhotep ruled peacefully for almost forty years, resting on the foundation of his conquering ancestors, who left him a far-flung and rich empire. His reign is known for its prosperity and great artistic achievements in building and sculpture. His chief wife, a nonroyal lady named Tiye, had at least six children. The oldest, Thutmose, died before he could inherit, leaving the second son, Amunhotep (Akhenaten), as the heir to the Egyptian throne.

This second son may have joined his father on the throne in a joint reign of some years, and it is this interpretation that holds in the Lord Meren series. Amunhotep IV changed his name early in his reign to Akhenaten, signaling a shift in religious emphasis, the nature of which is still being debated today. What is certain is that within a relatively short time, Akhenaten withdrew royal support from Egypt's king of the gods, Amun, in favor of a minor deity called the Aten, the sun disk through which life-giving light entered the world.

Around the same time changes in artistic style appear in Egypt—a so-called revolution that is hard for the modern reader to understand. In Egypt, as in the rest of the ancient world, art, religion, politics, and economics merged. There were no separate categories such as those we use for convenience today. Thus, when Akhenaten ascended the throne, and possibly before, he favored a new freedom and realism in artistic style that contrasted significantly with the old formal precepts of previous reigns. Many believe that this new style was a deliberate departure, perhaps Akhenaten's way of distinguishing himself and his god from all that came before.

As his reign progressed, Akhenaten seemed to grow more and more fanatical in his opposition to Amun. The king of the gods had benefited from royal patronage since—under the god's banner—Akhenaten's ancestors overthrew foreign rule and established the New Kingdom. The temple of Amun was rich beyond imagination, even owning foreign cities and slaves by the tens of thousands. Such a rich temple had to have been a rival to pharaoh's power. When Amun's position was threatened by a new god, perhaps the priests who benefited from that power fought back.

Whatever the reason, Akhenaten decided to uproot the royal court and government from the ancient capital of Memphis. He moved it away from the old gods, to a barren

site between Thebes and Memphis, and built a new city—
Horizon of the Aten. And there he remained, growing more
and more adamant in his persecution of Amun, until he died.

Akhenaten's chief queen was the fabulously beautiful
Nefertiti. This young woman played as prominent a role in
the reliefs of her husband's reign as did her predecessor, Tiye.
In fact, Nefertiti may have wielded a great deal of actual
power. However, we do not know this for certain. She bore
the king six daughters, and it is the affectionate scenes of the
royal couple with their children that are among the most
poignant in Egyptian art.

After the twelfth year of Akhenaten's reign, Queen
Nefertiti's figure mysteriously vanishes from royal monuments. The reason for her disappearance is not certain. It
could be that she died, but her status may have changed in
some other way. Whatever the case she was buried in the eastern desert in the royal tomb at Horizon of the Aten.

Akhenaten followed his beautiful queen to the land of the
dead a few years later. The pharaoh Smenkhare, who was the
son of either Amunhotep III or Akhenaten, may have ruled
briefly, but history knows the reign of the next king far better—that of the boy king Tutankhamun. Again it is uncertain
whether Tutankhamun (first known as Tutankh*aten*) was
Akhenaten's younger brother or his son. The boy succeeded
to the throne of Egypt when he was between the ages of
nine and sixteen and soon began a complete reversal of
Akhenaten's policies. Under Tutankhamun the royal court and
government moved back to Memphis, and Amun was restored. Tragically, Tutankhamun died young, between the ages
of nineteen and twenty-six after a reign of ten years, leaving
his successors to carry out the changes he began.

The bare recital of historical facts given above only hints at
the real mysteries facing Egyptologists to this day. Who were

Tutankhamun's parents? Why did Akhenaten become such a revolutionary? What really happened to Nefertiti? With so many questions, so many enigmas, a novelist has a wealth of material with which to create a historical mystery. *Drinker of Blood* weaves the story of Lord Meren's investigation of Queen Nefertiti's death with the story of her life. I suspect, however, that what I have created may not be as strange and exotic as the truth—whatever that might be.

DRINKER OF BLOOD

Prologue

Thebes, the reign of the pharaoh Amunhotep the Magnificent

If the guards caught her, she would be dragged back to the palace and whipped.

The palm-fiber rope bit into her hands as she shinnied down its length. Her bare feet plopped against the mud-brick wall before she dropped to the ground behind a sycamore. In the night's shadows the guards wouldn't see her rope dangling behind the tree trunk.

Pebbles clicked together under the weight of a heavy tread. She crouched low at the base of the sycamore. Her chest tightened with apprehension. It was Mahu, one of the royal guards. Mahu disliked children and wouldn't keep silent the discovery of a small intruder. If Mahu found her, he'd drag her to Queen Tiye and delight in telling the whole palace that the daughter of the queen's brother had been trying to escape the grounds like a baseborn criminal.

Demons take the man. Mahu was headed straight for her palm.

The girl pressed her linen-clad body to the tree trunk and prayed to Amun. She heard a tap. Mahu leaned his spear against the tree where she crouched. The guard fumbled with his kilt. An arc of liquid shot out, and a pungent odor signaled the reason for this stop on Mahu's rounds. She squeezed her eyes shut and held her breath until Mahu finished relieving himself and trudged by on his way past a reflection pool.

Rubbing her palms on her skirt to rid them of sweat, the girl melted from her hiding place into the cool perfection of pharaoh's private garden. She must be across the causeway and on the riverbank soon or Webkhet would leave. She paused beside an incense tree and scanned the path to the palace. Bordered by rows of imported shrubs, it was deserted. She sprang away from the incense tree with the grace and agility that were part of the reason she was in so much trouble. Anxiety and grief clawed at her as she let herself in through the door of a robing chamber.

Tomorrow Webkhet would be gone, leaving her alone to face the destiny others had planned for her. That thought urged her on through chambers shrouded in darkness, through the informal audience chamber with its paintings of bound captives and its throne of ebony and sheet gold, through the outer hall that bristled with columns, to the courtyard, and out a concealed door in the wall that rose twelve cubits high. Soon she was running down the causeway, her lungs heaving and her legs numb from the pounding of bare feet on packed earth.

Before she reached the bank, the girl turned aside. She scrambled along a track beside the river and away from the collection of royal barges moored at the quay. She trotted past the yachts of pharaoh's chief ministers, confident that the sailors on duty would take her for a peasant. It was her experience that without her jewels, slaves, and tutors, most people could not tell Nefertiti, daughter of Lord Ay and niece of the great royal wife Tiye, from any other twelve-year-old girl.

"Psst."

Nefertiti ducked behind a stack of clay jars and peeked in the direction of the sound. A low whistle floated across to her from the direction of a moored fishing boat. There, beached on the riverbank, lay a reed skiff. Beside it near the curved prow stood Webkhet.

"Nefertiti." Webkhet's voice floated in the breeze. "Over here."

Before her friend finished speaking, Nefertiti was at the prow.

Webkhet grinned at her. "I thought you weren't coming. It's so late."

"Aunt came to visit, so I couldn't get away." Nefertiti shivered even though the night was warm.

Webkhet nodded in sympathy. The daughter of a royal guard, she was familiar with the crowded and circumscribed living arrangements of pharaoh's family. Both girls climbed into the vacant fishing boat and sat down. They'd been friends for years, ever since Nefertiti had discovered how to escape her elderly nurse unnoticed and come upon Webkhet in the palace kitchen. They'd played, fought, laughed, and plagued the royal servants. With Webkhet, Nefertiti could yell and steal melons, run hard and quarrel, without fear of a reprimand from anyone. With Webkhet she was free of the fearful dignity required of even so minor a member of the royal family as she.

Once settled in the boat, the girls gazed across the river at the dark fields and the lights of the houses that perched between them and the desert. Nefertiti cupped her chin in her hand and sighed, giving way to misery.

"Aunt was hinting again. She asked if I liked Akhenaten, if I liked spending time with him. I think they've decided."

Webkhet patted her hand. "Who?"

"Pharaoh and Aunt. I think they've decided I should marry Akhenaten."

"How awful!" Webkhet squeezed Nefertiti's shoulders. "Do you dare tell them you don't want to marry him?"

Nefertiti sighed. It was questions like this that showed her how different her life was from Webkhet's.

"Would you deny pharaoh?"

Nefertiti received another squeeze of sympathy. No one she knew wanted to marry Akhenaten, prince and heir to the throne of Egypt though he was.

Akhenaten was so strange. He didn't like the gods. No one else in all of Egypt disliked the gods, but Akhenaten did. Nefertiti didn't understand why Amun, king of the gods, hadn't struck him blind—or worse—for his heresy. She'd listened to him complain about Osiris, god of death and re-birth, only this morning. Akhenaten was always mad at the gods, all except one, the Aten, whom he claimed for his own.

All girls married. It was the way of things. How else could men survive and have children who would care for them in old age? She had always known she would marry someone, but not her odd cousin.

Akhenaten's behavior was as strange as his appearance. Always sympathetic of heart, Nefertiti had never laughed at her cousin behind his back as many at court did. The young noblemen scoffed at Akhenaten's scrawny shoulders, sagging belly, and equine face. The ladies of the royal household were no kinder. Nefertiti despised those callous creatures who cared not that Akhenaten might perceive their contempt. There had been many times when she tried to distract his attention so that he wouldn't see a smirk or hear a derisive comment. Akhenaten might be odd, but he did have feelings.

Now Nefertiti could see that her pity and her attention had been what caught Tiye's attention and inspired the queen to consider her for her son. Aunt and pharaoh thought their plans a secret. They made the mistake of thinking their significant looks and prodding questions beyond the perception of a mere girl. Even Father thought her ignorant. With everyone bent on secrecy, Nefertiti had turned to her friend for comfort.

"If I have to marry him and be queen, I won't be able to see you anymore," Nefertiti said to Webkhet. "I won't be able to do anything interesting or fun. I'll be trained by Aunt to be queen, and she'll make me study forever."

"No more running off to sail on the river," Webkhet said with a pitying shake of her head.

They clambered out of the fishing boat, unhappy and apprehensive. Returning to the skiff, Nefertiti helped Webkhet push it into the water. Each must return home before someone missed her. Nefertiti watched her friend shove away from the bank with her paddle, seeing freedom about to sail away.

"What's that?" Webkhet pointed at something over Nefertiti's shoulder.

Specks of yellow light bobbed and danced across the causeway. Nefertiti caught her breath and counted. Ten, sixteen. She stopped counting. She jumped clear of the skiff and gave it a shove, sending the small craft into deeper water.

"Go," she said. Webkhet gawked at her. Nefertiti raised her voice in fear. "Go! They're looking for me. If they find you—"
She had no need to finish. Webkhet knew the danger.

Nefertiti's friend held out her hand. "Come with me. We'll run away together."

Nefertiti shook her head. She sloshed toward shore and turned back to the other girl.

"I must lead them away before they see you." With grim courage she steadied her voice to conceal the wreck of her hopes. "The gods protect you, Webkhet, my friend." She lifted her hand in salute before racing toward the line of guards that spilled onto the riverbank.

Webkhet's voice sailed after her. "May the gods protect you."

Lord Ay walked in the royal pleasure garden in pharaoh's palace. Beside him strode his indomitable sister Tiye, great royal wife, queen of Egypt. Ay had been summoned for an audience with the living god, only to find himself waylaid by the queen and taken to the gardens for a private talk.

Tiye had dismissed all her attendants. A slight woman with deep-set eyes that reflected a world of experience, Tiye walked with the swift, nervous gait of a much younger woman. When the last slave had vanished, Tiye took refuge from the sun beneath an aged tamarisk tree but walked back and forth in its shadows.

"Brother, you understand pharaoh's difficulty."

"Of course."

"You know that his many years of good living sit ill upon him. Although his wits are as sharp as ever, the king's health isn't as it should be."

Ay nodded. Pharaoh's teeth had rotted, and he suffered from his weight. Although no longer the embodiment of a great warrior and son of the king of the gods, Amun, pharaoh suffered far more from knowing that his heir, Akhenaten, was a strange and unpredictable young man whose wisdom was as questionable as his religion. Pharaoh had recently decided to cure his heir's strangeness and lack of training. As some heirs had done before him, Akhenaten was to share the throne with his father in a joint reign, and he was to be married.

"If your oldest had lived . . ." Ay's voice trailed off.

Tiye threw up her hands. "Regret is useless. Akhenaten is heir. Akhenaten! He won't even use his real name, no doubt because it's also his father's." Tiye sighed and turned to regard her brother with the solemn confidence he'd come to recognize.

"Pharaoh and I have decided upon a wife for Akhenaten."

Bracing himself, Ay heard the voice of his heart in his ears. He'd dreaded this decision, prayed to the gods to guide pharaoh's choice in a different direction.

"We've chosen Nefertiti."

"You know I don't want my daughter given to Akhenaten."

Tiye rolled her eyes. "Of course I know, brother. Haven't you shouted it at me for months? But Nefertiti is the only girl who possesses all the qualities needed in a great queen. She has composure, a clever heart, and that amazing beauty." Tiye put her hand on his arm. "And above all, she has a strong will. Egypt is going to need her, Ay. There is no one so well suited to guide Akhenaten without allowing him to suspect he's being guided."

"Has pharaoh said this himself?"

Tiye nodded and slipped her arm through his. She began to describe her plans for Nefertiti's training as they walked in the shade. Miserable, certain that pharaoh's decision was final, Ay hardly listened.

There had been another heir, an older boy who had been killed in a hunting accident. Ay had liked Prince Thutmose. Full of humor, clever like his mother, Queen Tiye, he had been a fitting choice to fulfill pharaoh's role as the warrior king of Egypt's far-flung empire. Nefertiti would have been suitable for Thutmose.

No one had ever paid much attention to Thutmose's weakling younger brother. Since birth, the boy named Amunhotep—who now insisted upon being called Akhenaten—had been afflicted with infirmity. It seemed that father and son conceived a mutual dislike from birth, perhaps stemming from the strength of one and the feebleness of the other.

Certainly the pharaoh Amunhotep never hid his distaste for Akhenaten's almost effeminate appearance. The lad had an oblong skull from which his fleshy lips and tilted, slanting eyes protruded. Ay pitied him, for every body part that should be large was small, and what should have been small was large. His ears were too big, as was his projecting jaw. His hollow shoulders were eclipsed in size by his protruding stomach, wide hips, and bulging thighs, all of which were balanced precariously on top of sticklike legs.

Alternately ignored and scorned by his father, Akhenaten had taken refuge behind his mother. Tiye, with a mother's great heart, had sheltered him from pharaoh's intolerance. The lad had also taken refuge in learning and religion, devoting himself to study and avoiding the arts of hunting and warfare so prized by his father. Ay suspected that it was during his years of sheltered study that Akhenaten conceived the bizarre notion that the sun disk, called the Aten, was the sole god. The Aten was the vehicle through which light entered the world, and that light, Akhenaten believed, was the true creator, the source of all life, the one god.

He'd listened once to the young man's beliefs, for Akhenaten thought about matters usually left to learned priests. According to the priests of Amun, the source of all creation was a mysterious and unknowable force, which they called the Hidden One, Amun. Akhenaten scoffed at this mystery.

"The sun's rays are the source," he said. "It's obvious. The sun causes crops to grow and cattle to multiply so that people may live. How absurd to overlook so plain an explanation for existence. The answer is the Aten—the source of heat and light."

Lately court rumor whispered that the young man denied the existence of all the other ancient gods of Egypt—Amun, king of the gods; Osiris, who rose from the dead to give hope of rebirth in the afterlife to all Egyptians; Isis, his sister, who had been responsible for bringing Osiris back to life. For century after century the towns of Egypt had worshiped their own gods, including Set, Montu, Hapi, the great Ra who was the sun. Aten had always been the god of the physical heat of the sun's rays, not a very special god at all. What was so unique about the Aten to pharaoh's strange son?

No matter. The problem pharaoh faced—that Ay and Tiye faced—was how best to train Akhenaten to rule Egypt well. He was a young man, set in his ideas, unschooled in diplomacy or governance of any kind. Tiye had suggested, and pharaoh had agreed, that making Akhenaten coregent was the best solution. So now father and son were to share the throne of Egypt and rule jointly. And his daughter was to be queen.

"Do you understand, brother? I'll be at her side, teaching, counseling, guiding. She will be safe."

Ay looked away from Tiye, over the high walls and gently swaying branches of the trees that sheltered the palace from the dangerous heat of the sun. "If she is married to Akhenaten, Nefertiti will never be entirely safe."

"Come," Tiye said. "Pharaoh is with the physicians and priests. He suffers from an ache in a tooth today."

They went into the palace, to the enormous golden doors that guarded pharaoh's apartments. The portals swung open under the strong hands of the king's Nubian guards. Taking shallow breaths, Ay walked with his sister toward the group of physicians and priests kneeling on the raised platform that held the royal bed.

The nauseating sweetness of incense combined with medicines burning in a closed room threatened to make Ay empty his stomach. He began to breathe through his mouth. The room was dark and patched with light from alabaster lamps. The dark blue of a water scene painted on the floor absorbed the light. A physician priest muttered charms and burned incense. Two more holy ones huddled over a yellowed papyrus with health amulets clutched in their hands.

Tiye went to her husband. He was sitting in bed, holding a damp cloth to his cheek. Ay knelt beside him, touched his forehead to the floor, and uttered homage.

Amunhotep's plump cheek was slightly swollen from his bad tooth, his body thickened from culinary indulgence, but his eyes glinted in the lamplight, and he'd been reading tax reports. Papyri were spread about the bed and littered the floor around it. A flick of pharaoh's hand caused all the physicians and attendants to vanish.

"So, old friend, we've made a mess of things. I by losing my oldest son, and you by not counseling me to kill Akhenaten years ago."

"Husband!" Tiye cried.

Amunhotep patted her hand. "You've lost your appreciation of my humor, little wife."

"This is not the time for jests," Tiye snapped, "and there's never a time for joking about our son's life."

Ay's head felt light with fear. There was no reply one could make when the golden one spoke of murdering his heir. It was a wonder the gods didn't burn him alive for hearing such words. Ay studied the leg of the bed. It was gold and shaped like the paw of a lion. He waited while Tiye and her husband squabbled with the ease of practice.

"So, Tiye told you of my decision, Ay. Nefertiti will guide my son and temper his strangeness with her wisdom."

"She is but a child, majesty."

Tiye waved her hand. "Nonsense. Girls are far wiser than boys at her age."

"Besides," pharaoh said as he refolded the damp cloth, "Akhenaten has seen your daughter again, for the first time in months, and is enamored."

Startled at the distaste he felt, Ay bowed low to conceal his expression. "I understand, divine one."

"Be done with your subservience, Ay. We've known each other too long, and I haven't the strength to suffer through it."

Ay bowed and managed a smile. They had always understood each other, pharaoh and he. From the beginning Amunhotep recognized Ay's gift for statecraft and lack of personal ambition. Ay was well aware that a pharaoh less perceptive, less secure in his own power, would have had him killed long ago.

"We take another gamble, my pharaoh, and this time with a twelve-year-old girl who has lived in obscurity, even if it has been in the royal household. You say the heir is fond of Nefertiti, but that doesn't mean he'll accept her guidance."

"By the time I've schooled her, he will," Tiye said as she began gathering the tax documents on the bed.

"They already deal well with each other," Amunhotep said through his compress. "Akhenaten is quite protective of her in his strange way." Amunhotep sat up straighter and leaned toward Ay. "Mark me. I'll undo the damage I've wrought upon the Two Lands by producing such a son. I'll do it through Nefertiti. Now silence your doubts. The physicians want to give me a potion, and I want to see the girl before I have to swallow that foul mess."

Tiye clapped her hands. The golden doors opened, revealing a slim girl standing alone. Light from the robing room beyond framed her in gold. Ay smiled at his daughter. She had her mother's loveliness as well as his athletic frame. Her delicate head sat upon a long, graceful neck like a heavy bloom upon a stem. Soon her face would lose the last of her child's plumpness and become startling in its refined and angular beauty. From her birth he had loved her for her unconquerable spirit and her entrancing smile. Now she had an air of sad dignity that caught at Ay's heart.

Although her expression was carefully blank, he could read her face like the hieroglyphs on a boundary stone. She had already been told. He would have liked to be the one to do that.

Ay watched with great pride and even greater fear as the guards pulled the doors shut, trapping his daughter inside pharaoh's bedchamber. She stood quite still, holding herself erect, arms at her sides, chin high. Ay experienced a thrill of approval. Her upbringing at court served her well; few approached pharaoh with their fear so well hidden. But Ay was her father, and he could see the little vein in her neck throb, saw her dread in the way she clenched her teeth to prevent her jaw from quivering.

Nefertiti walked forward and sank to her knees with the controlled movements of a born princess. Great, dark eyes touched the figure on the bed. For a moment the facade slipped, and Ay found himself looking at a frightened child. Young muscles tensed. Hands flexed in a barely visible movement. Then, at pharaoh's beckoning, Nefertiti came to kneel at his elbow. Ay squelched the urge to offer some word of reassurance to his daughter.

"You know what is required of you, child?"

Nefertiti glanced at him, and Ay nodded encouragement. "Yes, majesty."

Pharaoh grunted. "I'm going to die one day, you know."

"Yes, majesty."

Amunhotep smiled at her. "Thank the gods. No sniveling, and no protests that I'm divine and will live forever. Come closer. Are you frightened?"

"No, majesty."

"Don't lie. You're scared. You don't know what's going to happen to you."

Pharaoh called for a hot cloth. Tiye brought one, and the king put it to his swollen cheek. All the while, Nefertiti remained kneeling beside the bed with an easy familiarity that gave Ay some comfort.

Amunhotep moved the hot cloth so that he could speak unhindered. "Nefertiti, you're not a fool, so I know you're frightened. You should be. Akhenaten is intolerant and arrogant in his beliefs. I'm not saying his ideas about creation aren't sensible, but he goes too far. He'll cause much havoc if his excesses aren't controlled. I lay the task of managing him upon you. Tiye and your father will guide you."

It was a test of his will, but Ay held his tongue even though his daughter looked as if her ka—her soul—had flown from her body. The color drained from her face, making the lines of paint on her eyes stand out like the colors on a relief.

The girl wet her lips. "I know nothing of governance, majesty."

"Quiet, girl. I haven't the patience to argue, with this tooth plaguing me. You'll obey the commands I give you and prepare yourself to become queen of Egypt."

Nefertiti inclined her head, then lifted her gaze to stare straight into pharaoh's eyes. "I will be queen of Egypt."

There it was! Ay nearly smiled when he heard that defiant

tone, a tone that grasped pharaoh's scepters—the crook and the flail—and pulled them from his hands. She had always been part goddess, part night fiend, his little Nefertiti. Pharaoh was going to be surprised that his chosen tool was far from the docile innocent he assumed her to be.

Chapter I

Memphis, year five of the reign of the pharaoh Tutankhamun

His wife had always hated the night, for demons and lost spirits of the dead roamed in the darkness, but Bakht had always liked it. Night was the time of coolness, when Ra's solar bark vanished into the underworld. Besides, he'd never met a demon or disgruntled dead one while on guard duty in his many years as a royal soldier.

Bakht hefted his spear on his shoulder and paced slowly beside the perimeter wall of the royal menagerie. Beyond that wall and behind several others, far higher, lay the royal palace. Inside, surrounded by his most trusted bodyguards, the young king slept. He would need his rest, for the feast of Opet approached, a time of ceremony and celebration that would take pharaoh to Thebes. Bakht was looking forward to the days of feasting and merriment. His special place as a favored guard of pharaoh allowed him to be one of those to escort the king to the great city.

His bare feet slid over the packed earth, kicking aside pebbles. Bakht sniffed a pungent vegetable odor and stepped aside to avoid a dung pile. He glanced across the menagerie, a vast area filled with cages, biers, pens, and stalls and sheltered by palms, sycamores, and acacias. Accompanied by the rhythmic snarls of a male lion, Bakht walked by a giraffe pen. Far away from the peaceful animals lay the heavily reinforced domain of the predators—not just the lions but cheetahs, leopards, and Syrian bears.

Bakht heard his name called and turned to see the new guard, Khawi, approach. Khawi was young and in awe of his new responsibilities, and even more confounded by Bakht's position as the oldest regularly serving soldier at the palace. Ever since he'd learned that pharaoh often sent for Bakht to hear stories of expeditions to Nubia, raids against Libyan bandits, and other tales, Khawi had treated Bakht with the reverence due a great one.

Bakht tried not to grin as Khawi marched toward him with meticulous correctness. "Amun's blessings upon you, young one."

"And upon you, Guard Bakht." Khawi dipped his head and saluted at the same time.

"Admit it, young one. You thought this old man would forget to relieve you."

Khawi's eyes widened, and he shook his head vigorously. "Oh, no, Guard Bakht. Never would I think such a disrespectful thing."

Bakht took pity on the boy, who was no more than sixteen and far too naive for his own welfare. "Walk with me awhile, young Khawi. Someone's got to rid you of this habit of puppylike trust. It's a bad trait for a soldier, especially a royal guard." As Khawi fell in step with him, Bakht swept his arm around to indicate the menagerie, the pleasure gardens, the palace itself. "If you want to be like me and serve under many pharaohs—may they live forever—then you listen to me."

"They say you have served since the time of the father of Amunhotep the Magnificent," Khawi said with awe.

Bakht snorted, disturbing the rest of a red junglefowl. "Donkey-witted, that's what you are. I wasn't born until year nine of the Magnificent. But those were days of glorious happenings. I traveled into Nubia to serve the viceroy, and we crushed a mighty gathering of rebel tribes."

"Nubia," Khawi breathed. "Is it truly a savage and dangerous land?"

"Some of it."

Whipping around to face Bakht, Khawi gripped his spear in a stranglehold and danced from one foot to the other. "Tell me about the golden ones, Bakht. Tell me about the kings."

They had reached the ostrich pens. Pretending reluctance, Bakht rested his spear against a fence and spread his arms wide, stretching muscles that had grown slack with age.

"Please," Khawi said.

"I suppose I can spare a few moments," Bakht said as he leaned against the fence. "Of course, the Magnificent was the greatest of all. He built the mighty halls and gates of the Theban temples, and statues." Bakht pointed at the sky. "Great figures of himself as high as that star. Cunning as a crocodile, was the Magnificent. Chose the most brilliant ministers, the wisest and most beautiful of wives."

"The great royal wife Tiye."

"Ah, she was clever, was Queen Tiye. Played those cursed foreign kings against each other, kept them distrusting one another."

"Why?"

"So they didn't make trouble for Egypt, boy."

"But they did make trouble," Khawi insisted with the stubborn lack of tact of the young. "My father said that Pharaoh Akhenaten—"

"Shhhhh!" Bakht hissed and clapped the young soldier on the side of his head. "I was right. You have the wits of a donkey and the flapping tongue of a green monkey. Be off with you, and try to cultivate a clever heart before you get yourself into trouble."

Babbling apologies, Khawi scurried away. Bakht heard the main gate open and shut behind the boy as he resumed his rounds. His many years and his experience allowed him to take a familiar view of the family of living gods whom he served, but such an attitude was improper in a youth.

Muttering to himself of the carelessness of young ones today, Bakht trudged by the thick mud-brick walls of the rhinoceros enclosure without making his usual stop to admire the beasts. He would not allow the flapping tongue of Khawi to disturb his tranquillity. After all, he had survived three pharaohs—the Magnificent, the heretic Akhenaten, and poor Smenkhare, who had barely ruled before dying and leaving the throne to his brother Tutankhamun, may he have life, health, and prosperity.

Yes, he had survived, and prospered too, through serving the living gods of Egypt. And of those he'd served, the Magnificent had been the most interesting. He'd been the embodiment of the grandeur of Egypt. The Magnificent had been the first to advance Bakht, rewarding him for saving the life of a royal relative on that Nubian expedition. The Magnificent's eldest son, Thutmose, had been as gracious as his father. A pity he'd died. And of all his royal masters, Tutankhamun—life, health, prosperity—was the most charming. The golden one was full of curiosity about foreign lands and loved to send for Bakht and listen to tales of Kush, Libya, and cities like Byblos and Ugarit.

Now that he thought about it, of all the sons of the Magnificent, Thutmose had been the most tragic, and Akhenaten the most irritating and dangerous. Bakht could never reflect upon his service in the heretic's city without relief that he had lived to look back upon it. Had he not earned a stipend and a prosperous farm from his work in Horizon of the Aten, he would have left royal service. Even guarding the great royal wives hadn't made up for enduring the great heresy. Sometimes Bakht thought of Akhenaten's reign as an evil dream—the time when pharaoh cast out all the ancient gods of Egypt and forced the worship of the Aten, the disk of the sun. Certainly at the last he must have been possessed by a netherworld demon to have done what he did then.

Bakht rounded the corner of a pen containing hartebeests and rumbled to himself, "He's dead. Forget about him. Even his city is almost deserted."

Yes, the heretic was gone, and he could look back with pride at his many honors. Not the least of them was having served the most fascinating and clever of women, the royal wives. Of these, he had felt sorry for the foreigners, the Mitannian and Babylonian princesses sent to Egypt to seal alliances with pharaoh's fellow monarchs. They arrived full of their own consequence, proud of their blood and heritage, only to be met with Egyptian ignorance and sublime lack of interest in the greatness of other peoples. He had seen the great cities and temples of Babylonia and Assyria and thus could understand why these women felt equal to any Egyptian.

The foreign women were taken into pharaoh's household and given Egyptian names, households, and possessions, and after a while they seemed to forget their homes. Perhaps it was the greater freedom they found in Egypt that seduced them at last. Bakht often wondered at the lives of such exotic creatures as Babylonian princesses. Such beings were as far from him as the lives of the creatures in the menagerie.

Thinking about such mysteries relieved the boredom of standing guard over things no one with any sense would steal. What would a thief do with a giraffe in Memphis? It wasn't as if he could hide the animal. However, he would be entertained tonight, for tonight he was meeting an old friend near the baboon pit.

Bakht disliked the hairy, barking creatures with the doglike snouts and always hurried past their enclosure. Ugly animals. They had hands like the hands of a man, and eyes that seemed to look into his heart and understand his nature. With reluctance, Bakht directed his steps toward the baboons.

The creatures lived in an area bounded by a steep wall. They had more room than most people, as the menagerie overseer had found that crowding them resulted in nasty fights. Arriving at the foot of the steps that led to the top of the enclosure wall, Bakht looked around for his friend to no avail. Sighing, he used his spear as a walking stick, trudged to the top of the stairs, and sat down on the small landing. He could see groups of dark, huddled shapes, dozens of sleeping baboons.

Most of them were females and babies, brown with naked red faces and bottoms. Drab little things, they were, and the males were worse. The males had silvery gray capes of fur around their shoulders that made them look larger than they were. Nevertheless, the males possessed vicious canine teeth capable of tearing a man apart. Bakht didn't believe the overseer, who maintained that even the most aggressive baboon wouldn't attack a man unless there was no other choice.

What did it matter if baboons announced Ra with their cries and dances when he was born again in the eastern sky? Bakht had looked at them closely. They had low foreheads, tiny mad eyes, and dog snouts that made them look as though they wanted to rip his throat with their fangs. Glancing uneasily at the baboons, Bakht noticed that several big males had awakened and were moving toward him in the moonlight. He was glad the wall was steep, for they were excellent climbers.

Still, he regretted his impulse to sit here in full view of them. Baboons might be sacred to the god Toth, lord of the moon and inventor of writing, but Bakht preferred to keep clear of them. He peered into the darkness and spotted a male crouched nearby. The animal was looking at him. Suddenly the baboon started, gave a strangely human cry, and pulled back his lips to bare yellow teeth the size of Bakht's finger. Alarmed, Bakht stood, but the male wasn't looking at him anymore. Bakht turned and sighed as he recognized his friend coming up the staircase.

"Greetings. I was beginning to think you'd forgotten the meeting place."

His friend lifted a hand in response, and Bakht stood back on the landing to allow room for the other man to join him. As he came closer, Bakht noticed the hand that had lifted in greeting hadn't been lowered. There was something in it.

Frowning, he said, "What are you—"

He got no further, for his friend reached the landing, and the hand struck. The blow jolted the air from his body. He dropped his spear and grabbed his stomach when the pain hit—searing floods of agony, as though the baboon had sunk his fangs into Bakht's flesh. Hot liquid poured forth between Bakht's hands. Feeling foolish, he looked down at the blood flowing over his fingers, then up at his friend in time to see the dagger this time. It hurtled at him, sinking into his chest. Bakht's feeble attempt to ward off the blow cost him his precarious balance. When he stumbled to one knee, a blow to the side of his head sent him over the enclosure wall to land at the feet of the silver-caped baboon.

Stunned, Bakht barely heard the screams of the creature. He sucked in air and tried to stand, only to fall on his face. With one hand gripping his belly, Bakht pushed himself up to rest on one elbow. He opened his mouth to scream back at the baboon. The noise that came from his throat was a feeble whisper compared to the chorus of shrieks that assaulted him. More and more males joined the silver-caped one, and behind them came the females.

In terror, growing weak and dizzy, Bakht thrashed about on the ground, trying to get away. As he moved, he grabbed pebbles, sticks, anything he could use as a weapon, to hurl at his attackers. At last his back hit the enclosure wall. Bakht threw a rock at a furious mass of fur as it scampered at him. It screeched and retreated.

Summoning the last of his strength, Bakht cried out, knowing all the time that he would never be heard over the mindless screams of the baboons. His body was growing heavy. With one hand still pressed to the hole in his belly, his free hand scraped the packed earth, scooping up dirt. As blackness overcame him, he hurled the dirt in the snarling dog-face of the baboon that rushed at him.

Chapter 2

Memphis, reign of Tutankhamun

Lord Meren, hereditary prince and Friend of the King, sailed over the shoulder of his opponent to land flat on his back in the dirt. He sucked in air while trying to focus his vision on the sky, which looked the color of old linen in the first feeble light of dawn. A fine spray of dust coated his sweat-drenched body, and he cursed his own arrogance. The new charioteer might have only nineteen years, but he had the muscles of a rhinoceros and the stamina of a water buffalo. Now he was in the midst of a wrestling match in front of his charioteers and his son—Kysen—and he might lose. Ignoring the cheers of support from Kysen, his aide Abu, and others, Meren blinked to clear his vision.

He rolled to his feet as Irzanen approached. Emboldened by his success, the young man made his first and last mistake of the match. With a yell that proclaimed his impending triumph, he charged at Meren, leading with his right shoulder. Although he was breathing painfully hard, Meren smiled, braced himself as though he were going to take the charge, and let Irzanen come at him. The charioteer's bare feet slapped the ground, and at the last moment he lowered his head.

It was the move for which Meren had been waiting. He straightened from his crouch and whipped to the side as Irzanen pounded up to him. His foot lashed out, hooked the charioteer's ankle, and pulled. Irzanen crashed to the ground like a falling obelisk, and Meren jumped on his back. Grabbing Irzanen's arms, he bent them up and pressed them against his back. The younger man cried out and thrashed about with his legs, but Meren simply slipped a knee between them and nudged. Irzanen went still at once.

Shaking his head while their audience cheered, Meren moved his knee. "If you want to survive, Lord Irzanen, you must learn when to give way as well as when to fight." He released his opponent's arms and hauled him to his feet. "A wise heart is as valuable as strength."

Irzanen's chest was heaving. Rivulets of perspiration flooded his face. "I was too quick, was I not?"

"Swift of body, but not of wits." Meren wiped his forehead with the back of his arm and noted Irzanen's downcast expression. "And you almost bested me, but if you repeat that to the others, I will deny it."

Irzanen grinned as they were surrounded by charioteers. Abu offered advice and commiseration to the young charioteer while Kysen pounded him on the back and congratulated him for lasting so long against his father. Meren accepted a wet cloth from Reia, one of his most trusted charioteers. His face was buried in the cool material, but he looked up when he heard a groan.

He hadn't hurt the youth; he was certain of it. The charioteers had drifted away to form more wrestling groups, but

Lord Irzanen was still at his side. He was looking across the practice yard, which was bounded by the barracks and stables in Meren's Memphis residential compound. Meren followed the direction of Irzanen's gaze and saw his middle daughter, Bener, following his eldest, Tefnut. Evidently Bener had been watching the contest, but now she was walking away, down the graded path that led through the formal gardens to the town house. Meren turned his gaze back to Irzanen, who was beginning to resemble a sick bull.

Perhaps it was his bulky muscles that fostered this impression. Certainly the young man was pleasing of appearance. Meren had long ago realized why the offspring of the nobility and royalty so often presented the features and bodies of gods. Noblemen, unlike commoners, could choose from a host of well-made young women. Generations of such pairings produced beautiful children. Irzanen had inherited the long-legged, almost Nubian stature of his father, Prince Minnakht, and the symmetrical features and wide mouth of his lady mother. His hair, cut short in the military manner, curled like the tresses of a Mycenaean Greek, but he was saved from the impression of femininity by his forthright manner and a certain endearing clumsiness that came from having grown nearly half a cubit in one short year.

A sigh brought Meren's attention back to the young charioteer. Meren decided it was best to know what was taking place. He hadn't noticed Bener taking special interest in this lad, but she was so clever of heart and so skilled in circumspection that Meren had to be constantly alert.

"Is something wrong, Irzanen?"

The young man blinked and dragged his gaze from Bener's disappearing figure. "Naught, lord. I, that is, I didn't—"

"Find your tongue, Lord Irzanen."

"I didn't realize Lady Bener watched the practice matches, lord!"

Meren tried not to smile, but Irzanen's discomfort was too much for him. Seldom did young men blurt out such awkward statements to him. It was well known that Meren prized his daughters dearly and tolerated no interference with them from his charioteers. Most were sons of noblemen, and he chose them from the recruits of the elite chariot cavalry of the king. They served him in his capacity as the Eyes and Ears of Pharaoh. Places with him were valued and fought over not only because of Meren's reputation as a warrior and confidential inquiry agent of the king, but also because of his personal relationship with Tutankhamun. Yet despite their privileged position, Meren had always made sure the charioteers understood the dividing line between their service to him and pharaoh and the private life of his family.

He had been lucky for many years. Tefnut had married Prince Sunero when she was fourteen without engaging herself in any dalliance with the charioteers. The heart of Bener, who was sixteen, was serious. Quick of wit and far too complex of character for her own good, Bener had seldom expressed prolonged interest in young men. It was his youngest and most beautiful daughter, Isis, who worried him.

A black shroud settled over Meren's spirits at the thought of Isis. His heart had been wounded a few weeks ago, when she had, through her selfishness, nearly cost him his life. Since then he had been trying to summon the courage to confront Isis about her dangerous behavior, but he had yet to bring himself to speak to her. Isis avoided him, thus aiding his delay. She was ashamed, he could tell. But how long she would steep herself in remorse was a question he couldn't answer.

This time it was his own sigh that signaled a return to the present. Meren frowned at Irzanen. Presumptuous puppy.

"Don't stand there gawking like a heron after a fish," Meren snapped. "Knife practice."

Stalking away from the sorrowful Irzanen, Meren joined his son at a leather target set up near the stables. Kysen handed him a bronze knife, a plain weapon with an edge as sharp as his grandmother's tongue. Kysen threw his own, blade first, into the target from fifteen paces away. Meren cast an irritated glance at Irzanen across the practice yard, then signaled Kysen to move nearer the target. A large space separated them from the nearest buildings, and they were alone for the moment.

"The merchant is coming?" Meren asked softly.

Kysen paused in the act of pulling his knife from the target and glanced around the yard. "Prince Djoser is bringing him, as you instructed—he thinks we want to buy horses. But I still believe that searching for the murderer of a long-dead queen is madness."

"We've sailed this route before, Ky." Meren hefted the knife in his hand, testing its balance. "Whoever the evil one is, he already knows we've found out that Queen Nefertiti didn't die of a plague but was poisoned. If we don't find him, he'll find us and kill us. There will be no more argument."

Kysen inclined his head, and Meren thanked the gods he had at least one person with whom to share this burden. The difficulties in trying to find out who poisoned Nefertiti were countless. He could do nothing openly without the risk of warning anyone who might be guilty or those who would welcome a chance to stir up trouble for a rival for pharaoh's friendship.

He began by trying to find and question the one most likely to have administered the poison, the queen's favorite cook. The woman and her husband were killed before he could talk to them. Her sister might have been of help, but her wits wandered so much that he had yet to get much sense from her.

Kysen had set inquiries afoot through his nefarious friend Othrys, a Mycenaean Greek pirate. Othrys sent out his agents in search of information, only to have them disappear or return dying. From these experiences the pirate provided the names of three men powerful enough and audacious enough to have dared to kill a queen and risked incurring his own enmity.

Now, although Meren had sent his own scribes and servants on various missions of inquiry, he was being forced to deal with the three men first while waiting for more facts. One of these three—Dilalu, Yamen, or Zulaya—or someone who commanded one of them had become a hidden and dangerous enemy. This hidden one didn't want to be found; he killed rather than be discovered. This alone was proof of his guilt.

Meren believed, however, that there was a good chance that someone else, someone far more exalted, was the true hidden one, the man ultimately responsible for Nefertiti's death. None of the three had been closely associated with the queen's household. Ordering and accomplishing the death of a queen—such an act of sacrilege and temerity—would require someone daring, someone like Dilalu, Zulaya, or Yamen. But to conceive of the idea—the murder of the wife of the living god of Egypt—took far more power than any of those men seemed to have.

The situation was confusing because of the limitations upon his usual power to investigate. He would have to cultivate patience while his servants worked slowly and unobtrusively. The last thing he wanted them to do was attract attention and provoke curiosity among the officials and government workers in this intrigue-ridden city. Meanwhile, he shouldn't make his son suffer just because he was frustrated. Kysen was worried about him. He smiled at his son.

"I'm being as indirect as I can, Ky. Dilalu may be a merchant of weapons, but he thinks I'm interested in him for his reputation as a breeder of horses."

Tossing his knife in the air and catching it, Kysen gave a sharp laugh. "He could hardly think the Eyes and Ears of Pharaoh in need of extra daggers or spears."

"My heart's thoughts are as yours." Meren rubbed the scar on his wrist. It was bothering him again. "Have I ever told you about Queen Nefertiti?" He slipped his knife into a sheath at his belt.

"A little. You said Isis is almost as beautiful."

"Ah, but Nefertiti was raised and trained by pharaoh's mother, the great Tiye. Unlike your sister, she knew the importance of duty. I never saw two women more skilled in diplomacy, and Nefertiti, may she live forever with Osiris, needed all her skill to remain in her husband's favor while convincing him to do things that were best for Egypt."

Kysen held his knife by the blade and threw it into the target. The weapon stabbed deep in the straw-stuffed leather, and Meren shook his head.

"That close to an enemy, you'll have no time to pull your knife, reverse it, and take a throwing stance. Here, watch."

Meren grabbed his knife from its sheath by the handle. His arm sailed up, forearm in front of his face. He threw the knife in a slashing, diagonal movement. It smacked into the target, the handle shuddering a bit with the impact.

Turning to Kysen, he said, "You see? Less throwing time, less exposure to your adversary. About these three men Othrys thinks might be interfering with our inquiries into the queen's murder."

"Father," Kysen said in an aggrieved tone, "sometimes

you're confusing when you make these sudden shifts of conversation."

"Forgive me." Meren gave his son a pained smile. "Too many years spent trying to baffle courtiers and enemy ambassadors. What I was trying to say was that there were many at court who might have wanted Nefertiti dead."

"Not the newcomers Akhenaten brought in to serve the Aten."

Meren nodded. Tutankhamun's older brother, Akhenaten, called the Heretic, had forced Egypt to abandon her old gods in favor of his choice—the Aten, the sun disk. The priests and temples of the old gods had been disestablished, and their endowed riches diverted to the Aten in the care of new men willing to participate in the heresy. Egypt suffered from the resulting disharmony and chaos to this day. The priests of the old gods, especially Amun, king of the gods, hated Akhenaten's very memory, and all who had supported the heretic.

"The priests of Amun? Would they have done such a thing?" Kysen asked.

Meren shook his head. "In the last years before she died, Nefertiti had contacted them and begun to work for a reconciliation. They wouldn't have killed their hope of resurrection." He watched Kysen throw his knife by its handle. "Of course, there were rivalries in the royal household among the women. There always are, and one can never tell when such rivalries will poison the wits of an ambitious secondary wife or ignored princess."

Kysen's head jerked around, and he stared at Meren. "Not one of his daughters."

"No, most likely a lesser princess. But I can think of no woman who would be in a position to gain from Akhenaten by Nefertiti's death. However, the queen did take a disliking to some courtiers who sought pharaoh's favor. I remember she held ill opinions of Prince Usermontu and Lord Pendua. But neither seems to have benefited from her death."

"In a way that we can perceive," Kysen said.

Meren's wide mouth quirked up at one corner. "Correct."

He threw his knife again, hitting the target in the center. Grabbing the hilt, he paused in the midst of pulling it free from the leather and studied the wooden handle. The knife was one of the sacred weapons that slaughtered the enemies of the sun god Ra in the underworld, thus allowing him to rise each day and bring light to the world.

"After I deal with Dilalu, we must go over what my scribes have gathered from the old records," Meren said.

He glanced over his shoulder to see the fiery orb of Ra crest the trees that sheltered his town house. At the same time, Zar, his body servant, walked around the stables and came toward him. Meren nudged Kysen.

"Prince Djoser must be here with the dealer in weapons. Tell Zar to bring them here."

Turning on his heel, Meren went to the stables. The low mud-brick building housed the teams of thoroughbreds that pulled the chariots driven by Meren and his men. In the first stall, a luxurious box finished in hard plaster and strewn with fresh straw, stood his favorite pair—Wind Chaser and Star Chaser. Brothers, they worked together as one, and Meren had raised them himself. Seldom did a day pass that he didn't take them out to the desert for exercise. If he couldn't, one of the other charioteers made certain they were kept in shape.

Star Chaser whinnied and stuck his head over the wooden gate in the stall. Wind Chaser pivoted and thrust his nose in Meren's face. Meren fed them handfuls of the grain they craved. The two were dish-faced, with great, low-set eyes and tapered muzzles; their flexible nostrils snuffled at him. They were dark, dark roans, their obsidian-black manes and tails grown long in the absence of warfare. Meren was proud of their refined and graceful features and fine-boned strength. They had charged with him into battle countless times, never wavering, never losing courage.

As he stroked their soft muzzles, Meren settled into a private realm of tranquillity, summoned by the feel of delicate skin and the soft rumbling sounds Wind and Star made when they talked to him. He answered in a low murmur as he stroked Wind's neck and laid his cheek against Star's jaw.

Kysen's reluctance to delve further into the death of the queen had kindled his own foreboding. Since discovering the murder, Meren had been suffering from evil dreams. Were they messages from the gods, or were they scraps of old memories?

Akhenaten had killed Meren's father for refusing to adopt the Aten as his sole god. He'd tortured Meren, suspecting him of the same treachery, and only the intervention of Ay had saved the devastated youth. Meren rubbed his wrist against Wind's neck.

It was beginning to itch, as it often did when he was agitated or when he was reminded of those nightmare times at the heretic's capital, Horizon of the Aten. He closed his eyes and tried to fend off the images of that dark cell, but he saw again Akhenaten's foot, soft and scented with oil, in its golden sandal from his position beneath the royal guards on the floor. He glimpsed the white-hot brand in the shape of the Aten. The metal formed a sun disk with sticklike rays extending from it and ending in stylized hands. It descended and pressed into his wrist, and Meren's body went rigid with agony.

"No."

His own voice jolted Meren back from the realm of apparitions. Turning his face, he buried it in Star's neck. Wind nudged him, jealous and impatient. The soft nose on his shoulder tickled, and Meren laughed unsteadily.

Someone blocked the light from the door. Immediately Meren shifted into the guise of courtier and King's Friend. Without looking, he said, "May Amun bless you, Prince Djoser."

Djoser was the son of Amunhotep the Magnificent and an Egyptian noblewoman. A scholarly man with a misguided ambition to be a soldier, he was slight, with thinning hair concealed by a court wig that lay about his shoulders in intricate braids. Djoser's arched brows and open-mouthed expression combined to give an impression that the prince was constantly startled. He wore a fine pleated robe and broad collar of alternating gold and carnelian beads and seemed embarrassed when he took in Meren's plain kilt, sweating body, and lack of ornaments or eye paint.

With an uncertain step he entered the stable, followed by a stocky man no higher than Meren's shoulder who walked with a cocklike strut. No doubt the visitor thought his gait stately, but the effect was that of a waddling pyramid block. Dilalu the merchant smelled of expensive unguents. Meren detected the scent of sweet flag, juniper berries, and myrrh. Beneath these lurked the odor of stale wine. In his arms Dilalu carried the fattest tabby Meren had ever seen. It watched Meren with flat-headed malice as Dilalu's stubby, beringed fingers stroked its fur.

Djoser stopped before Meren and bowed. "Lord Meren, Friend of the King, count, and hereditary prince, I present the merchant of Canaan, Dilalu."

Meren nodded, a slight inclination of the head that expressed his superior station in life. Dilalu bowed low with the fat cat in his arms and spoke with a manner and tone that called up visions of ox fat melting in the sun.

"Great lord, mighty of power, a humble man am I to be

summoned into thy presence. May the blessings of the Lady of Byblos be upon thee."

"Indeed," Meren murmured as he stroked Star Chaser's withers.

He let silence lengthen, a method by which he'd disturbed many an evildoer. This first meeting was but to whet Dilalu's appetite with the prospect of a connection near pharaoh. Only after the weapons seller was drooling at the possibility of much Egyptian gold would Meren begin inserting the point of his knife into the cracks in Dilalu's ramparts. Holding out his hand, he let Wind Chaser snuffle it. When Star began to toss his head, Meren spoken again, causing Dilalu to jump and his cat to hiss.

"I have heard of the quality of your thoroughbreds, merchant. I wish to purchase a fine pair for my eldest daughter in celebration of her first child. The birth should take place in three months' time."

Dilalu's stubby fingers dug into his cat's fur. The animal growled, and the fingers lifted. Then, as if he suddenly woke from sleep, the merchant launched into a speech that had obviously been practiced beforehand.

"O mighty of power, blessed of Baal, O puissant prince, unbounded is my humility at being blessed with a commission from your noble self. Great is my fame; it is true. The old pharaoh, may he live forever, and his great royal wife knew the value of my steeds. I have provided mounts for all the great kings of the world—the king of the Hittites, the king of Babylon, many, many great kings. General Horemheb and General Nakhtmin order my horses for the chariotry of Egypt. Indeed, one can see my fine thoroughbreds from the Delta to the southern lands of Kush."

Dilalu stopped, but only because he'd run out of breath.

"The living Horus, his majesty Tutankhamun, would admire my horses, should they be driven by the noble Lord Meren."

While listening to Dilalu, Meren had knelt down to inspect Wind's hoof. The man was already sweating with anticipation. Meren stood and looked at Dilalu with curiosity. The man's tongue was slippery as wet granite, which was no doubt of great use to him when selling mountains of weapons to petty kings in Syria.

"Are you the one who provided mounts to pharaoh in Horizon of the Aten?"

Dilalu bowed again, nearly crushing the cat in his arms. The animal spat and struggled. It finally jumped to the ground and began to stalk around the stables.

"Perhaps the great lord has seen the matched black stallions of the old king. Pharaoh drove from his palace in the northern city down the royal road with them countless times."

"Yes," Meren said softly. "I remember."

"And I provided the great royal wife with a white pair."

"I remember a mare called Swiftness."

"The finest, O mighty prince. The queen allowed me into her presence to praise the animal."

Affecting indifference, Meren scooped up a handful of grain from a bucket and fed Wind and Star. Dilalu gave Prince Djoser an uneasy look and burst into florid speech again.

"O mighty lord, whom pharaoh has made powerful, I have added horse to horse, bow to bow, shield to shield, for the armies of Egypt. And I long to serve the upright Lord Meren. I have other animals from afar—leopards, green monkeys, gazelles, onagers, and parrots." Dilalu ventured a few steps nearer his quarry and gave Meren a sideways glance that started at the top of his black hair and ended at his ankles. "I even have slaves from across the sea, blond ones from the wild north lands."

"What I want from you, merchant, is first choice from

among your finest mares and stallions, and perhaps I will need a pair of hinnies."

"O mighty prince, I breed my hinnies from royal stallions and the gentlest of female donkeys."

Giving Dilalu a blank stare, Meren turned to Prince Djoser. "The merchant may speak to my steward about payment. Pray come with me and taste some new Syrian wine my trader has just brought back, my friend."

Meren and Djoser left the stable. Dilalu scooped up his cat and scurried after them, his long woolen robe a bright blot against the white-plastered walls of the buildings. Zar was waiting to escort the merchant, and Meren didn't look at him again as he engaged Djoser in conversation. When Dilalu was gone, Meren walked toward the house with his friend. The first meeting had been everything he'd planned. Dilalu had already revealed his presence at Horizon of the Aten and his acquaintance with Nefertiti.

"My thanks for bringing the merchant," Meren said to Prince Djoser.

Djoser smiled and ducked under the branch of an acacia beside the walk. "He'll try to cheat you."

"Is that not the way of merchants?"

Djoser frowned, as if troubled. "But you could have gotten horses by sending your trader to any of the breeders in Egypt, Meren."

"Ah," Meren said smoothly, "but this Dilalu has the finest, the horses favored by the royal family, and I want the best for my eldest daughter, who is about to bear her first child."

"Still—"

"And how much greater the value of the gift if one attends the details of its acquisition personally, my dear friend."

Djoser brightened. "I never thought of that."

Having shared an upbringing with the children of the royal

palace, Meren wasn't surprised at Djoser's blindness. He stopped beside the long reflection pool that decorated the approach to the house as servants scurried toward them bearing trays and ostrich feather fans.

"This personal attention, it is a practice I learned from Queen Nefertiti. She used to choose gifts for her daughters herself. But enough of miserable merchants."

"I agree," Djoser said. "Men like that are never of much consequence."

"Your words have much truth," Meren said as he picked up a bronze goblet from a tray. "And dealing with that one has left a bad taste on my tongue."

Chapter 3

Thebes, joint reign of the Pharaoh Amunhotep III, the Magnificent, and his son, Akhenaten

Nefertiti dashed through a maze of palace rooms cluttered with guards, servants, courtiers, and slaves, her gauzy, pleated robes billowing around her long legs. Her majesty, Queen Tiye, would scold her later for her unseemly haste, but word had come that her new husband was upset. The queen had made Nefertiti's duty plain—as wife to pharaoh's heir, she was to control Akhenaten's intolerance and mystical tendencies. A daunting prospect for a girl of twelve.

As she approached her husband's quarters, Nefertiti slowed to a fast walk. Her hands shook as she contemplated the task before her. Akhenaten's heart was filled with strange notions, ideas that drove his father into rages the moment the two exchanged more than a few words. Amunhotep was still horribly offended that her husband insisted upon being called a name of his own invention rather than the name he shared with his father.

Because of Akhenaten's bizarre behavior, Nefertiti had lost her old life of obscurity, her quiet manner of living, and worst of all, her friend Webkhet. Wives of pharaohs didn't have intimate friends among the guards' families. She still missed Webkhet. Last night, after a spell of crying, she'd resolved to put her longing for her friend aside. Feeling pity for oneself was unqueenly and cowardly. This had been one of Tiye's first lessons.

She didn't share pharaoh and Tiye's belief that she could influence Akhenaten and lead him away from his more fanatical tendencies by the power of her beauty and the tranquillity of her spirit. Nefertiti had found it impossible to remain tranquil when Akhenaten was submerged in one of his mystic trances. And when he erupted into rage, he was even more frightening than his father.

Nefertiti slowed to a sedate walk outside the audience hall called the Bull Chamber. She knew it was important to be beautiful. It was one of her greatest tasks. The gods had blessed her with an almost perfectly oval face, delicate brows, and eyes the shape of large dates. Her bones were fragile, and her neck so long that the extra weight of her headdresses seemed to threaten to snap it.

Akhenaten loved her fine skin, made golden brown by many hours spent beside her husband in the worship of the Aten. He was fascinated by her mouth. The lower lip was full, while the upper was short and slanted down. It intersected the upper to form corners that disappeared into tiny hollows. Yes, it was one of her greatest tasks—being beautiful. Nefertiti wasn't certain it was an enjoyable one. People seldom took account of her heart; they were too busy looking at her face.

Smoothing her braided wig, Nefertiti patted her face, which was damp with perspiration. Her hands were still shaking. Ignoring the guards that bracketed the double doors, she waited while her breathing slowed. She could hear raised voices coming from the audience chamber. Her father, Lord Ay, was in there.

At least she would have his supporting presence to give her courage. Nefertiti nodded to the guards, who opened the doors. Inside she walked past four wooden columns painted in black and red and across the rectangular chamber to a dais. Under her feet lay paintings of bound captives, the traditional enemies of Egypt: Libyans, Nubians, Asiatics, and blond savages from across the northern sea. Pharaoh always trod on his enemies, to ensure Egypt's safety.

On the dais, under a canopy of gilded cedar, her husband, Akhenaten, sat attended by Lord Ay and Humay, one of the countless powerful priests of the god Amun. Akhenaten slouched in his chair of ebony and sheet gold and squinted at the priest. Nefertiti gazed up at Akhenaten's face. It was long, with lips too full and a mouth too wide for its narrow chin. But his eyes dominated his face—slanting, larger than expected, and filled with black fire, they looked as if they could shrivel one's ka when they burned as they did now.

Nefertiti crept up to the group slowly, hoping to divine the reason for Akhenaten's ire before she was noticed.

"He has no right to be offended," Akhenaten was saying, every word a sneer. "The fool is but a priest."

Humay's eyes widened. "He is the high priest of the greatest god of Egypt, Amun, the Hidden One, the king of the gods—"

"That's not true!"

Akhenaten's voice boomed off the walls and evoked a shocked silence. Humay gaped at the prince, then cast a terrified look at Ay, whose visage remained blank.

"I have heard the voice of the True One," Akhenaten said in a calmer voice.

As he launched into a description of his beliefs, the prince grew less angry but more excited. Nefertiti glanced at her father. An accomplished horseman, Ay still retained the figure of an athlete and charioteer. With a start, Nefertiti suddenly realized that her father resembled the ideal warrior pharaoh more than her husband ever would.

The contrast between the muscled form of Ay and the warped figure of the prince was painful, given the general's greater age. Where Ay's shoulders and thighs bulged with strength gained from constant exercise, from hefting spears and bows and riding bareback through the desert, Akhenaten's body was hollow. His shoulders were sunken and rounded. He was thin, his muscles soft from lack of use, and his bones too finely made.

What was more unfortunate, his hips were as wide as a woman's, and his belly looked as though he'd given birth to several children. Although Akhenaten had always been frail, that didn't stop him from getting what he wanted, for Akhenaten's heart was strong in will and intelligence. Unfortunately for Nefertiti, it was also filled with chaos.

Akhenaten had finished his lecture. "Go back to the high priest and tell him what I have said." The prince straightened in his chair and caught sight of Nefertiti, and in less than half a breath his mood changed from mystic irritation to pleasure. He smiled at her.

"My beautiful one has come." He rose and held out his hand to her. "Go away, both of you."

The priest hurried out of the room. Ay bowed to Akhenaten, turned, and passed his daughter. As he neared her, he gave Nefertiti a smile of encouragement. She merely stared back at her father with large, startled eyes. Seeking composure as she put her hand in Akhenaten's, she studied the painting of a rampant bull that formed the central decoration of the audience hall. Black and white, the creature reared ten cubits high against a background of mountains in blue, yellow, and red. Akhenaten squeezed her hand.

"Come, beautiful one. Let us forget these troublesome and ignorant priests of Amun. We'll go outside and receive the blessing of the rays of the Aten."

They sat at the edge of a pool stocked with fish and brimming with water lilies. Akhenaten brought a goblet of wine with him but set it aside. The sun reflected bright sparks off the stone of the pool. Nefertiti's eyes ached from too much light, so she kept them lowered. The heavy curtain of her wig provided some protection from the glare.

Akhenaten seemed unaffected by the brilliance. He lifted his face to the sun. His eyes widened for a moment before they were forced closed by the rays of the orb. Seated side by side, they absorbed the light and heat.

"I know you dislike my fighting with the priests," Akhenaten said.

"The way of Egypt is as old as the world, my husband."

"But I have been chosen to give Egypt the Truth, so that the misguided ways of old may be corrected."

Nefertiti frowned. She had listened to Akhenaten's version of the truth many times.

"Why, husband? Why must you be so—so different?" She bit her lip, for she sounded like a confused child even to herself when she was trying so hard to be a mature woman.

Akhenaten looked away from her, and a long silence settled over them. Nefertiti grew uneasy, afraid that she had offended. But then she saw Akhenaten's face. He was remembering something that caused great pain, and shame. Her husband, the son of the great Amunhotep the Magnificent, was ashamed.

Speaking slowly, as if every word cost him in courage,

Akhenaten turned to her. "You are my wife. You must know everything so that you understand the Truth." Akhenaten waited for her to nod before going on. "I wasn't much older than you when the Aten revealed the Truth to me. I was alone on my estate near Abydos. Father was still keeping me hidden. He wanted no part of a sickly weakling, and he didn't want the people to see me. He knew I'd never be a great athlete and warrior, so he kept me hidden, as if I'd committed some horrible sin. I used to pray to the false gods to make me strong, or at least to give me some sign of their favor. It never came."

Akhenaten stood up and lifted his hands to the sun. "One day I was well enough to drive in my chariot, and I went out alone. I got lost in a desert valley. I knew someone would come looking for me, so I stopped and sat on a flat rock. It was midday and so, so hot. I thought of Father. He would never have gotten lost, not the magnificent Amunhotep."

Nefertiti peered up at her husband and pharaoh. Akhenaten was communing with the sun and seemed to have forgotten her. The silence stretched out. In a sudden sweep Akhenaten brought his arms down.

"Father made me hate myself, may his soul be damned. It was his fault I couldn't even find my way across my own lands. Father wanted me to die." Akhenaten turned to Nefertiti. "I finally realized that out on that rock. And I decided to give Father his wish. I was going to stay out in the desert until I died. The sun's rays were so powerful they went into my bones. I let them bathe me in death. It wasn't long before I felt suffused with brilliant, white light and heat. My ka left my body then and floated up high on the boiling air, higher and higher until it joined with the sun, and my true father, the Aten, revealed himself to me at last."

Always practical, Nefertiti asked, "What did he say?"

Akhenaten blinked at her. "Why, that I'm his son. That I

am the embodiment of the Aten on earth. That the Aten is the one source of power of the universe, creator of all. The Aten brings life, makes mountains, causes rivers to flow. The Aten is fertility and passion; everything comes from him." Large hands waved at Nefertiti. "After the Aten revealed the Truth to me, I understood why I was different. I'm the embodiment of creation. I am the masculine and feminine force. I am the Aten on earth, and all must recognize me as such. So you see, beautiful one, we don't need all these false gods. They're really all imperfect reflections of the Aten. The people don't need Amun. They don't need Osiris. They'll pray to me for eternal life. It is I who can give it to them in the name of my father, the light that comes in the sun disk."

Again Nefertiti returned to mundane matters. "If the Aten is so powerful, why did he let all the other gods usurp his rights?"

"Nefertiti!" Akhenaten glowered at her. "Men imagined those gods. They don't exist, I tell you."

Pharaoh's voice rose. Nefertiti leaned away from her husband, suddenly frightened by the molten obsidian of his gaze.

"You will honor my words," Akhenaten ground out. "I am the son of pharaoh; I am the Aten personified. You'll believe because I wish it."

Akhenaten stared into Nefertiti's eyes. Unwilling, she stared back into the eyes of chaos. Her throat and mouth went dry. She felt as if she were a gazelle in the mouth of a lion. She was being choked by powerful jaws. Without warning, Akhenaten's mood changed. He straightened, smiling.

"Don't worry." The king sat back beside Nefertiti again and took up his goblet. "You'll see the Truth in time. There is no other possibility." Akhenaten put the goblet in Nefertiti's hand. "This is a sacred wine I made with the help of an old sorcerer priest of Ra. It's full of magic herbs and touched with the rays of the Aten himself. I use it to help me commune with my father. Only take two sips."

Nefertiti took a small drink. It was wine. Wine and something else that burned her mouth. The fumes from the goblet got in her throat and nose. She almost sneezed as she took a second sip. Akhenaten took the cup back and drained it. He said something, but Nefertiti was listening to the buzz in her head. It reminded her of a honeybee. It was a buzz in emptiness, like a bee in a deserted tomb. She swatted at the bee. Akhenaten caught her hand.

"We will praise the Aten, beautiful one. Say the words with me."

Nefertiti found that she could repeat the words of praise, even though it was hard to stand with her arms raised to the sun as Akhenaten did. Unfortunately, it was a long hymn with many phrases saying there was no other god. Akhenaten enjoyed repeating that he was the only one who knew the Aten. When they reached the portion in which the gifts of the Aten were listed—all beasts, trees, herbs, birds, ships, roads, fish— Nefertiti yawned.

It seemed to her that each word took hours to say. She was sure her mouth moved more slowly than cold honey. They praised the Aten's power over the animals and plants, over man, water, and earth, all to the accompaniment of that entombed bee in Nefertiti's head. The buzzing grew louder and hurt her ears, but Akhenaten's voice cut across the sound and made it stop. Nefertiti sighed, then drew back as her husband's face loomed at her.

"Now you see, wife. My father does love me, for my father is the Aten."

Nefertiti gave another deep sigh. Her tongue was getting too big for her mouth. She licked her lips. "Your father is pharaoh."

"No. He's the Aten." Akhenaten steadied her with a hand on her arm. "My father the Aten has spoken to me of you. You are the embodiment of all that is good in our family of god-kings. Beauty and strength, my Nefertiti. It's no accident that you and I are as we are. We complement each other. The Aten has given me another Beautiful Child of the Sun."

By now Nefertiti's head felt too heavy for her neck. Her skin burned and yet felt numb. How this could be, she wasn't sure. She was dizzy and tired, and bored with communing with the Aten. The Aten was everything, according to Akhenaten, but at the moment Nefertiti considered the sun disk to be an enemy. It burned her eyes and made her heart race.

Akhenaten was in the middle of a sentence. Nefertiti made a shushing sound and sank down on the pool ledge. She leaned over the water, dipped her hands in it, and fell in. The coolness was such a relief that she decided to stay under the surface until the sun went away. The last thing she remembered before she went into darkness was Akhenaten's hands cutting through the water in search of her.

Chapter 4

Memphis, the reign of Tutankhamun

Late on the morning of his meeting with Dilalu, Meren was standing in the wake of a breeze created by the undulation of ostrich feather fans wielded by royal servants on the loggia of the royal palace. From the shade beside a slender column carved in the shape of an elongated water lily, he listened only partially while the old overseer of the audience hall went over plans for the feast of Opet with pharaoh.

This was the daily gathering of the king's ministers and councillors. They stood in groups about the loggia, deep in discussion, some in argument. Maya, the treasurer, who loved ceremony and merriment, was one of the few paying heed to the overseer of the audience hall, along with the king's uncle and chief minister, Ay. Prince Djoser's presence was a courtesy on the part of pharaoh, and perhaps an attempt to find a vocation more suitable to the young man than soldiering. He was standing beside a table loaded with roasted duck and pigeons and sharing jokes with Lord Pendua.

The two military men, Generals Nakhtmin and Horemheb, formed another enclave, guarding a tall, curved wine jar set in a stand and draped with garlands. Ordinarily Meren would have been drawn into conversation, for he liked both Maya and Horemheb, but his meeting with Dilalu weighed on his heart. He stared out across the court, in which lay an azure reflection pool large enough to carry several pleasure boats. Ancient sycamores and palms formed shady avenues around the water, while beds of exotic flowers were interspersed with rows of spice trees.

A black shadow caught Meren's eye. Beside the reflection pool and a patch of sunlight, Sa, the king's black leopard, lifted his head. Golden eyes opened and stared at him. Sa's tail flicked lazily back and forth, as if he were debating whether Meren was prey or not. Meren whispered the cat's name. Sa blinked, then yawned and got up, padding slowly to a shady spot under a myrrh tree.

Sa made Meren think of the merchant's cat. A greater contrast he could not imagine. Yet as he recalled the encounter with Dilalu, Meren grew more and more uneasy. Kysen's pirate friend Othrys had been wary of Dilalu, and according to his son, there was little that frightened Othrys. The fool who had presented himself before Meren wouldn't frighten a bean goose.

The scattered councillors began to move. Meren dragged his thoughts back to matters at hand. Pharaoh had called his name. He walked back to the king, who was seated on a chair of polished cedar decorated in red sheet gold. Bowing low, he took his place beside Ay while Maya shuffled through a stack of papyri on a nearby table.

"About this matter of the Hittite," the king said. "My majesty sent a royal messenger to King Suppiluliumas as you insisted, Meren."

"Thy majesty is wise," Meren said.

The king's young face, usually impassive when dealing with matters of government, flushed. His dark brows drew together. "My majesty likes not having to explain myself to that barbarian."

"His emissary was killed by an Egyptian, majesty."

"I wanted to kill Mugallu myself." The Hittite emissary had insulted pharaoh, and Tutankhamun hadn't forgotten.

"Yes, golden one, and thy patience is wondrous."

The king glared at him in frustration. "My patience is forced on me by you, Meren. I have no choice in the matter."

"Majesty," Meren said with the reproving tone of a father, "you have chosen the wisest course, which is not the same as having no choice."

"It is with you and Ay here to remind me of my duty night and day."

Tutankhamun's fingers were wrapped around a jeweled pen case. He slapped the cylinder against his palm, and Ay hastened to distract the king with a matter of property ownership to be settled between two princes. Meren schooled his features so that he didn't betray his amusement. The golden one seldom allowed his temper such freedom before his less intimate councillors.

Egypt was fortunate to have Tutankhamun, who embodied the ideals of what pharaoh should be in both body and character. Tutankhamun's face was as handsome as his mother's, the great and powerful Queen Tiye. He had inherited her large, dark eyes, heavy-lidded, thick-lashed pools that reflected a ka too sensitive for the burdens of a god-king. At the same time and despite his youth, the king's courage was unquestioned. Indeed, Meren was having a difficult time restraining pharaoh's desire to test himself in battle rather than in training exercises.

Meren felt a pang of sympathy for the boy. Not yet fifteen, Tutankhamun had inherited the throne of Egypt when he was only nine, after the divisive reign of his heretic brother. Having come of age lately, Tutankhamun found himself caught up in the aftermath of Akhenaten's disastrous policies. He had to control the virulent hatred of the priesthood of Amun, who lusted after the riches and power of which the heretic had robbed them.

Corruption had spread, plaguelike, among temple personnel and government officials, threatening Egypt from within, while the Hittites perched at the edge of the northern empire, ready to strike. Such were the burdens of pharaoh, a youth who walked with the dignity of his ancestors, the pyramid builders, and possessed a compassion born of grief for the dead brother and sister-in-law whose names he dared not speak.

While Ay was talking to pharaoh, Horemheb wandered over to lean against a column near Meren. "You've had reports about this troublemaker among the petty kings of the north?"

"The one called Pilsu?"

"Aye, that's the one."

The king turned to Meren again. "Ah, you're together. Then we will speak of the disturbances among the towns near Ugarit."

Horemheb nodded. "We have read the reports, majesty."

"So, does this carrion threaten the trade routes?" the king asked.

"Not yet, majesty. At the moment Pilsu busies himself by stirring up discontent among the chiefs of the towns."

Tutankhamun sighed. "Another of these interminable disputes."

"As long as they squabble among themselves, they have no

time or strength to give trouble to thy majesty," Meren said smoothly.

"Just see to it that Pilsu grows no stronger than he should," Tutankhamun said. "I'll not have trade interfered with."

Horemheb bowed. "Thy majesty's word is accomplished."

"Do you think Pilsu is a tool of the Hittites?" Meren asked the general.

"Have you heard it?" Horemheb countered.

"No, but it wouldn't be the first time the Hittites have fed the fires of a petty dispute and then interfered on the pretense that their interests were threatened."

They both looked at the king, who cast an inquisitive glance at Ay. The old minister shook his head. Everyone went silent. The king picked up a token from the game board sitting on the table beside his chair. Toying with the carved ivory, he spoke slowly.

"Perhaps it's time my majesty recalled one of the royal spies from the north."

Meren exchanged a wary glance with Ay. Summoning an agent from his sphere of duty was a great risk.

"Majesty," Ay said, "when such a one is recalled, there is always a chance——"

Tutankhamun slapped the ivory game piece down on the table and gave a sharp sigh. "I know that. I've seen what happens." The king turned suddenly to Meren. "Have I not, Eyes?"

"Indeed, majesty." There had been times when the king escaped Ay's vigilance and exposed himself to peril, involving Meren along the way.

"Then my majesty has spoken. Ay, recall one of your own at once."

"Yes, majesty."

"Now, what remains?" the king asked.

Ay shook his head, as did Horemheb. No one else seemed ready to speak until Maya looked up from a stack of papyri in his hands.

"A small matter, golden one. Last night a royal guard was killed in the menagerie."

At this remark, the councillors broke up into groups again. No one was interested in the death of a common guard. Maya was rolling the papyri and placing them in a document case when the king spoke.

"Which guard?"

"Oh," Maya said. He furrowed his brow and glanced at the document case. "Oh, yes. He was called Bakht, majesty."

Meren was thinking about Dilalu again. Something wasn't right, and he was going to find out what it was. At once. Tonight. He would send Kysen to the foreign quarter of the city.

"Meren!"

Waking from his deep concentration, Meren bowed to the king again. "Majesty."

"I said that this Bakht was pleasing to me. For years he has told me stories of his adventures in Nubia and in the north. He has—had even gone across the great sea to the Mycenaean Greek cities. Maya says he was killed in the baboon pen. He fell in."

"A terrible accident, majesty."

"Bakht didn't like baboons, Meren."

"The males can be fierce, golden one."

"I don't understand why he would be there," the king insisted. "Bakht avoided them."

"If he was afraid of the baboons and happened to fall into their pen by accident, his screams might have enraged the males."

Tutankhamun looked unhappily at Meren. "I suppose you're right."

"I am sorry, majesty."

"Still, my majesty will rest better once you have inquired into the matter. And Maya, Bakht is to have a good embalming. Let the priests of Anubis be informed."

The council session broke up with a wave of the king's hand. Not wanting to be waylaid by pharaoh and forced to set a date for taking his majesty on a military expedition, Meren slipped inside the palace. He hurried through corridors made bright by the exquisite wall paintings of the king's artisans.

Since discovering that Queen Nefertiti had been murdered, Meren had been trying to recall the events surrounding her death. Unfortunately, his heart had been scoured of many memories of that time. His years at Horizon of the Aten had been filled with fear. He'd been so young when his father had been killed—eighteen. The fear had acted as a burnishing stone on papyrus, polishing away unwanted ugliness.

Now, when he needed those memories, he was finding it difficult to reconstruct them. He was thinking of writing what he did remember in a secret record. The act of writing usually helped him recall tasks he had to complete; it might help his memory. He could always destroy the record. He would have to destroy it, for it would be too dangerous a thing to have about him for long.

Walking past lines of royal bodyguards, Meren found his way to his chariot in the forecourt of the palace and took the reins from a groom. Wind and Star, responding to his voice, trotted down an avenue lined with sphinxes. Now that his duties at the palace were over for the day, he could plan how best to find out more about Dilalu.

Whatever the method, he didn't want the merchant to know he was being scrutinized. Kysen was the best man for that task. His adopted son had been born to a commoner family of artisans from the royal tomb makers' village in Thebes. His accent wouldn't betray him in the unsavory sections of the city known as the Caverns. While Meren could pass himself off as many things, he had difficulty hiding his aristocratic origins from native Egyptians. In addition, he was too well known in Memphis. No, skulking around the dissolute taverns and perilous streets of the Caverns was an activity at which Kysen was far more accomplished.

Abu, Lord Meren's aide, slid along a dark street, his back pressed to a wall that seemed to consist mostly of cracked plaster or exposed and crumbling mud bricks. He dragged with him an odorous little man who squealed and grumbled with every step.

"I was coming, me. Would I ignore the command of the great Lord Kysen? Got lost, I did. Terrible twisty and winding is these lanes."

Abu paused long enough to cuff his charge on the ear. "Close your mouth, Tcha. The gods alone know how such a babbling dung-eater came to be a thief."

"Thief! Tcha is no thief. Ask Mistress Ese. Ask anyone."

"Another word, and I'll stuff you in a refuse heap and undertake this task myself."

Evidently Tcha believed Abu, for he clamped his mouth shut and allowed himself to be dragged through the winding, cramped, and littered streets. They hurried down an alley. On one side rose the high wall of a house that marked the beginning of the foreign district. At the corner of the house a shadow separated itself from the darkness in front of Tcha, who immediately yelped. The shadow lunged at him, and a hand fastened over the thief's mouth.

Kysen shoved the struggling Tcha against the opposite wall

of the alley and hissed, "Silence, you simpleton! I don't enjoy touching you, but I'm not letting go until you're quiet."

When Tcha nodded vigorously, Kysen stepped away from him and tried to make out the thief's features in the moonlight. He could see little, but he knew Tcha, an emaciated little wretch who more resembled an embalmed corpse than anything alive. With his bowed legs and scars from numerous punishments from the authorities, Tcha was a leather-skinned, gap-toothed witness to the harshness of the life of a poor Egyptian. Kysen sniffed and took another step away from the thief. Unlike most Egyptians of whatever wealth, Tcha seemed to dislike bathing. Kysen knew that in daylight Tcha's body would be covered with dirt that seemed to have ground itself into his skin, while his hair would lie in greasy plates issuing from the crown of his head. They would snake over his ears and forehead, and down the back of his neck.

Kysen said without much rancor, "I told you to meet me here at full darkness, Tcha."

"Got lost."

Abu loomed over the thief. "You know every crack in every wall of this city."

"I thought you would be eager to be allowed to rob a rich man without fear of arrest for once."

Tcha began to sidle away from Kysen. "O great master, gracious of heart, divine of beauty, my poor talent is of no use to one so powerful."

Abu reached out and clamped a hand around Tcha's neck. Tcha squawked but stopped trying to get away.

Kysen contemplated the scrawny shadow that was the thief. He'd contacted Tcha after his father returned from the palace this morning. The little burglar had been astonished and then greedily pleased that he was to be allowed to rob a merchant's house. He'd agreed to pilfer Dilalu's correspondence in the process. What had happened in the intervening time to put Tcha in such fear?

Kysen darted forward and whispered to Tcha. "You've found out who Dilalu is, haven't you?"

"A merchant. He's a merchant, by the blessings of Amun."

"Correct," Kysen said. "So there's nothing to fear. Bring him, Abu."

Kysen led the way through the streets of the foreign quarter. Here lived traders from the Greek islands and mainland cities, artisans and merchants from the city-states of Byblos, Tyre, Ugarit, and the great lands of the Tigris and Euphrates river valleys. They passed several noisy taverns, encountering shrinking and cloaked figures that vanished as soon as they appeared. Finally they came upon a quieter street. Its only waking inhabitant was a fat, flat-headed cat sitting beside a porter asleep in a doorway. It hissed at them and stalked away in search of a feline fight.

Kysen slithered down a passage beside the cat's house and around the back of the building. There rose a pungent and mountainous refuse heap. At the foot of an exterior staircase, Kysen halted and grabbed Tcha by the arm.

"This is the house. To your work." Tcha squirmed but Kysen tightened his grip and bent down to whisper in the thief's ear. "Listen to me, you carrion feeder. You'll do as you agreed, or I'll send you to the granite quarries."

As he'd expected, the threat of actual work, especially such taxing labor, caused Tcha to become as docile as an aged donkey. The wretch nodded, and Kysen released him.

"Remember, confine yourself to a few metal vessels or jewels."

Kysen watched the thief remove a linen bag from the recesses of his kilt. Tcha hesitated only a short time before scrambling to the staircase. Kysen signaled to Abu, and they melted into the darkness beyond the refuse pile.

Waiting in nighttime always seemed longer than waiting during the day. Kysen pressed his back against a wall and slid down to crouch beside Abu, whose gaze swung in an arc, watching for any hint of trouble. Kysen's back and legs were growing numb when Tcha's head popped over the roof coping. He rose as the thief scrambled downstairs and launched into a foot-pounding run. When his quarry darted past, Abu stuck out his foot. Tcha hit the ground with a smack, but would have jumped to his feet and kept on running if Kysen hadn't grabbed him. Releasing his captive when Abu fastened his hand around Tcha's neck, Kysen snatched the linen bag.

"Empty. Tcha, you're too miserable for the quarries. I'm sending you into the desert—"

"Lord," Abu said. "The wretch is frightened. More than usual, that is."

Kysen peered at Tcha, who was shaking as if he were on some foreign snow-topped mountain. Dropping the bag, Kysen folded his arms and spoke calmly.

"What happened?"

"Merciful Amun protect me." Tcha whimpered and seemed to melt onto the ground, where he groveled at Kysen's feet. "Let us flee this place at once, lord. At once!"

"Not until you explain."

Constantly glancing at the house of Dilalu, Tcha said, "I went up to the roof, me. Like always. There was another sleeping porter there, but I always slide through a roof vent or a window if it's large enough. I got inside through the door this time, and then—merciful Amun." Tcha moaned and began to rock back and forth on his haunches.

"Curse you, Tcha, get on with it," Kysen said. Tcha's fear was beginning to affect his composure.

"Know why there's only sleeping porters on guard? Because inside there's black giants!"

For a moment Kysen's thoughts stilled. Then he asked, "Do you mean the merchant has Nubian guards?"

Tcha's head bobbed so rapidly Kysen was certain it would snap off his neck.

"They was awake. All of them! I went down the inside stairs and nearly ran into them at the bottom, but Amun was watching and slowed my steps. I saw them before they saw me. Dozens of them, all armed with knives and spears and bows and axes and—"

"Tcha!" Kysen snapped.

"Yes, lord."

"Exactly how many did you see?"

Tcha held up his fingers and counted silently. "Eight."

"This—this merchant has eight Nubian bodyguards?" Kysen didn't listen to Tcha's reply. Dilalu employed mercenaries, which he took care to conceal from everyone. "Is that all you saw?"

Tcha whimpered again and said, "Yes, master."

"Then we cannot get inside the house," Abu said.

Kysen rubbed his chin while he thought, then he motioned to Abu. The charioteer snagged Tcha by the arm and followed. Kysen crept back toward the back stair. Once he realized where they were going, Tcha tried to dig in his heels, but his efforts were useless against Abu.

Kysen stopped between the refuse pile and the stair. He gazed up at the reeking mountain thoughtfully. "Abu, Dilalu is an Asiatic."

"Aye, lord."

"Then he uses the wedge-shaped script of the Asiatics, inscribed upon clay tablets." Kysen turned to Tcha. "Thief, you will search the refuse heap for clay tablets."

"But the Nubians!"

"Will not show themselves unless forced to do so. Therefore I would encourage you to be both quick and quiet."

"But—"

Kysen gave a sharp sigh. "Tcha, if you don't do as you're told, I will do what I've been tempted to do since meeting you. I am going to throw you in the Nile to rid your insect-like body of that foul odor. Of course, you'll probably be eaten by crocodiles before that happens."

Tcha danced from one foot to the other as he regarded his persecutor. Evidently he perceived Kysen's determination, for he darted to the refuse mound and began searching through the fetid contents.

"Fear not," Kysen said. "Abu and I will keep watch. If the Nubians come, just burrow into the filth. You should blend in quite well."

Chapter 5

Thebes, the joint reign of the pharaohs Amunhotep III and Akhenaten

Nefertiti stood in her chariot outside the great Sun Temple, waiting for her husband to finish his consultation with the royal architects. Wind whipped her robe around her legs and threatened to topple her high crown. It was dusk, and a day spent arguing with the priests of Amun had tired her. They hated the Sun Temples, all four of them, thrusting as they did against the sacred precinct of Amun.

It seemed a lifetime since she had married Akhenaten, and yet she was only eighteen. Eighteen and a failure. For although she'd become queen when Akhenaten ascended the throne to rule jointly with his father, she had yet to bear a son. Three daughters. Three beloved daughters. Failure. And even more important, she hadn't been able to prevent her husband from taking more and more outrageous steps in his journey toward chaos.

But how could she have foreseen that Akhenaten's elevation to the throne would feed his heresy? Instead of making him the incarnation of Amun, as had happened to all his predecessors, Akhenaten's kingship proved to him that the Aten's plan for him had become manifest. The Sun Temples were one result.

Massive, open, decorated with reliefs in Akhenaten's new style, they were her husband's announcement of his new religion. He even had a sed-festival to mark his revolution. Gone were scenes of pharaoh worshiping his father Amun, who gave him life. On the walls she and Akhenaten were depicted worshiping the Aten. There was even a series of piers on which she and her little Merytaten were depicted making offerings to the Aten.

The Sun Temples disturbed Nefertiti. Oh, pharaohs had built temples since the beginning of the Two Lands, but not like this. Not covered with reliefs that abandoned the graceful precepts of Egyptian artistry. She and Akhenaten were shown with elongated faces, protruding buttocks, exaggerated hips and thighs, and spindly legs. Akhenaten had explained to her how the natural power of the Aten was reflected in this style. She could understand his wish to depart from the formality of the usual temple reliefs, but to go to such an extreme . . .

She had questioned the wisdom of the Sun Temples, tried to convince Akhenaten to build them elsewhere, to no avail. She had tried to mediate between him and the priests of Amun. Her efforts had postponed a formal break for a while, but Akhenaten had never been a tolerant man.

When the priests of Amun refused to change, her husband recalled her advice about building elsewhere. To Nefertiti's astonishment, he decided to build a new city. For the past several years the vast resources of pharaoh had been concentrated in a barren spot in the middle of nowhere. Thousands of laborers, artisans, and architects scrambled to create Akhenaten's planned capital, which he called Horizon of the Aten. Soon the whole family would move there, along with the courtiers and government.

Faced with his son's absolute determination, Amunhotep had decided not to object to the move. Perhaps he'd simply grown tired of fighting with his son. Tiye and Nefertiti both tried to keep them from quarreling, for the confrontations took a toll on Amunhotep's health.

Nefertiti sighed and glanced around her. The court in which her chariot stood was filled with royal attendants. Outside she could hear the clatter of chariots, the clop-clop of donkeys, and the ceaseless tread of bare feet as the rest of the city went about its daily routine. Finally she saw Akhenaten emerge from the temple. He joined her in the chariot, taking the reins from a groom, and set the vehicle in motion. Soldiers ran ahead and behind them, clearing the way. Nefertiti smiled at her husband, but he was glaring at the chariot teams' ears and muttering to himself.

"Is something wrong, husband?"

"The high priest of Amun, he was there lurking behind a statue. He thrust himself into my presence!"

"How odd."

"He dared to argue with me again."

"If you would only be patient, husband."

She jumped as Akhenaten roared at her. "No! It is not for me to be patient. I am pharaoh. I am the son of the Aten, living in truth. My word is truth. If these blasphemers persist in their lies, I'll kill them."

Akhenaten was panting as he guided the chariot. His face had turned carnelian, and his eyes burned like the Lakes of Fire in the netherworld. She had to distract him, or he might actually have the priests executed. Placing a hand on his arm, Nefertiti made her voice hard and sharp.

"I am angry too, husband."

"What have you to be angry about?" he snapped.

"I am angry that so many cause you pain. I would banish all who do so. It is not fitting that your peace be disturbed constantly."

Distracted, Akhenaten gripped the reins with one hand and leaned down to kiss her cheek. "My little warrior. I think you would charge into battle at the head of my armies if I allowed it."

"I would, husband."

Nefertiti found herself enveloped by Akhenaten's free arm, her face pressed against a gold-and-turquoise broad collar. At last she was released. Akhenaten wasn't smiling anymore, though. His eyes were bright with unshed tears as he watched the way ahead.

"You are my champion, little Nefertiti, my love. You alone can I trust never to surrender. You are my general of armies."

She smiled and kissed his cheek, only to be startled by another abrupt change of mood.

"And I'll reward you as you should be rewarded!"

"I need no more jewels, Akhenaten."

"No, not jewels, beloved." He beamed at her while he glanced at her head and neck. "No, you shall have an ornament befitting your warlike spirit. You, my queen, shall wear a war crown."

"But that is the crown worn by pharaoh," Nefertiti protested. "It is a battle symbol."

"That's why you shall wear one I design for you, my little warrior."

She knew better than to argue. Once an idea became fixed within his heart, Akhenaten tended to consider it a divine inspiration. She had grown in wisdom since marrying him. Far better to save her influence for persuading her husband to stop his newly appointed ministers from commandeering a whole granary full of wheat intended for the mortuary temples of Thebes.

Akhenaten glanced down at her again as they neared the quay where the royal barge waited to take them across the river to the palace. "Truly, Nefertiti, you grow in beauty and dignity each day."

She smiled at him. She had learned the art of appearing regal from Queen Tiye; her body was wrapped in gauze, electrum, and precious stones. Green malachite and kohl paint emphasized her eyes. Never did she forget her duty to be beautiful, for Akhenaten's affection was founded upon her appearance. Once, such knowledge would have dismayed her. Now she understood her husband better. To him, her beauty balanced his lack of it, and having so beautiful a wife enabled Akhenaten to say to the world, Look, this magnificent woman loves me; in her eyes I am worthy.

Nefertiti turned away to look at the Nile. Sometimes her heart hurt with pity for Akhenaten. His ka seemed to contain a lost and lonely little boy who never grew older, who never learned to master his pain, and who searched endlessly for relief. Being the wife of such a man was hard; being the wife of such a man who was also pharaoh seemed impossible. She grew weary of her role as his mooring rope, of the constant need to be strong and beautiful.

The chariot stopped, and Akhenaten conducted her to the royal barge through a sea of kneeling onlookers. Once they were on board the gilded vessel, it drifted majestically away from the quay. Nefertiti enjoyed standing at the rail and watching the river traffic. She and Akhenaten surveyed great oceangoing freighters, smaller river boats, the pleasure yachts with their trailing kitchen boats, and the swarm of fishing boats and tiny skiffs.

She glanced over her shoulder when she heard a shout. A boat was being rowed alongside the barge, and a priest of Aten scrambled up a rope to the deck. Carrying a leather document case, the man hurried to Akhenaten, folded his body, and touched his forehead to the deck.

"Ah, Penno, you've finished. Give them to me."

Nefertiti drew closer, wondering what could have been so urgent that the priest would chase after pharaoh in so hasty a manner. Akhenaten unrolled a long sheet of papyrus. She could see that most of the text consisted of lists. She glimpsed a section given to property in the delta. There was a whole page devoted to workshops and another to storehouses holding gifts and spoils of war. She glimpsed another papyrus devoted to property in Upper Egypt, including fields, herds of cattle, and goats. Another section listed personnel—overseers of estates, scribes, soldiers, herdsmen, and a vast array of artisans. A separate sheet detailed foreign possessions, from gold mines in Nubia to whole towns as far north as the Orontes River above Byblos. Nefertiti's gaze caught the number of orchards—over four hundred—the hundreds of thousands of head of livestock, the scores of ships, and the tens of thousands of laborers.

The sheets over which Akhenaten was poring had to be a compilation of the vast riches of the temple of Amun. It couldn't be an accounting of the possessions of the Aten temples, and pharaoh had more riches. Nefertiti turned away to gaze out at the setting sun. This list had been composed by Penno, a prophet of the Aten, not by the Second Prophet of Amun, to whom such an administrative task would have fallen ordinarily.

Why did Akhenaten need a separate list? She already knew the answer. Her husband had broken with Amun, denied his existence, true, but even Nefertiti hadn't guessed the extent of his ruthlessness toward the priests and the god who had defied him. Although the day's heat had yet to give way, she felt a chill spread over her body.

Akhenaten rolled the papyri and handed them to Penno with a satisfied smile. "Excellent. You may begin writing the decrees. My majesty will choose those who will oversee the transfers."

Penno bowed himself out of the royal presence. Nefertiti waited until he was out of hearing range, then dismissed the attendants who fanned them. Waving the royal bodyguards away, she linked her arm through Akhenaten's and gently pulled him next to her. They gazed out at the west bank. The barge was approaching the royal harbor, and she could see waiting ministers and the tiny figures of her daughters, dancing with impatience on the quay. There wasn't much time.

"Akhenaten, you're diverting the revenues of Amun?"

"Of course," he replied as he waved at their daughters. "Did I not say I would?"

"I hadn't realized your decision was set."

Akhenaten looked down at her with a slightly hurt expression. "After your zeal on my behalf, are you surprised? You said—"

"I have no patience with those who offend you, my husband."

She was rewarded with a royal smile.

"However—" The royal smile vanished, but she continued. "However, if you close the workshops, transfer the fields and orchards, divert all the revenues, many will suffer."

"The priests of Amun have had the benefit of my majesty's patience for years," Akhenaten snapped. "They'll have it no longer."

Here was the test of her diplomacy. "Of course, husband.

But it isn't only a question of the priests. There are the families of the priests."

"They should have considered that before defying me."

"Perhaps, but then there are the artisans, the field laborers, the scribes, the—"

"They can work for the Aten."

"Some, perhaps, but there are only a few Aten temples, and they won't be able to use all the labor of those displaced." Akhenaten's face was growing stiff with resistance, so she hurried. "Think of the thousands upon thousands of people who will be cast out, and with them their families and those who served them. Each pr—each worker represents many more who will suffer."

Akhenaten pulled his arm free and confronted her. "All must learn the price of defying pharaoh. By the Aten! Never was a pharaoh so disobeyed. That's why I'm building my new city. I need a place of truth, unsullied by the abominations and falsehoods with which Thebes and Memphis are contaminated."

"This is true, husband, but in withdrawing to the new city, you cause great disruption to those left behind. What will happen to the people of Memphis once pharaoh's patronage is diverted to this place where no city ever was?"

Akhenaten shouted, "Enough!"

She pressed her lips together, folded her arms across her chest, and met his wrath with her own growing irritation. Tiye would have scolded her, but Nefertiti was disgusted with her husband's callousness. After years of diplomatic maneuvering, her patience was at an end. Pharaoh was the shepherd of his people. It was his divine duty to care for them, not make their lives harder than they already were. Nefertiti's eyes narrowed, and she felt her cheeks redden. Without warning, Akhenaten threw back his head and laughed.

"By the Aten, little wife. You're the only one in all of Egypt who dares glare at me. Come, we mustn't quarrel." Akhenaten planted a kiss on her hot cheek.

She would have objected to this sudden end to their conversation, but the barge was docking at the royal quay. Allowing Akhenaten to guide her to the gangplank, she eyed him surreptitiously. His manner was excited, cheerful, and something else. She noted his rapid breathing. By the gods, her defiance had excited him.

As she stepped off the gangplank, Nefertiti was mobbed by her daughters. While she greeted each little girl with a kiss, her thoughts chased each other in a furious attempt to assess this new development. Perhaps Tiye had been wrong. If her defiance excited Akhenaten, might she be able to use it as well as her charm and tact to bring him to see reason?

Lifting the naked and chubby Ankhesenpaaten, Nefertiti followed her husband as he made his way toward the royal palace. She gave half her attention to the happy chattering of her two oldest daughters—Merytaten and Meketaten—and pondered this new discovery. Dared she use defiance as a tool? It had served the priests of Amun ill. But she was Akhenaten's queen, whom he called mistress of happiness, fair of face.

Suddenly she remembered the two colossal statues of himself that Akhenaten had recently shown her. Twice normal size, each was a nude, elongated monster with the feminine attributes Akhenaten insisted upon. A narrow, triangular skull supported the pharaonic headcloth and diadem. The eyes were mere slits, separated by a long, thin nose. The only fullness in the face came from the lips, which protruded with a roundness that was blatantly sensual.

Those statues represented confusion to her. Akhenaten had explained their symbolism, but Nefertiti remained unconvinced. As the son of the Aten, Akhenaten was the font of all regeneration; he was both male and female. Well, pharaoh could be anything he wished, she supposed. But to her, those composite stone creatures represented confusion more than anything else. Akhenaten was confusing, and his reactions to defiance unpredictable. Neither his father nor Tiye had made progress with him by argument. Could she?

Nefertiti felt a tug on her ear. Her youngest was playing with one of her heavy gold-and-carnelian earrings. Disentangling tiny fingers from the jewel, Nefertiti handed the child to her nurse and hurried to catch up with Akhenaten and her older daughters. A quick glance over her shoulder showed the glint of the sun off the electrum-tipped poles and gold-encrusted doors of the temple of Amun.

The dying sunlight caused the facade of the pylon gates to burst into flame and then grow dim. Turning away, Nefertiti shivered. Soon her husband would extinguish the brilliant flame of that place. And she was very much afraid that from pharaoh's sacrilege, misery would flow like the waters of Inundation.

Chapter 6

Memphis, reign of Tutankhamun

The morning after Kysen looted Dilalu's refuse heap, Meren stood under the small loggia attached to his office on the top floor of his town house. The air was suffused with moisture, a sign of Inundation, for the Nile had swelled over its banks to flood the fields of Egypt and deposit its fertile gift of new soil. It was almost dawn, and he could see silver mist floating above the river. The vapor obscured the east bank except for the tallest palms, but its ephemeral cloud was no barrier to the croak of toads or the occasional bleating of goats.

Meren glanced at the bundle of papyri in his hand, but he was distracted by the sight of Bener striding into the granary court, her household records under her arm. She proceeded to direct his steward in the distribution of grain for the day's baking. A splash from the reflection pool deflected his thoughts. He could see Kysen's young son, Remi, toddling around the edge of the water. The child bent down and slapped the water again, causing a duck to squawk and flap its wings and Meren to smile. Isis scurried from the direction of the women's quarters and scooped the child into her arms with an ineffectual admonishment.

Meren's smile vanished. Isis was still avoiding him. Twice now he had lingered after an early-morning meal in the hope that she would remain behind with him rather than hurry away. He'd spoken kindly to her, had done so for days, without response. Isis, his most beautiful and willful daughter, had lost her pride and seemed filled with shame. Meren had never been blind to Isis's lack of humility, but this bent-necked, cringing remorse gave him pain.

The murmur of voices from his office reminded him of his duties. He hadn't yet had time to do more than receive the reports of the men he'd sent to various offices in search of records from Nefertiti's household. He went inside and collapsed on his chair on the master's dais, the focal point of the long room. Stacks of document cases and rolls of papyrus littered the elegant chamber. They obscured the delicate wall paintings and leaned against slender wooden columns.

All three of his scribes had been diverted from their search for old royal records to pursue two tasks he'd given them. Kaha, the best translator of the wedge-shaped characters used by the Asiatics, sat on the floor in the middle of several small piles of clay tablets, deciphering Dilalu's discarded correspondence. Dedi and Bekenamun, called Bek, strode about the office and dug through the piles of documents strewn over every surface. Most of the records had been borrowed from various government departments like the treasury, the chamberlain's office, and the army. Meren had instructed his scribes to trace the career of the military officer known as Yamen.

It seemed years ago, although it had only been weeks, since Kysen had brought word of the three men suspected of being the mastermind behind Nefertiti's murder—Dilalu, Yamen, and Zulaya. Kysen's account of the fear the names of these men inspired hadn't alarmed Meren until his son told him that even the Greek pirate Othrys gripped his sword and spoke of them in a whisper. Othrys was the kind of man who dined on his enemies' entrails and drank their blood.

"Lord."

Meren looked up to find Kaha standing before him with several clay tablets in his hands. "What have you found?"

"You said, lord, that this Dilalu is a dealer in weapons?"

"He also trades in exotic animals, horses."

Gripping a small rectangle of clay, Kaha pointed at a mound of tablets on the floor behind him. "Yes, lord. Those are bills of lading for such items. And the tablets next to them are records of stores of copper arrowheads, spear points, and so on." Kaha held up the rectangular tablet so that Meren could see the lines of angular script. "This, however, is not."

Meren noted the gleam in Kaha's eyes. The youngest son of a minor lord, he was known for his facility with languages.

"Out with it, boy."

"Lord, this is a letter from the chief of a town near Gaza, specifying the number of troops he requires for his payment to Dilalu. Not weapons. Troops. Nubian bowmen." Kaha thrust the tablet under his arm and proffered two more. "These had been damaged. Parts of them are missing, but from what I can decipher, each is to one of Dilalu's customers at the border between the empire and the Hittites. They give the cost for several services—providing weapons, providing infantry, providing chariotry."

Meren heard a crackling sound and looked down to find that he'd crumpled the documents in his hands. He forced his fingers to release and smooth the papyrus.

"So," he said quietly, "Dilalu isn't just a merchant of weapons."

Gathering the tablets in his hands, Kaha smiled proudly and shook his head. "He's a mercenary."

"A clandestine mercenary squatting in pharaoh's capital and sending forth chaos throughout the empire," Meren replied.

Kaha's smile faded.

"You know this matter is not to be spoken of," Meren said.

"Of course, lord."

"Destroy those tablets—no, wait." Meren smoothed his palms over the documents in his lap. "Put them in a records box, Kaha, and hide them."

"But where, lord?"

"Go to the foreign minister's office and put them in the midst of the correspondence from the reign of Amunhotep the Magnificent, may he live forever."

"But the Magnificent ruled for many dozens of years, lord. There is more correspondence there than there are water drops in the Nile."

Meren was shuffling through his papyri. "What? Yes, I know. Don't forget to mark the storehouse and the location of the box within it, or we'll spend years trying to recover it."

"Aye, lord. Lord?"

Meren stopped perusing documents and looked at the young scribe.

"I never would have thought of the foreign records storehouse. How does one acquire such, such—"

"Guile?" Meren asked.

Kaha cleared his throat. "Artfulness," he said with certainty.

"I suppose it's a gift from the gods," Meren said as he ran his finger down a line of hieroglyphs. "That and spending so much time at court."

"Yes, lord." Kaha went back to his tablets with a contemplative expression.

Before Meren could begin to ponder the implications of the scribe's discovery, there was a knock at the door.

"Enter," he called.

When the door swung open to reveal the rounded form of his oldest daughter, Meren dropped his papyri to the floor and went to greet her.

"Tefnut, my rotund little gazelle." He took both her hands and kissed her cheek, leaning over his daughter's large belly. "Are you certain there are still three months before the birth?"

Her face flushed with the exertion of climbing stairs, Tefnut grinned at him and responded breathlessly, "I'm certain. Father, I've something to discuss with you."

"Come sit down."

He led Tefnut to his chair and found a stool for her feet, which were swollen. Tefnut groaned and pulled at the skirt of her loose gown. Kaha brought a tray with a water jar and cups. While Meren poured, Tefnut regained her breath.

"I've missed you, daughter."

"In this large household?" Tefnut swept her arm around, indicating the sprawl of the family town house, the gardens and service buildings, the barracks of the charioteers. "You're too busy to miss me, Father."

Meren handed her a cup. "When you are gone, part of my heart is missing."

Over the rim of the cup, Tefnut's eyes widened, and she swallowed hard. Her surprise was the measure of his guilt. Meren had only recently come to the understanding of how inattentive he'd been toward his daughters. Heedless of their need for his approval, he had given them over to the care of nurses and then his sister after his wife died. In the years that passed, he'd given them brief encouragement, kissed them when they were hurt or especially clever, and sent them on their way. His reward had been to see hopelessness in their eyes. Now he was trying to amend his neglect.

Tefnut seemed speechless, so he went on. "You are my eldest, the first to capture my heart with your toothless little smile."

"Toothless!"

"All babes are born toothless."

"Oh." Tefnut's eyes glittered with unshed tears.

"Daughter, I know you never understood why I adopted Kysen. You resent him, and it's my fault."

Shifting in her chair, Tefnut shook her head. "I don't resent him anymore, Father." She placed a hand on her belly and smiled. "Having this child within me has given me a little wisdom, I think. All parents need a son to carry on for them. Daughters go out of the house, to begin families of their own, to become mistress of a new house. Sons remain behind."

"Do you know how hard it was to see you go from my house to one of your own?" Meren grabbed the water jar and filled another cup.

"I'm sorry, Father."

Sighing, Meren picked up the cup. "It's the way of the world. Where is that big hippo of a husband of yours anyway?"

"Sunero has gone to the docks to buy cedar and spices for us to take home. Which brings me to what I wanted to discuss. I want to take Isis with me when I leave."

"You're leaving already? You just arrived."

"No, I'm not going yet, but when I do, Isis should come as well." Tefnut leaned forward and put her hand on his arm. "I've spoken to Kysen and Bener, and they agree. Isis needs time to grow in wisdom and time to forget her disgrace. She can't do that here with you."

"But I have forgiven her!"

"Which only increases her shame, Father."

Meren threw up his hands. "I don't understand her. She goes from extreme to extreme, from being swollen with pride to prostrate with contrition."

"True," Tefnut said, "but once she is away from the scene of her disgrace, I think she'll begin to sail a more steady course. She just needs calm waters in which to guide her skiff, Father."

Giving his daughter a wry smile, Meren said, "Perhaps you're right. And at least she'll be away from all her admirers. I've had offers of marriage from three men of my acquaintance since I returned to Memphis. But I can't allow Isis to choose a husband until I'm sure she won't drive her mate to insanity."

Tefnut laughed and clutched her belly. "Ooo! I think I woke the babe."

Forgetting about Dilalu and the army officer Yamen, Meren lost himself in wonder as Tefnut guided his hand to feel the kick of his second grandchild. Only two. He was thirty-four and had only two grandchildren. Men his age usually had many more. But Tefnut had been slow in conceiving, and Kysen was divorced from his wife. Bener had so far refused to marry the candidates Meren had suggested, and Isis wasn't ready. Meren was discussing likely husbands for his middle daughter with Tefnut when the summons came from the palace. The king commanded the presence of the Eyes and Ears of Pharaoh.

The king was touring the royal workshops near the palace when Meren responded to his summons. As he left his town house, the scribe Dedi had thrust a thick set of documents in his hands and requested that he read them. Meren held them now as he strode down the avenue between long lines of workshops. The air was filled with the din of hammering and the shouts of workmen. He walked around a stack of cedar logs that had just been delivered from Byblos. The long, straight wood was valued in Egypt almost as much as gold. It was used in rich furniture and in the great warships and royal barges that made Egypt the maritime power that she was.

Although the stack of logs was high and represented a royal fortune, Meren paid it no heed, for he had glimpsed what Dedi had written on the first document. It was a summary of his and Bek's searches into the career of the officer Yamen. The man was the son of a minor noble of Imu, a nome capital in Lower Egypt. Being a younger son and not possessed of a fortune, he'd spent most of his life in the army. Yamen had been fortunate, however, in that his father was a friend of General Nakhtmin, and the general had promoted the young man's interests, assigning him to important jobs in his service.

Yamen had held titles such as scribe of accounts of the division of Amun and scribe of recruits before being assigned to the general's staff. Meren leafed through the documents behind Dedi's summary. The last ten years or so had seen Yamen's rise in importance. He now regularly undertook missions of inspection as a royal envoy to foreign vassals of the empire. Yamen was now a "king's messenger to all foreign lands," but still attached to General Nakhtmin's staff.

Meren pulled an old report from the stack of documents, his footsteps slowing as he walked past a joiner's workshop. The report was a list of rewards. Yamen had received plots of land, gold cups, even the Gold of Valor, yet there was no indication that the officer had ever taken part in battle.

Returning the summary, Meren read that Yamen often had been sent to assess the need when an Asiatic vassal requested

gold, troops, or weapons to defend his city. Bek had noted in
the margin of the summary that three times out of five,
Yamen affirmed the need for pharaoh's generosity to the vassal. And when the aid was sent, the trouble always vanished
immediately.

Meren curled the set of papyri into a roll and tapped it
against his palm. In his experience the majority of requests for
aid were unjustified, the result of the acquisitive nature of
pharaoh's vassals. If Yamen was sending so much aid, there
was a good chance of collusion with the vassal prince or governor. Which meant that the envoy was getting paid for his favorable reports.

And there was something else odd about Yamen's career: he
always seemed to land in positions with access to valuables, or
to information about the movement of goods or men. Most
interesting of all, Dedi reported that Yamen was being considered for the position of royal herald and might be granted
the right of *amakhu*, the right to burial at pharaoh's expense.

"Pharaoh!" He'd forgotten what he was doing.

Meren came out of his reverie and looked around the
workshops. Rolling the papyri tighter, he set off in search of
the king. He walked swiftly, turned a corner, and saw the king
standing in front of a shoulder-high weighing scale set in
front of a guarded building—a precious-metals storehouse.
Only Karoya, pharaoh's chief bodyguard, accompanied the
boy. To the right of the scale stood a scribe recording
amounts of gold and silver. Meren joined the group and
bowed to pharaoh as the scribe's assistant steadied the plumb
bob with one hand and the balance beam with the other.

The scribe piled rough yellow nuggets on one pan, while
the chief goldsmith added weights to the other. On the
ground lay a basket of extra weights. Some were shaped like
domes, others like ox heads. One was formed in the image of

a hippo. Meren watched the goldsmith add an ox head to his side of the scale. The pan was still higher than the gold.

"Not enough," the king said. He reached for a stone ox head and put it on the pan next to the other weights. The pan tipped, then slowly settled into balance. "Excellent." Tutankhamun turned to Meren. "Ah, there you are. You're late, Meren. It's not like you."

"Forgive me, majesty."

Around them the hammering, sawing, and yelling rose, and the king smiled. "I forgive you, Meren, because it's not often I catch you in even a small fault."

The king signaled for Meren to walk beside him as he left the gold storehouse. Leading Meren and his guard, Tutankhamun crossed a path to the other side of the workshop district. When they reached a particularly noisy area near the main workshop of the master stone carver Thutmose, pharaoh stopped. Karoya turned his back and moved a few paces away to stand with his legs braced apart. He folded arms the size of oxen over his chest and glared at anyone who came within forty paces.

"Come closer," Tutankhamun said to Meren. "I don't want anyone to hear."

"Yes, majesty."

Meren moved as near as he dared, within a small stride of the king. To go closer risked arousing curiosity and provoking gossip. His efforts were foiled when the king closed the distance between them to half a pace.

In a loud whisper, the king said, "Maya says that all the secret tombs are complete and that my brother's whole family is safe in the royal cemetery in Thebes." Tutankhamun glanced around, his eyes guarded, his jaw muscles twitching with tension. "I put Akhenaten and Nefertiti with my mother. You were right. It was the only place that might be safe from those who would destroy them."

"Thy majesty is wise."

"You think it a good choice?"

That strained look had come into the boy's face. Meren felt a pang of sympathy for the king. It hadn't been long since someone had broken into Akhenaten's tomb in Horizon of the Aten and desecrated the king's body.

The news had devastated Tutankhamun. His memories of Akhenaten were of a somewhat eccentric brother old enough to be his father. Nefertiti had been a second mother. The idea of someone hacking at Akhenaten's body was horrific. If his body was destroyed, his soul would have no place to lodge, and it would wander, homeless and desolate. Eventually it would perish. It was this possibility that impelled Meren to conceal from Tutankhamun the extent of the damage done to the heretic pharaoh's body—and the fact that Nefertiti had been murdered while the boy lived with her.

"Thy majesty has made the best of choices, for Queen Tiye was revered by all. Few would look for Akhenaten in her house of eternity, and no one would think of desecrating it."

Meren was rewarded for his assurance by seeing the fear and tension drain from the king's young features. Letting out a long breath, Tutankhamun resumed his tour of the royal workshops. As they passed, artisans paused to kneel and touch their foreheads to the ground. By pharaoh's order, however, they resumed their work immediately. Tutankhamun was constantly trying to avoid ceremony, to the dismay of Ay and his courtiers.

"I have just had more reports of people absconding with conscripts," Tutankhamun said as they walked up to a jeweler's studio. Dozens of artisans sat before stone slabs, cutting inlay from chunks of lapis lazuli, turquoise, and other precious stones. "The priests of Amun waylaid thirty-two laborers bound for the temple of Ra in Heliopolis. There were more reports, but I am more troubled about something else."

"The stolen gold, majesty?"

"Maya told you."

"He said that the Nubian gold expedition was attacked in the desert and lost much of its shipment."

Pharaoh scowled at Meren. "And if I'd been on that expedition, I could have gotten that battle experience you've been promising me for months."

"It's too near the time of the feast of Opet, golden one."

"You always have a good excuse to keep me away from battle, Meren, but I'm not going to be patient much longer. As soon as I have report of a suitable opportunity, you and I are going on a raid against bandits."

"I know thy majesty wishes to prove himself in battle, but—"

"I won't listen, Meren. You've trained me yourself. Am I not a good warrior?"

"Of course, majesty. But—"

Tutankhamun held up his hand. Meren shut his mouth and trained a severe look on his king. Few would dare give such a look to the living god, but Meren had served the king since he was a child.

"None of this is why I summoned you," the king was saying. "I have heard a rumor, Meren. One concerning you."

"There are many such, majesty. They outnumber the grain in the royal storehouses."

"This one is different. It is said that you tried to seduce Yia."

Meren stopped, his jaw coming unhinged. "Who, majesty?"

"Princess Yia, wife of Prince Hunefer."

"How can I have seduced her, golden one? I don't even remember her."

A mischievous smile flitted across the king's face. "Prince Hunefer complained of it to me last night. He says they were at the feast of welcome you held for Tefnut and Sunero, and during an acrobatic performance, she vanished and so did you."

"Hunefer has the wits of a gnat," Meren said with a snort. "He lives in constant fear that his wife will betray him. And I know why."

"Why?"

Ignoring the king's smirk, Meren said, "Because Hunefer has no chin and very little forehead. He looks like a green monkey in a kilt, and he knows it."

No longer able to control himself, Tutankhamun burst into laughter. Karoya, who was ahead of them, turned his head briefly in surprise, and Meren glimpsed the curl of his lip. Even the stone-faced Nubian was laughing at him! Fuming, Meren crumpled the papyri he was holding and trudged beside the king toward the chariot workshop.

"Don't scowl so," the king continued. "You're the one who is always admonishing me for my gravity."

Relenting, Meren gave the king a smile he usually reserved for his children. It disappeared with Tutankhamun's next question.

"What have you discovered about the death of my old guard in the menagerie?"

"The guard?"

The king halted and stared at him. "You forgot?"

Blinking, Meren shook his head. "The guard. Yes, the guard. I've entrusted the inquiry to my aide Abu, majesty. No doubt he has already gone to the embalmers to inspect the body."

"I remember Abu," Tutankhamun said slowly while he fixed a steady gaze on Meren.

"If thy majesty desires, I will go myself."

"No, no. I trust Abu." The king began to walk again. "Then you will have something to report soon."

"Yes, majesty."

"You won't forget? You've been distracted lately, Meren."

"One does not forget the commands of the living god, majesty."

"Platitudes, Meren. You really are not yourself. Are you overburdened?"

"No, majesty."

"Then what ails you?"

"Naught, golden one. Perhaps I am a little concerned with my youngest daughter."

"Isis," the king said with a nod. "I know."

Meren said nothing. No discussion was necessary, for the king was privy to all that had occurred the night Meren almost lost his life to Eater of Souls due to Isis's carelessness. He preferred that the golden one assume that his distraction was due to family problems; he didn't want to reveal his suspicions about Queen Nefertiti's death. Pharaoh had far too many burdens for a youth, the burdens of a vast empire, an intrigue-ridden court, and a kingdom still in turmoil in the aftermath of heresy. He didn't need the unhappiness of suspected murder added to the load he carried.

Looking down at the crumpled papyrus roll in his hands, Meren remembered Yamen. He would contrive a meeting with the officer at once. Even if the man had nothing to do with the queen's murder, he was worth watching. As Meren was the Eyes and Ears of Pharaoh, it was his responsibility to ferret out such sources of corruption.

They were making their way back through the workshop complex in the wake of Karoya's majestic progress when a royal messenger came running up to the king and threw himself at pharaoh's feet. He presented a folded message.

Opening the papyrus, Tutankhamun read swiftly and looked up at Meren with a grin. "At last! Bandits are reported north of the great pyramids. They're raiding villages, and I should have word of their movements in a few days."

"No doubt they've already fled the area, majesty."

"No. These bandits are bold. They raid several villages on successive nights before running away. Be ready to leave at any time, Meren."

"Yes, majesty."

It had come. He had run out of excuses to delay the boy, and now he must fulfill his promise. Meren rubbed his head, which was beginning to ache. He didn't want to think of the possibilities, but in his imagination, he could see himself returning from the raid with the king's lifeless body in his arms. There was no heir, and Tutankhamun was adored. The kingdom would be plunged into chaos.

"Be of good cheer," the king said. "How dangerous can a passel of barbarian thieves be?"

Chapter 7

Memphis, reign of Tutankhamun

Several days after his expedition to Dilalu's house with the pungent Tcha, Kysen was in a desert wadi along with a dozen other noblemen. He breathed the cool morning air in deeply. Around him teams of horses snorted and pawed the rocky ground where the hunting party had gathered.

He, his father, and many of their friends had come to this barren place in the eastern desert of Memphis at Prince Djoser's request, to join in his gazelle hunt. Meren had almost refused to go and witness yet another of Djoser's awkward attempts to prove himself skilled at killing. Then Kysen had suggested that the hunting party would afford the excuse to meet Yamen for which they'd been searching. It was better than contriving a visit to General Nakhtmin's headquarters, for Meren seldom paid such calls. His own duties kept him far too busy.

Kysen caught his father's eye. Meren was talking quietly with Prince Djoser, and as he finished, the prince called to a man holding the reins of a team of white stallions. Meren turned away and began a conversation with the head groom while Djoser brought the stranger and his chariot over to Kysen.

"Kysen, may the blessings of Amun be with you, and many thanks for joining my party."

"I'm always honored by your invitation, Djoser."

"I present Yamen to you, Kysen. He has hunted with me before, but never when you have been along. He's known for his driving skill, and I thought to give you an advantage by making him your driver."

Kysen inclined his head in regal acceptance of the compliment. It had taken him years to learn the attitude appropriate to the son of the hereditary prince and Friend of the King, Lord Meren. In the thoughts of his heart he was still a bruised and dirty little boy running in the streets of the tomb makers' village in Thebes and trying to forget his father's latest beating.

"Yamen," he said. "Have I not heard of an officer of the army called Yamen? Yes, a recipient of the Gold of Valor."

"The lord Kysen does me honor to remember," Yamen said.

The man wasn't what Kysen had anticipated. He had expected a man of his father's years, an oily, ingratiating serpent and place seeker. Yamen appeared much older than Meren, whose sharp features bore few of the lines of age. Perhaps it was that Yamen's hair had deserted him except for a thin fringe of closely cropped hair that circled his skull. The dome of his head was well-shaped, no ugly scars or protrusions, and he had a sharp little nose that balanced the dome.

Yamen was short, like a peasant whose farm yields enough grain to survive but not enough to thrive. But the lack of height was deceiving. His body was slight but wide of shoulder and obviously blessed with sinewy strength. Kysen decided that the man ought to be able to handle a pair of stallions with ease. Indeed, Yamen appeared to be everything Meren's inquiries had revealed he was not—a brave and experienced warrior.

"Have no fear, Lord Kysen."

Surprised, Kysen could only repeat the word. "Fear?"

"I know how I appear to the world," Yamen said with a wry smile. He spread his hands and chuckled. "A little man dwarfed by the horses and by his companions. I'm not the image of a hero one beholds on the walls of great tombs and monuments. But I've killed a few lions, and none can best me in a chariot race."

In spite of himself, Kysen had to return Yamen's grin. He'd never have supposed that this corrupt officer would have the grace to laugh at his own shortcomings. Now that he thought of it, Kysen had met few of noble birth blessed with this quality. His father had it, but Meren was different from most highborn and pampered courtiers. Something had happened to his father—Kysen suspected at the heretic's hands—that had burnt to ashes any false sense of magnificence.

"Then we'll be the first in the hunt," Kysen said.

Yamen slapped one of his white stallions lightly on the shoulder. "I can promise it. We'll be driving the best team in Memphis."

Kysen took his bow from a servant while Yamen hopped into the chariot with practiced ease. He joined the officer in the vehicle. Checking the spear case and quiver mounted on the side of the vehicle, Kysen heard the clatter of hooves all around them as the party set out. Already dust rose from the chariot wheels and wafted into his face.

Djoser drove through the moving vehicles to their side and shouted, "The chief huntsman says the gazelles are headed for the next valley. We'll wait for them to enter it before giving chase."

Kysen surveyed the desert terrain while they drove. Limestone cliffs rose in the distance to the north and south. Once the air grew hot, hawks would appear, coasting on invisible waves, watching for the slightest movement. The chariots slowed as the chief huntsman pointed at the gazelle herd, disappearing into the valley ahead. Barely visible in the dawn light, the animals picked their way across the rocks.

Kysen glanced at the hunting party. Many were charioteers, highborn, trained in the hard traditions of the imperial military and proud of their skill. He could hear them teasing Djoser for proposing to use nets to trap their quarry.

Yamen raised his voice over the clatter of the chariots as they drove alongside Djoser's vehicle. "Come, Djoser. Our friends are right. Using nets and dogs isn't sport. Let us test our skill."

"You'd give chase without the dogs?" Kysen asked as he braced his feet on the floor of the chariot.

"Is such a hunt beyond your skill?" Yamen asked with a challenging grin.

Kysen touched the dagger of bronze and gold thrust into his belt. "Not if it isn't beyond yours."

They approached the valley entrance slowly. Rock cliffs closed in on either side of them. They jutted up to the sky, sheer as the walls of a pyramid. The howl of a jackal echoed down the valley from them. One of the noblemen uttered a charm of appeasement to Anubis, jackal god of the underworld.

The gazelles were still well ahead, and there was much discussion as to who would lead this netless chase. Finally Yamen spoke loudly.

"I wager my new foal that Kysen and I can bring down the first animal."

Silence fell among the men, who glanced at each other in surprise at the value of the wager. Kysen met his father's stare with a slight smile. He could tell that the officer's obtrusive manner and arrogance were beginning to annoy Meren. His father started to speak.

"Why should there be a wager—"

"A wager it is!"

Kysen looked over his shoulder at the speaker, Lord Tharwas. He should have known Tharwas would match the wager. He was a friend, but Kysen wasn't blind to his rashness.

"It's arranged, then," said Djoser. "Kysen and Yamen will lead."

Yamen drew in his reins while Kysen shook his head ruefully and knocked his bow. The rest of the party dropped back. Kysen braced his feet. One hand gripped his weapon; the other held on to the chariot rail.

He waited, relishing the cool silence, the threatening quiet of the desert his people called the Red Land. He put his hand over the eye-of-Horus amulet at his neck and prayed for strength and skill, clasped the chariot rail again, and nodded to Yamen.

The officer slapped the reins; the vehicle lurched forward and gained speed. Kysen could hear the pound of hooves as the team broke into a gallop. He narrowed his eyes against the wind and sand and set his legs as he felt Yamen's body lean to guide the horses around a boulder. Surprised, he realized that the two of them had the ability to speak to each other without words that was essential between driver and bowman. He hadn't thought to find himself attuned to this corrupt man.

Ahead the gazelles flew with speed born of terror. Beside him Yamen moved a leg so that Kysen was between it and the chariot wall. With this mute warning Kysen had time to cling to the rail with both hands. The chariot jolted and spanned a crevice in the valley floor, then regained speed so quickly that Kysen gave a shout of joy. The swiftness and the excitement of the chase sent fire racing through his veins.

Yamen laughed and plied his whip. They drew closer to a young straggler. Together he and Yamen took up the shooting stance, Yamen using his body to brace Kysen as he let go of the chariot to draw back an arrow. Careful to draw all the way even with his ear, Kysen steadied himself in the chariot, waited for the animal to take a long leap, and let the arrow fly. It hit the gazelle, and the creature plunged to the ground with the arrow embedded in its abdomen. Kysen drew another arrow from the quiver mounted on the side of the chariot while Yamen aimed their vehicle at another target.

Suddenly the gazelles veered right. Delicate hooves scrambled across the rock and sand. The herd leaped across the path of the chariot, and Yamen hauled at the reins. The stallions screamed, and the chariot bucked. Clutching the railing, Kysen swore and glanced around the desert. Prey never ran toward predator.

Heart thudding in his chest, he scanned the rocks to their left while Yamen struggled to control the rearing horses. On a ledge above them there was a blur of yellow and brown. Kysen turned toward it without thinking and raised his bow. At the same time he let out a war cry. The tawny mass came hurtling at him. He released his arrow, but the thing kept coming. It landed on him, taking the chariot with them in a crash to the ground. The horses screamed, and Yamen shouted.

Somehow Kysen managed to draw his dagger while flying to the ground. He landed on his back, and the air rushed from his lungs as he was buried beneath fur and muscle. He stabbed with the dagger, even though he knew it was useless. Expecting to be torn apart by teeth and claws, he felt a jolt that shook the body on top of him. A bony foreleg smashed into his head, and he lost control of his body. He breathed in the smell of blood before darkness claimed him.

"Kysen."

Kysen tried to ignore the voice that pestered him. He was asleep, and it was too much effort to wake up. The voice raised in command.

"Kysen, listen to me. Breathe deeply."

Someone was shaking him and splashing water in his face, and people were making a great noise all around him. For long moments his thoughts seemed like sleepy crocodiles paddling through muddy water in the heat of the day.

Then he remembered. "The lion!"

His eyes popped open as he tried to rise. His arms flew up to protect his face. Meren grabbed his jaw and made Kysen look at him.

"The lion is dead, Ky."

Chest heaving, his face damp more from a cold sweat than from the water his father had splashed on him, Kysen nodded. Meren's hand left his face. Kysen managed a smile to reassure his father, whose own features were graver than an embalmer priest's.

Yamen pushed between Djoser and Tharwas to beam at him. "Well done. We killed the beast together."

Kysen sat with his forearms on his knees and closed his eyes against the morning sun. When he opened them, he was surrounded by hunters. A few wore anxious expressions. Most grinned at him. Yamen straightened and let out a shout that was taken up by the men waiting with the horses. Kysen felt a chill run through him, a chill of pleasure. These men were saluting him. With a jolt he realized that they no longer thought of him as Meren's low-born adopted son. When had that happened, and why hadn't he noticed until now?

Yamen was still grinning at him. "Behold, Kysen."

The hunters parted to reveal the carcass of a young male lion. He could see his arrow protruding from the animal's chest. A javelin was sunk deep in its back. Meren offered his hand. Kysen grasped it and rose, and together they walked over to the body. Yamen joined them and pointed at several gashes in the lion's fur. They were black with old blood. A part of the animal's muzzle had been ripped away, exposing the bone.

Yamen grasped the blood-flecked mane. "He must have lost a battle with another male."

"Such injuries would drive him mad with pain," Meren said. "I don't think he would have charged otherwise."

Kysen tried not to think of those gaping jaws and curved, yellow teeth.

Yamen slapped him on the back. "You don't look well. You should sit down. He landed on you hard enough to flatten you like a papyrus sheet."

Kysen sat on a rock. Meren brought an earthenware canteen and made him drink. About them the hunters busied themselves checking reins and examining horses for injuries. Glad not to be the object of everyone's attention, Kysen watched Yamen direct several men in binding the carcass for transport back to Memphis. Then he heard Meren whisper.

"I should kill him at once."

Startled, Kysen glanced up at the lean, elegant figure of his father. "Why?"

Meren's gaze—hard as pyramid stone and cold as obsidian—was fixed on Yamen. Without taking his eyes from the officer, he handed Kysen his dagger. It was stained with the lion's blood.

"He couldn't have known the lion would be there," Kysen said.

Meren shot a severe look at Kysen. "You defend him?"

"There's nothing to defend. It was chance that the lion hunted the same quarry that we did."

"I like it not that the first time we seek out this corrupt army officer, he nearly gets you killed."

Kysen began rubbing his dagger with sand. "If he'd wanted to kill me, he would have let the lion have me."

There was silence while Meren continued to shred Yamen with a razorlike gaze. "There is another possibility."

"Yes?"

"He deliberately sought danger in order to impress us."

At Kysen's skeptical look, Meren went on. "Think for a moment. The man is a place seeker and a purveyor of corruption, and this is the first time he has been invited to hunt in a party of great men, in a group of which I'm a part."

"You think he wanted to catch your attention."

Meren nodded almost imperceptibly. Then he smiled. It was a smile that had seen rivers of blood on the battlefields of the empire, a smile that lurked in dark alleys and behind sacrificial altars.

"And if he has put himself to so much trouble, we should reward him," Meren said.

"We should?" Kysen wiped the dagger on his kilt and sheathed it.

Meren didn't answer. He raised his voice and called to Yamen. By the time the officer was with them, Meren's features had assumed one of the countless masks Kysen had come to recognize. A twinge of pity caught him by surprise as he watched Meren turn upon his victim that disarming and gracious smile that had been the downfall of greater men than Yamen.

"I haven't yet thanked you for saving my son's life, Yamen."

The officer made a low bow. "I but assisted Kysen, lord."

"Without your javelin, I'd be dead," Kysen said.

Meren nodded. "And without your skill with the chariot, you'd both be lion's meat." Hauling Kysen to his feet, he grasped the arms of both men, held them high, and shouted to the hunting party. "Lion killer!"

The men gave an answering shout. "Lion killer!" The nobles matched the shout with a salute of dagger and spear.

Meren released them and turned to the officer. "Come, Yamen, ride back with me. I would know more about the man to whom I owe so much."

Left to himself, Kysen went over to the team of white stallions, which had been examined by the grooms and pronounced fit. Had Yamen seen the lion and aimed the chariot for it? A shiver rippled through his body. From his record, Kysen had assumed the officer to be cowardly and corrupt, but what kind of madman risked being savaged by such an animal? What ambitions demanded so perverse an impulse? Or so desperate a distraction.

He got into the chariot and drove it over to Meren's. Yamen stood beside his father, smiling. Kysen had seen that same look of glutted satisfaction. Where? Ah, on Isis's pretty face. He'd seen her smile like that when she'd attracted the attention of yet another handsome courtier.

Just then his father laughed at some comment Yamen made. It was an easy, musical laugh that sent warning trumpets blaring in Kysen's ears. Such ease of manner, such charm and courtliness. With that remarkable ability of his, Meren had sensed danger. The laugh, the manner, told Kysen that Yamen's fate had been decided. Deserved as that fate might be, he found himself pitying the man who had just saved his life.

Chapter 8

Thebes, the independent reign of the pharaoh Akhenaten

The hawk had flown to the sun. That was the way one re-ferred to the death of a living god. The royal family had left the isolation of pharaoh's new city and returned to Thebes for the funerary ceremonies of Amunhotep the Magnificent. Egypt grieved, not only for the old pharaoh but for herself.

On the evening after the Magnificent was sealed in his tomb, Nefertiti sat in her personal sailing vessel and watched the black waters of the Nile flow by. Painted red, green, and gold, the boat slid across the water like hot oil on polished granite. Streams of golden light from the boat's torches marked her progress along the canal toward the quay in front of her father-in-law's mortuary temple. The hawk had flown to the sun, and one of the strongest foundation stones of Nefertiti's life had vanished.

So much had happened in the past few years. Fulfilling his promise, Akhenaten had taken her, the family, and the entire government of Egypt to his newly built city, Horizon of the Aten. Her husband's choice of a site for his capital was in keeping with his unpredictability. Instead of selecting a place where there were green fields, a place with access to the busy cities of the delta or the all-important Nubian territory, he chose a barren, empty plain.

Lying between Memphis and Thebes, this plain was startling in its vastness, stretching as it did from the Nile to the distant cliffs of the eastern desert. And it was drab. No starkly beautiful desert reds and creams here, just pale tans and grays, and only the sky offered any color. On the opposite bank lay fields, scattered and sparse. To Nefertiti, Horizon of the Aten was a place of emptiness.

In the past few years Akhenaten had closed many of the old temples, especially those of Amun and his goddess wife, Mut. All work on the Theban Sun Temples had ceased, and Nefertiti feared that many of her predictions were coming to pass. Word reached her from Memphis and other places of the suffering of the displaced and neglected.

She had overcome her disappointment at failing to bear a son, to carry on the royal line; and now she had just learned she was to bear another child. Her daughters were growing from precocious little top-heavy creatures into slim girls. Merytaten, the oldest, already copied the manners of her mother and spoke with becoming gravity and stateliness to her royal father. She and her sisters were golden orbs lighting Nefertiti's days.

The children had provided comfort during the long fading of Amunhotep the Magnificent. Not long ago, the old man had succumbed to a disease of the mouth and gums and to corpulence and old age. To the last, Queen Tiye remained at his side, refusing to allow him to give way to pain and desperation. He left behind a kingdom swirling in a whirlpool of dissent, and two younger sons, the children of his old age. The youngest was but an infant, and Nefertiti had taken over his care when Tiye gave way to despair upon her husband's death.

Despair. Nefertiti frowned as she stared at the oars plied by the sailors in a rhythm coordinated by drumbeats. As well as she knew Akhenaten, she couldn't have predicted that years of argument and impotent commands by his father would fail to dissuade Amunhotep's son from his radical course. The old pharaoh had even enlisted the support of his other wives in the fight, but that only gave Akhenaten a violent distaste for the most vocal of them—poor Tadukhipa of Mitanni.

Nefertiti was afraid that Akhenaten's resentment of his father had spilled over to contaminate Tadukhipa and the whole kingdom of Mitanni. She had warned Queen Tiye and Amunhotep, but the prejudice had already crept into Akhenaten's heart. This was an evil happening, for Mitanni had been an ally to Egypt and served as a bulwark against the encroaching Hittites. Sometimes Nefertiti suspected that if his father had hated Mitanni, Akhenaten would have loved the kingdom.

Shortly before Amunhotep's death Nefertiti had taken over the queen's network of messengers, spies, and informants, with Akhenaten's agreement. Worn out with nursing her husband, weighed down with grief, Tiye had given Nefertiti lists of cities and agents and sent all messengers to her successor.

"Pay attention to any word from Rib-Addi, king of Byblos, and all that comes to you regarding Aziru of Amurru," Tiye had said. She handed Nefertiti yet another list. "These are the chiefs and small kings who can't be trusted. They will prostrate themselves before pharaoh and spout all sorts of servile blandishments in order to convince Akhenaten to give them gold and troops."

"Yes, Aunt."

"Watch the trade routes, Nefertiti. Trade is vital, and any who interfere with it must be crushed. However, it's often a simple matter to quell unrest. Demand that the vassals near the trouble solve the problem. It's far easier for them to round up bandits than they'd have you believe."

Thus had she inherited another royal task, one for which Akhenaten had little liking. And now Amunhotep the Magnificent was dead, and the strongest curb on her husband's bizarre nature had vanished. Tiye said that they were fortunate that Nefertiti had borne children to steady him somewhat. Nefertiti wasn't so certain.

It was true that his attitude toward her had changed after the girls were born. Before, she had been his beautiful and amusing younger companion. When Merytaten came, he fell in love with the babe. He was already enamored of the mysteries of nature, and the force of creation became much more personal to him with the births of his own children. Akhenaten's wonder grew to include and envelope Nefertiti as well. Then his fascination with her had taken an unpredictable turn.

Akhenaten proclaimed her the fount of life for his new religion, the royal spouse of the Son of the Sun. He'd given her a new title—Exquisite Beauty of the Sun Disk. She remembered how, more and more, he had brought her forward during royal ceremonies and state occasions. Nefertiti found that her husband listened to her as an equal rather than as an entertaining child. The change had irritated her as much as it gratified her. She was no cleverer after becoming a mother than she had been before the girls' births.

With the growth of her influence over her husband came added risks. She'd become the focus of court intrigue. Noblemen who had barely noticed her now fawned over her as they had over Queen Tiye. Such hypocrisy was even more irritating than Akhenaten's unaccountable change of attitude. Sometimes, after days spent navigating the white-water rapids of the court, Nefertiti longed for the peace and obscurity of her childhood.

Most of all, she longed for the comfort of Amunhotep's presence. The old pharaoh had been so kind to her. He'd encouraged her to be brave, assumed that she was as clever of heart as his wife, protected her from the more dangerous members of his lascivious and jaded court. As long as Amunhotep had been alive, she had been merely Queen Nefertiti, wife of the junior ruler. Now she was much more. She was the great royal wife, She Who Was Pure of Hands, Great King's Wife Whom He Loves, and Lady of the Two Lands, beloved of the great living sun disk.

Being the great royal wife meant that she was no longer an apprentice. She was queen of Egypt, and the future seemed as unpredictable and dark as the river's black water. Nefertiti sighed when her sailing vessel gently bumped the quay. Her chief bodyguard, Sebek, helped her out of the boat. Half Nubian, with the height of a temple column and a face like a brooding jackal, Sebek didn't approve of this night visit to the mortuary temple on the west bank, but Nefertiti needed comfort. She was not yet twenty-one, mistress of an empire, wife of a man whose ideas and actions threatened his own kingdom.

She needed solace. Facing the grand facade of the mortuary temple, she walked down the paved avenue toward the pylon gate that marked the entrance. Sebek was at her heels, grumbling. Chosen by Tiye, he was a mature warrior, a commander of infantry and charioteers, and looked upon Nefertiti with a fatherly concern that sometimes grew irksome.

Nefertiti ignored Sebek's muttering and paused before the soaring images of the dead pharaoh that guarded Amunhotep's pylon gate. Carved of magic-stone, they represented pharaoh seated in majesty. They towered above her so high she could barely make out their eyes. Not that it would matter, for the statues stared ahead over her and everyone else below.

Sebek snapped an order at the two guards who accompanied them. Despite his glowering disapproval, Nefertiti was determined to make a food offering. She hoped to entice her father-in-law's spirit with a few dessert cakes made by the chief cook of the House of Rejoicing. Then he would appear as the ba, the human-headed bird, that manifestation of the deceased's personality that traveled between the tomb and the netherworld. Now that the king was no longer plagued by disease, he could enjoy the sweets he'd loved so by taking the form of the ba bird.

It took her a while to get past the astonished priests on duty, but at last she entered the dark cella that contained the offering table. With her box of cakes in one hand and a lamp in the other, she approached the slab of alabaster. Sebek waited at the door. Nefertiti scowled at him, and the warrior turned his back. Placing the lamp on the floor, she set the box on the altar and recited a spell. She had to get the words right. It was important in magic to repeat words of power in their exact order. She finished without a mistake and sat down on the floor before the altar to wait.

Nefertiti wrapped her arms around her bent legs and concentrated on the low relief behind the offering table. It portrayed Amunhotep in his prime, as Nefertiti had never known him. The artist had made Amunhotep's nose too long.

Nefertiti could smell the scent of flowers, bouquets and wreaths from the funeral. Beside the altar lay a scrap of material. She picked it up. It was from a mourning tunic, one of the blue-white linen garments made by the women of the royal household. At the funeral the women mourners had cried, thrown dust and ashes on themselves, and rent the tunics.

The frayed linen brought back too-clear memories of the funeral. The ritual of burial had been a shock. Although preparing for the afterlife occupied a great deal of one's lifetime, Amunhotep's funeral taught Nefertiti that the utilitarian business of mortuary endowments and collecting funerary furniture afforded little protection from the reality of death. Seeing her father-in-law's mummy on its boat-shaped bier had frightened her. Until then she had managed to remember Amunhotep as a vital, laughing man who delighted in good food and the caress of a woman. Now he was a thing of gold and precious stones, an unbearably remote product of metalsmiths and carpenters. The face created by those strangers was the face of cold eternity.

During the ceremonies she had kept her eyes averted from the mummy until her aunt threw herself at the foot of the coffin and screamed. Nefertiti had never before heard Tiye so much as raise her voice. Aunt was the essence of serenity, always in control. She had ruled with her husband, helped plan great temples, and tricked foreign ambassadors with aplomb.

Nefertiti sat in the dark chamber with her arms clutching her knees and tried not to remember her aunt's screams, but the memory forced its way to her heart. Tiye's grief had been terrible to witness—the great royal wife, mighty of strength, lay shattered. Tiye's disintegration, even more than Amunhotep's death, shook Nefertiti's world and left her more frightened than she had ever been. The death of pharaoh was awful but could be endured; her aunt's grief was a nightmare.

Drawing in a breath, Nefertiti let it out slowly and pressed her fingertips to her forehead. Her greatest worry had been that Akhenaten would interfere with the king's proper burial ritual in the name of his new god and thus deny the old king eternal life. He'd promised Tiye a traditional burial, but Akhenaten often changed decisions.

Her fears had been for nothing. Akhenaten officiated as priest, performing the ceremony of the Opening of the Mouth so that Amunhotep could eat, drink, and speak again. Her husband even attended the banquet after the funeral without treating the family and courtiers to a harangue about the Aten. Nefertiti was anxious to leave Thebes before being in the city of Amun aroused Akhenaten's fanaticism.

Nefertiti shifted her position so that she rested on one hip. The lamplight flickered. A shadow shaped like a wing moved across the face of the offering table. Nefertiti got to her knees and reached out with one hand. Was it the dead king's soul, come in bird form to visit her?

Suddenly a shout made her whirl around to face the door. As she moved, the wing shadow vanished. The shout had come from another room. Sebek too was looking in the direction of the shout, his hand on the scimitar at his belt. There was another shout, louder this time. Alarmed, Nefertiti ran out of the cella. Sebek launched himself after her, and they raced through the temple until they reached the outer hall. Great papyrus-bundle columns flanked an open court, where a crowd milled around two men.

Sebek thrust an arm in front of Nefertiti. "I'll go first, my queen." He gripped the hilt of the scimitar and walked up to the group of men. Nefertiti was close at his back. Sebek stopped beside a young priest at the edge of the crowd. "Make way for the great royal wife Nefertiti."

Shaved heads turned. Backs bent, and bodies scuttled to the side. They made their way to the crowd's center, where two men were shouting at each other as if they were in a beer tavern. Nefertiti recognized Wadjnas, chief priest of the mortuary temple. The man's face was contorted with fury, and he clutched the folds of a hastily donned robe. A wig sat awry his bald head until he clamped it straight with his free hand.

Wadjnas roared at the man facing him. Mery-Re. What was the high priest of the Aten doing in pharaoh's house of eternity? That was the question Sebek voiced in Nefertiti's name. The arguing ceased at once, and there was a moment of quiet while the men bowed low before Nefertiti. Although both men appeared startled at the presence of their queen, Wadjnas recovered first.

"Majesty, this—this *heretic* is going to erase the names of the gods. He says pharaoh ordered it. He says he will even wipe out the name of Osiris."

Nefertiti heard a mass intake of breath from the other priests. Her insides churned, and she waited for the gods to rend Mery-Re into small pieces. Osiris, renewer of life, the god who died and had been reborn—such a blasphemy could not be imagined. And yet these newcomer priests seemed confident in their sacrilege; she could see their puffed-up conviction in their faces. For years Akhenaten had been recruiting obsequious men whose sole qualification for membership in the Aten priesthood was a blind acceptance of his religious decrees. This was the result.

"The divine Son of the Sun orders the names of the usurpers to be expunged," Mery-Re said. "They are an abomination to the Aten." He motioned to the men at his back.

Nefertiti glanced at the hammers and chisels in the hands of the Aten priests. She noted their armed escort. Mery-Re was watching her. What could she do? Pharaoh's word was absolute. A cold fog invaded her body. While she hesitated, the soldiers corralled Wadjnas and his followers in one corner. Mery-Re directed his men to a wall depicting the judgment of Amunhotep's soul. Amunhotep stood before Osiris, while

Anubis and Toth weighed his heart against the feather of truth. A priest pointed his chisel at the name of Osiris. Nefertiti cast a glance of appeal at Sebek, but the warrior lifted his hands in an unaccustomed movement of helplessness. The priest drew back his hammer.

Even now pharaoh might be undergoing judgment. The mist that shrouded Nefertiti's thoughts evaporated. The hammer arced toward the chisel. Nefertiti shouted, leaped at the priest, and caught the hammer in mid-swing. Pulled off balance, the man dropped the chisel. Nefertiti jerked the hammer out of his hand.

"You won't destroy pharaoh's ka." The priest shrank from her as she dropped the hammer.

Mery-Re swept toward her, two soldiers at his side.

"Thy majesty is misguided, distraught. Take the queen back to the palace."

The soldiers and Sebek moved toward each other as Nefertiti drew herself up to her full height. She stared at Mery-Re as if he were a maggot on the tip of her sandal.

"Mery-Re, you sniveling place seeker, you forget your lowly station."

"Nefertiti!"

It was Akhenaten. Nefertiti was left standing in a sea of crouching figures. Pharaoh stalked to her, followed by a squadron of charioteers bearing swords.

Coming close, Akhenaten took her hand and searched her face. "What are you doing here? You're pale. Are you well?"

"Yes, majesty." Nefertiti stared into her husband's black eyes. "Majesty, did you order Mery-Re to wipe out the gods' names?"

"Of course," Akhenaten said as he gazed about the temple. "Words in stone make for permanent lies. The Aten's name shall replace all gods. What are you doing here?"

"I came to visit pharaoh's ka."

"Then you shall witness the beginning of reform. Mery-Re, begin."

Without thinking Nefertiti raised her voice. "No!"

Akhenaten had been surveying the temple walls with a preoccupied, hungry look on his face. At Nefertiti's shout, his eyes widened. He looked down as if to be sure that word had come from her.

"No? Did you say no?"

Akhenaten took Nefertiti by the shoulders and pulled her close so that he glared into her eyes. She put her arms on Akhenaten's shoulders and braced herself. She had gone too far this time. Either her husband would listen, or pharaoh would denounce her and send her away in disgrace. Nefertiti lowered her voice so that only Akhenaten could hear.

"Husband, you promised Queen Tiye you wouldn't interfere with pharaoh's provisions for the afterlife. Please don't make the gods angry." Nefertiti gasped as Akhenaten shook her.

"Blasphemy! There are no gods to make angry. Say it."

Nefertiti twisted the shoulders of pharaoh's robe in her fists. Anger began to replace her fear; she had always hated being bullied. Akhenaten became her unreasonable husband rather than pharaoh. She pounded Akhenaten's chest and spit out the words of a long-dead king.

"He is a fool who makes light of the judges of the dead."

Nefertiti was released suddenly, causing her to stumble. Akhenaten made a frustrated sound and snatched her arm. Nefertiti shied away as her husband thrust his face down into hers.

"The little hawk has talons," the king said.

The temple was so quiet she could hear her own breathing. Akhenaten was still glaring at her, but she refused to let him frighten her. Lifting her chin, she scowled at him. Her risk was rewarded. She could see him respond to the challenge of her defiance. He was still angry, but beneath the anger was excitement.

"By the Two Lands, you're as stubborn as my father ever was. I'm trying to save his ka."

Nefertiti jerked her arm free and poked a finger in her husband's chest. "If the Aten is all-powerful, why can he not see into your father's heart and judge him accordingly?"

"We've spoken of this many times before, Nefertiti. Father denied that the Aten was the one god."

There was no arguing with Akhenaten. No appeal to reason or the ancient ways would affect a man who knew he was the arbiter of all things. Nefertiti imagined her father-in-law's ka annihilated by the monster Eater of Souls in the Hall of Judgment. A silent cry went through her. *Osiris, help me.* She gazed up into Akhenaten's angry countenance. The wide, fleshy mouth looked as big as the maw of a demon. Moving so that her body almost touched Akhenaten's, she lifted her head so that her lips were near his ear.

"You promised," she whispered.

"What?"

"You promised you'd leave pharaoh's temple alone. Didn't you mean what you said?" Akhenaten released her arm, and Nefertiti moved back a step to gaze up into his black eyes. She kept her voice low and slightly rough. "I always thought I could trust you. I believed in you. How can I believe in you if you do this to your father?"

Her voice seemed to drain the anger from Akhenaten's countenance, leaving only excitement and affection. "You must believe in me."

"Then help me believe," Nefertiti said. "Keep your promise."

Nefertiti nearly cried out when Akhenaten took her hand

and asked in a tone that was half teasing, half menacing, "Do you defy me?"

"No. I've never done that." Nefertiti made herself meet her husband's eyes, even though she was sure Akhenaten could see how much she hated to plead.

Akhenaten studied her until Nefertiti thought she would scream from the tension. Then he laughed softly.

"Mery-Re, return to the palace. I've changed my mind."

Nefertiti watched the high priest gather his men and retreat. Disapproval was blatant in his stiff posture.

Sebek came up beside her while pharaoh moved away to speak with Wadjnas. "I feared for you, majesty."

Nefertiti said nothing. She was still shaking from the risk she'd just taken. Once angered, Akhenaten could be vindictive and cruel. Although never its victim, Nefertiti had seen the results of pharaoh's wrath.

"My queen, are you well?"

"Yes." She pressed her shaking hands together. "I—I prayed for help from Osiris, and he came to my aid."

"Yes, majesty."

Nefertiti heard the warrior's skeptical tone. Sebek had never ventured an opinion about pharaoh. Such a liberty was not to be contemplated.

Sebek glanced over Nefertiti's head. "My queen, his majesty summons you."

Akhenaten waited at the entrance to the temple. His white robes stood out against the darkness of the stone around him. He lifted his arm; his eyes beckoned. Summoning her patience and her shredded composure, Nefertiti went to join her husband. As Akhenaten guided her outside, she couldn't help wondering if he would forget his desire to wipe out the name of Amun.

Chapter 9

Memphis, reign of Tutankhamun

Two chariots stood in the forecourt of Meren's town house. A line of servants on their way to the docks carried boxes and wicker trunks past the double reflection pools and out the front gates. Two Syrian girls, the personal maids of Tefnut and Isis, scurried after the group headed for Lord Sunero's yacht. It was already hot this morning as Meren helped Tefnut into the chariot beside her husband.

She leaned down and whispered to him, "Try not to worry, Father. I'll write so that you'll know how Isis fares."

"I'm not certain this is the best course," Meren replied.

Sunero gripped the reins of the chariot with one hand and steadied his wife with the other. "Leave it, Meren. You can't rush healing. Such things take many weeks and months. And you're not going to change your decision after I've had that mountain of parcels and boxes stuffed on board my yacht. I swear Isis has taken half the contents of your house."

"Not quite half," Meren replied with a faint smile. "Although Bener would agree with you." He touched Tefnut's hand. "Take care, little daughter."

Tefnut pressed a hand to her belly and said, "Father, you're the only one who would refer to me as little."

"I would, too," Sunero said.

"Anyone would look small next to you, husband. You're as tall as an obelisk."

"And as majestic," Sunero added.

"Ha! Certainly as noticeable."

Meren listened to the couple's exchange as they drove down the avenue to the gate. He returned their waves as they left the grounds, thinking how easy they were with each other. Had he and Sit-Hathor ever been so free with each other? After all this time, he seemed to remember only the pain of missing her and the emptiness in his heart, the emptiness he was afraid to fill.

Chastising himself for descending into another dark mood, Meren watched Kysen and Bener take leave of Isis. The chariot driver waited in the shade of the loggia while the family conversed, and a groom held the reins of the horses. Bener was talking gravely to her younger sister. Occasionally Kysen would offer a terse comment or pat Isis on the hand. Isis hung her head and listened, nodding and saying little. Seeing no improvement in her spirits, Meren sighed and realized he'd been right to agree to this visit. The old Isis would never have listened meekly to advice from her siblings. She would have given a derisive sniff and left them in mid-sentence to go her own way.

Meren joined his children beside the second chariot. As if by prearrangement, Bener dragged Kysen back to the house on the excuse that she wanted his opinion of a newly brewed batch of beer. Meren tried to catch Isis's eye, but she turned away to stroke the neck of one of the horses. Meren took the reins from the groom, who melted away to stand at the chariot driver's elbow.

"Will you at least bid me farewell, Isis?"

She glanced at him before staring at the horse's neck again. "Of course, Father. May the gods be with you while I'm away."

"And with you, my little one."

When Isis didn't answer, he sighed. "Isis, you can't live in shame forever. I'm tired of seeing you skulk about the house like a sick little jackal. You made a terrible mistake, but I know you never intended harm, and I forgive you. Now you must forgive yourself, and I do wish you would make haste about it, for I don't think I can bear this miserable humility of yours much longer."

Isis stared at him, and her mouth went slack with astonishment. "You don't hate me?"

"I love you," Meren snapped. "You would have known that had you not pretended to be asleep when I tried to see you in your room last night or had you not been avoiding me all this time."

"No," Isis said with a shake of her head. She stroked the horse's withers. "You have to hate me."

Uttering a gasp of exasperation, Meren dropped the reins and wrapped his youngest daughter in his arms, squeezing hard before releasing her. Isis gawked at him as he picked up the reins again.

"I don't have to hate you, but it seems you must hate yourself for a while longer."

"But—"

"But you're not going to do it in front of me," Meren said. He took her arm, guided her into the chariot, and signaled the driver. "I have made sacrifices for your safe journey, my Isis.

Have mercy on Tefnut and try not to sulk so much. Your frowns will curdle the spirits of the child in her womb."

"What I did—"

Meren handed the reins to the driver and stepped away from the chariot. "Farewell, daughter. You are always in my heart."

The chariot jumped into motion, and Meren waved to Isis as it clattered down the avenue. His last glimpse of her was of a wide-eyed, lithe, and beautiful young girl staring at him in astonishment.

When she was gone, Meren walked to the loggia and paused to lean against a column. Behind him the polished cedar of tall front doors gleamed even in the shade. The solar orb cast glittering fans of light across the reflection pools. Once again his thoughts turned to his investigations. Dilalu had returned with a small caravan of horses with which he tried to tempt his noble customer. During that interview the merchant had hinted of his extensive trading contacts and the ease with which he obtained rare items, and dropped the names of several of his more warlike customers. Meren assumed that the oily foreigner was testing his openness to the clandestine purchase of arms.

He'd spun Dilalu in a web of sweet anticipation of profit, but said nothing definite. In the meantime there was Yamen. Kysen had persuaded him to delay dealing with the officer when Meren expressed a desire to reach down his throat and rip out his spine. Now he realized he may have allowed his terror over Kysen's near-death to influence his view of Yamen. He would invite the officer to the house for a meal with several other military friends.

Meren was headed inside to summon a messenger to go to Yamen when the sound of more chariots made him turn. To his surprise, Maya, the royal treasurer, and General Horemheb

came into view. Preceded by several attendants, their chariots
sent pebbles flying as they drove up to the loggia. Grooms
rushed to see to the horses, and Meren's steward and servants
hurried to attend the guests.

Only a formal greeting was possible until Meren led his
friends into the reception hall, where Bener and Kysen waited
with refreshments. Once pleasantries had been exchanged, a
look from Horemheb caused Meren to dismiss his son and
daughter. He could see Bener's curiosity, but he gave her a
warning glare, and she vanished.

Meren refilled Horemheb's goblet with beer from a strain-
ing vessel and handed it to the general. "Whatever brings you
here must be momentous to draw both of you to my house
so early."

Maya exchanged glances with Horemheb. Meren had always liked the treasurer. Born into an old noble family, Maya
had never been one of those men ready with a vicious tongue
and betrayal in his heart. His love of efficiency had claimed
advancement for him when his lack of ambition might have
hindered him. Maya's real interest was gossip and meddling in
the lives of his friends for their own good. He swore that
Meren was too serious, too wary, and vowed that his friend
spent too much time in royal service and not enough in his
own. He'd given Meren the name Falcon long ago, saying that
it described his predatory attitude toward pharaoh's enemies
and his vigilance in defense of the king.

"Well," Meren said. "What have you come to say to me? If
you're going to try to arrange a match between me and another
of your cousins, Maya, enlisting Horemheb's aid won't help."

Maya popped a date in his mouth and held up a finger.
"Ah, speaking of matches, my Falcon. Are you mad to try to
seduce Princess Yia? Of all the women at court, Hunefer's

wife, by the gods! Pharaoh, may he have life, health, and prosperity, is not pleased."

Scowling at his friend, Meren didn't answer at once. Although somewhat younger than Meren, the treasurer had a face that looked like the wind-scoured floor of the desert. Scarred by some childhood illness, the skin of his cheeks was stretched tightly over thin bones. He had a narrow-lipped mouth and eyebrows that seemed to form a horizon supporting an expansive forehead, upon which lines had been grooved as if by a master jeweler. Nevertheless, the entirety of his features combined to fascinate. Perhaps this was because of Maya's artless charm and easy manner, and perhaps it was because his eyes always seemed lifted at the corners from mirth. However, charming though Maya might be, Meren had no intention of allowing his friend to intimidate him into a meeting with yet another eligible relative.

"I have spoken to his majesty about Yia already," Meren muttered.

Horemheb's voice rumbled forth. "Damnation, Maya. You're delaying on purpose. Get on with it." He rose from his chair and put a hand on Meren's shoulder. "I don't believe any of it, my friend."

"Any of what?" Meren looked at Maya, who was studying another date as if it were made of gold. "Maya." The word came out sharply, for Meren's temper was shorter than ever after seeing Kysen nearly killed because of Yamen and saying farewell to Isis.

"All right," Maya cried. He bent and rummaged through a leather document case he'd brought with him, producing a thick roll of papyri. He held them in his lap with both hands, as if afraid the documents would start flapping their sheets and take wing.

When the treasurer stopped again, Horemheb threw up his

hands and made a disgusted sound. "You're a coward, Maya. I'll tell him. We've found that Nubian gold that was stolen." The general walked around to face Meren, his arms folded over his chest. "It was discovered at your country house outside Abydos. The mayor of the city heard rumors that it was there and applied to Maya to investigate."

It had been years since Meren had been taken off guard in such a way. Baht, his country estate, the home of his childhood, was a place of peace and rustic charm. He found himself staring at his friend and blinking like a sleepy cow.

"I had to do it. It's my duty to—but you know this. And that's not all, Falcon." Maya was on his feet now, holding his documents against his chest like talismans. "The new steward at your delta estate near Tarrana has absconded with a boat full of conscripts assigned to the temple of Amun in Thebes. He says it's your custom to do this, that you've been doing it for years. He only got caught because he's new and was stupid enough to try to steal from the king of the gods rather than a minor deity."

Rising from his chair, Meren went past his friends, down the steps of the master's dais, to lean against a painted column. His gaze rested upon a graceful wall painting of dancers and musicians at a feast.

"Meren?" Horemheb's voice came to him from the dais. "Falcon?"

He turned, shaking his head. "Have you told anyone other than pharaoh?"

Maya shifted uneasily. "We told Ay."

Meren nodded. Of course they would have spoken to Ay.

"We know there is some explanation," Horemheb said. "You had some reason for doing these things, something to do with your duties as Eyes and Ears of Pharaoh."

"No," Meren said.

"What do you mean, no?" Horemheb demanded.

"Oh," Maya said with a groan. "I knew it. He's going to be noble, offended, and disdainful. Look at him. He isn't going to tell us anything."

"There is nothing for me to tell," Meren said with an irritated look at Maya. "I've done nothing."

"You didn't take the conscripts or the gold?" Horemheb asked. "Then what were they doing in the possession of your servants?"

Meren strolled up the steps of the dais, faced the general, and in a light tone said, "Do you really think I will allow you to question me? We're old friends, Horemheb. You should know better." He whirled around at the feel of Maya's hand on his shoulder.

"Falcon, if you had nothing to do with these crimes, say so, and we'll punish the guilty servants. That will be the end of the matter."

Brushing off Maya's hand, Meren went to a table and picked up his beer goblet. With his back to his friends, he said, "You'll punish no one."

"I have to do something," Maya said, wringing the papyri in his hands.

Meren didn't answer. He was thinking furiously. He'd never indulged in the corruption so common among some councillors and great men. Such grave transgressions had to be deliberate, which meant that someone wanted him disgraced. Why now? Such traps could have been sprung years ago. But years ago he hadn't contacted men he suspected of killing a queen.

"It's no use," Horemheb said. "He's going to be stubborn, and that cursed pride of his is going to keep his mouth shut."

There was movement beside him, and Meren found Maya regarding him with apprehension.

"Listen to me, Falcon. I know your name has always been as clean as new linen, but you have enemies at court. Prince Hunefer would love to see you brought down, especially now. His cronies, those such as Lord Pendua and Prince Usermontu, would all rejoice should you be cast aside by pharaoh. You must do something."

"I'm grateful to you both for coming to me," Meren said, "but I have no intention of answering such absurd charges."

"My Falcon, you must, and soon. Pharaoh commands your presence tonight at the evening meal."

Horemheb stomped down the dais stairs and joined them. "I don't suppose you'll talk to us now, so that we can return to pharaoh with something other than your silence. No, I didn't think so." Horemheb drew closer so that Meren had to look him in the eye. "Damn you, Meren. Being the Eyes of Pharaoh has warped you. This is no time to keep secrets."

Meren met Horemheb's troubled gaze with a bland mask of unconcern, then turned his back on his friends. "In this case, I have no secrets to keep. Good day to you both. I'm sure I'll see you this evening."

Not moving until he was certain the two were gone, Meren then sprang into motion and raced out of the reception hall. Walking swiftly through the grounds, past the pleasure gardens, he crossed the practice yard. There he signaled to Abu and Kysen, who were examining a new team of hinnies that had just been delivered by Dilalu's grooms. They met in the central room of the barracks block. Several charioteers were there, mending harnesses and going over reports from the Memphis police watch. Meren dismissed them. He snatched up a chariot whip and began to twist its leather in his hands. Kysen and Abu were both looking at him in alarm.

"What's wrong, Father?"

"Lord?"

Pacing the length of the room, Meren yanked the leather hard, causing a snapping sound. He could feel a rage building in his heart. A cauldron of liquid metal bubbled in his chest, burning away all reason as it churned, feeding on its own heat until his only recourse was action—foolhardy, dangerous action.

"Father!"

Kysen was in front of him, his hand on the whip. Meren looked down to see his hands tangled so tightly that the leather cut into his skin. He stared at them, the conflagration in his heart still scalding his wits. His son pulled at the leather, loosening it. He had freed one hand when Bener opened the door, stepped in, and slammed it behind her. The bang cut through Meren's fury, and he fastened his gaze on his daughter.

"What's wrong?" she asked.

"Go away," Kysen said as he freed Meren's other hand. "This isn't a matter for women."

They both went silent when Meren spoke in a rough voice. "Let her stay."

At the sound of his voice, Kysen and Bener dropped their combative stances, and Abu drew nearer. Meren began to twist the whip in his hands again.

"Father, tell us what happened."

"It has to do with Maya and General Horemheb," Bener said.

"Were you listening again?" Kysen demanded with outrage.

Bener drew herself up. "Don't speak to me in that accusing tone."

"Silence!" Abu exclaimed. So seldom did the aide exert his authority that both shut their mouths at the same time. Abu turned to Meren and held out his hand for the whip. "Lord, give it to me. Your hand is bleeding."

Meren felt mild surprise as he noticed the crimson line across his palm. He relinquished the whip and leaned against one of the pair of columns in the room. Slowly, keeping a distance between the words and the rage they provoked, he told his family and aide what had passed. When he finished, no one spoke. Bener began to pace as Meren had, her head bent, her hands clasped behind her back. Kysen scowled at the opposite wall while Abu rubbed his chin. Then Bener stopped abruptly.

"It's Hunefer," she snapped. "That evil pig dung. He's afraid he'll lose his wife, so he's spreading these lies."

Kysen rolled his eyes. "Hunefer isn't clever enough to have designed these traps. This isn't just a case of rumor, Bener."

"I know that!"

Meren squeezed his eyes shut as their voices rose. He couldn't speak freely with Bener in the room. She didn't know anything about the murder of Nefertiti, and for her protection, he couldn't tell her.

"Bener, we're to go to the palace tonight," he said. All argument ceased. "Do you think your clever heart is up to the challenge of a visit to the great royal wife?"

A mischievous grin was his answer.

"Are you certain? You know she's an enemy, and she'll try to trick you into betraying any secrets you might hold."

"I think she regrets her intolerance," Bener said. "My friends and I have noticed a great improvement in her manner lately."

Meren raised one brow. "How fortunate."

He was skeptical of Ankhesenamun's change in character. It was more likely that she realized she'd come near to getting herself accused of treason with all her plots against her own husband and had decided upon a more conciliatory approach.

"Very well," he said. "Bener will see what news she can gain from the queen. Abu, you will go to Baht and handle this matter of the Nubian gold. Take men with you and find out how it got into my house. My sister must be frantic if the estate has been invaded by pharaoh's emissaries and soldiers. Send Reia and Simut and the rest of the men to the delta to deal with this new steward who has taken it upon himself to steal for me."

"Yes, lord, but that will leave few here on duty."

"Leave two men. That will be enough. Lord Irzanen and one other."

Abu inclined his head. "And what of the matter of the royal guard Bakht?"

"Bakht?"

"The royal guard who was killed in a fall into the baboon pen in the menagerie, lord."

"Ah, yes."

"There are suspicious aspects to his death," Abu said. "His wounds didn't seem to me to be ones from the fangs of a monkey."

"Have you ever seen such wounds, Abu?"

"Not from a baboon, lord."

"We'll deal with the guard when you return," Meren said. He turned to Bener. "Daughter, if the charioteers are to journey so far, they will need provisions."

"I'll see to it at once," she replied.

Meren walked with her to the door and opened it for her. "I am blessed to have a daughter whom I can trust with such secrets."

"Don't worry, Father. I'll keep my lips closed. And I can deal with the great royal wife, too."

Meren shut the door after her, turned, and sank against it to regard Kysen and Abu. "You understand what this means?"

"We've frightened someone," Kysen said.

Abu threw the whip onto the table. "Dilalu or Yamen."

"Perhaps," Meren said. "Whoever it is, we must find out quickly. I can't leave Memphis. It would look like a guilty retreat. Kysen must stay with me for the same reason." Meren went to Abu and put his hand on the man's shoulder. "I must leave this in your hands, old friend. And there's no one I'd trust more."

"I understand, lord."

"Find out who was on duty when the gold appeared. Find the ones responsible, and then——"

"Find their master."

"Yes," Meren said.

"But be careful," Kysen said. "Remember what happened to Othrys's men when they asked questions."

"I have no intention of being poisoned," Abu said with a grim smile. "We'll leave at first light. And, lord?"

"Yes, Abu."

"None of the evildoers will escape."

"I need them alive."

"Of course, lord."

Abu left them alone, and Meren started pacing again.

"Father, you have to tell pharaoh now. Once he knows you're looking for Queen Nefertiti's murderer, he won't listen to the lies or believe the traps."

Meren paused, throwing up his hands. "Don't you see, Ky? It's too late. If I tell him now, it will appear as if I'm making up some fantastic tale to save myself. The man who told us of the murder is conveniently dead, and he died on my ship. My ship. Who can vouch for my words? My own son? A tavern owner? A Greek pirate? None of you will be believed as disinterested witnesses." Meren sighed. His head throbbed, and he rubbed his temples. "The king trusts me. He calls me friend. He won't condemn me because of some baseless lies."

"Maya and Horemheb didn't come solely on their own account, did they?"

"No, Ky, they didn't. If pharaoh had believed the reports, if the accusations had been against anyone else—" Meren lifted his gaze to the troubled eyes of his son. "No, he sent them to warn me. And for that I will always be grateful. He doesn't know it, but the golden one may have saved my life and yours."

Chapter 10

Near Memphis, reign of Tutankhamun

Less than a week after the visit from Maya and Horemheb, Meren crouched behind a half-finished mud-brick wall. He, the king, and the royal war band had concealed themselves in a hamlet on the outskirts of the Nile flood plain north of the great pyramids. He prayed to Set, god of storms, that the only cloud in the sky wouldn't cover the moon and deprive him of a good view of the bandits. On his left was Mose, the second of the royal Nubian bodyguards who were like the king's shadows. A little way off he could hear Karoya's quick breathing. Between Karoya and Meren the living god of Egypt crouched, tense and exultant at the prospect of battle.

The king's personal bodyguard and war band were scattered throughout the ramshackle settlement. Tutankhamun had forbidden Meren and Horemheb to bring more than these closest companions. They were hidden behind the lean-tos, huts, and debris piles that surrounded the animal pen. Down the hamlet's only path, out of sight, Horemheb waited with the scout who had tracked the raiders. The bandits were headed toward the village, traveling slowly by night across the windswept desert.

It had come suddenly, this journey to the near wasteland at the edge of the desert. Word that the raiders had been located had come by royal messenger the night he'd been summoned to that evening meal at the palace. Wary, certain that whoever was trying to ruin his name was also responsible for Nefertiti's death, he had entered the vast pleasure garden of pharaoh in the company of Kysen and Bener. At once his children had left him to circulate among the small group of diners, gleaning what they could from court gossip.

Meren wished he was back at the palace now instead of crouching in the dirt behind a pile of bricks that had been situated too near the animal pens. He smelled goat and donkey dung. In the royal pleasure garden there had been far more pleasant scents—incense, the perfume oils used by the courtiers, the scent of water from the reflection pools.

He preferred the gardens to the grandeur and opulence of the palace. Climbing vines covered the walls, and the royal gardeners kept the beds filled with native and foreign flowers. Best of all were the trees. Cultivated for generations, they lined the many paths throughout the garden and formed a thick canopy of green overhead—sycamores, fig trees, persea, acacia, yew, tamarisk, and willow. Entering the pleasure garden was like entering the idyllic netherworld of the gods.

That night, however, he'd hardly noticed the greenery. The number of those invited to dine with pharaoh had been small. Meren saw the queen and her confidante, Princess Tio, talking to Bener. Maya was there lounging in a pavilion, in conversation with Kysen. He didn't see Horemheb. Barely noticing the gentle laughter of the women, Meren found the king sitting on the ground at the edge of the reflection pool.

Although this evening was to be free of ceremony, Meren sank to the ground and bent low.

Tutankhamun dismissed the slaves fanning him. "Rise, Meren. We're alone, so you can explain to me at once what you've done to make someone try to destroy your name."

"Majesty?"

Raising his eyes to the stars, the king addressed them. "Do you see? Even now he is surprised that I understand him. After all our years together, he still thinks me a babe."

"Thy majesty has grown in wisdom like the god his father."

"Meren, I've had to endure an audience with the Hittite ambassador today, as well as judge five disputes among the temples and my nobles and condemn a nobleman to the gold mines for embezzling royal grain. And now I hear that my Eyes and Ears is involved in corruption. Don't test my patience, just tell me whom you've threatened in my service. Someone is trying hard to ruin your name. What have you done?"

Meren met pharaoh's gaze and found himself startled by the assessing quality in those large, heavy-lidded eyes. "I've done nothing, golden one. Nothing more than usual, that is, but I'm grateful to thy majesty. The golden one hasn't asked me to defend myself against these charges."

"Would you have done so, had I asked?"

"It isn't possible, majesty."

"Why not, if you're innocent?"

What words could he choose that would prove his innocence? That was a question he'd been asking himself since learning of the false charges. The evil had already been done. Until he knew more, he could only protest his innocence and his ignorance, two qualities for which he'd never been known.

"Meren, you're not listening."

"Forgive me, majesty."

"I said that I know you. You're involved in some intrigue, something that has been troubling you for a long time. Do you think I haven't noticed? I've never seen you distracted in my majesty's presence." The king handed Meren his wine goblet. It was gold with a fluted bowl and narrow stem. "Besides, you don't need conscripts or gold, or if you do, you know you have only to ask and I'll give anything you wish."

"I am humbled by thy majesty's generosity."

"And since this is so, I ask again. What is wrong?"

Meren's gaze skimmed across the surface of the reflection pool. Torchlight danced over the water, and a swan paddled by.

"I—I am unable to answer thy majesty."

Tutankhamun sat up straight and looked at Meren in astonishment. "And if I command you to answer?"

"Please don't, golden one." Meren returned the king's stare with a grave one of his own. They remained as motionless as a tomb painting, while Meren wondered how far he could test the boy's faith in him.

"Very well, Meren. I can see that you're gravely troubled. After all you've done for me, I can at least have patience a while longer."

Meren bowed his head. "Thank you, majesty."

"You worry me."

"For that I am most sorry, golden one." Meren hesitated, but continued when the king sent an inquiring glance his way. "There is something I must ask, majesty, although I have tried your patience sorely."

"You ask little of me. I can endure it."

Now Meren felt his mouth go dry. He fought back visions of his father's death, visions he thought he'd banished forever.

"Should thy majesty come to believe that I have done evil—" He stopped, closed his eyes for a moment, and then began again, using a more courtly phrase. "Should I be banished from the grace of thy majesty's favor, I beg that my family not be forced to share my fate as—"

"Stop!"

All conversation in the garden ceased. Karoya, who was never far from the king, moved uneasily and gripped his spear.

Tutankhamun ignored everyone and began again. "You're frightening me."

"I don't wish to, golden one."

"Are you trying to make me unsure of you? Why would you ask such a thing if your name is true and honorable?"

He couldn't explain. How could he tell the boy that his greatest fear wasn't ruin at the hands of his enemies? What he most feared was that his family would be made to suffer as well. After Akhenaten killed his father, Meren had been dragged into the morass of pharaoh's enmity. His cousin Ebana had fared far worse, losing both wife and son.

He had to say something. "I can only swear before the mighty Amun and all the gods that I am true to thy majesty."

That oath had done little to assuage the king's apprehension. Meren shifted his position behind the brick wall. His legs were growing numb. It hadn't helped that, in an attempt to change the subject, the king had asked about the investigation into the guard's death. Upon learning that Abu had been sent out of the city without finishing the inquiry, Tutankhamun had been irate. Eyes flashing with temper, he'd almost ordered Meren to bring Abu back, but a royal messenger had interrupted him. Hearing of the raiders caused all else to flee the royal heart.

Now it was the king's turn to shift his weight and pound at numbed muscles. Meren checked the positions of the war band. Karoya, Mose, another Nubian called Turi, and two others formed a wall around the youth, all that could be hidden behind the wall. The king moved again.

Meren remembered the wait before his first battle. "It shouldn't be long now, majesty."

"Good," Tutankhamun replied. "Every time a nomad chief or a bandit leader decides to raid, I get a fresh inundation of half-dead peasants throwing themselves at my feet, begging for asylum, begging for food, and bringing the raiders closer to the Nile. At last I'm going to see these bringers of chaos for myself."

"These villagers have been most unfortunate," Meren said as he glanced around the newly built houses. "One of the women told me that twice before they have fled the raiders. They've left behind the houses they lived in for generations, the graveyards of their ancestors, the men who died defending them. All that's left of a once-prosperous village is a band of women, children, old men, and youths. There isn't a male over the age of thirteen left."

"Except for that young potter," the king said, his voice vibrating with restrained anger. "He'll soon die from losing that leg."

Meren peered over the wall into the darkness. No movement yet. He listened to the whispered banter among the war band. Most had been raised in the palace along with Tutankhamun. They'd trained together, studied together, lived together, so that they formed a close-knit unit. Each knew the movements and skills of the other, and all would die for pharaoh.

Meren especially trusted the two oldest—Hety and Raweben. The youngest, like pharaoh, had fourteen years. With these companions, pharaoh's training had been hard. Meren had agreed with Ay and Horemheb that the boy wasn't to expect royal treatment from them during training. He had been an equal. He received the same blows for negligence. He had run the same races around the palace walls. Their weapons and tasks had been his, except that they had been seasoned in battle while the king had not.

From across the village came the yowl of a cat, Horemheb's signal.

Meren picked up the bow that lay beside him. "They come." One of the goats in the pen bleated. "Remember to wait until they're all within the camp before shooting."

A long howl sounded; then a pounding of hooves and the clash of metal signaled the raiders' attack. Expecting no resistance, the bandits clattered into the center of the hamlet, swords waving wildly. On foot and on horseback they circled the animal pen. Before the intruders could attack the deserted dwellings, Horemheb gave a shout. Meren let fly his arrow and watched it strike the chest of a man waving a stolen scimitar encrusted with gold.

A horse screamed and went down with an arrow in its leg. One of the thieves had the wits to shout a command to take refuge. Tutankhamun aimed his bow at this man. With satisfaction Meren watched the king single him out; five bandits had fallen, but a score remained, and they'd be less trouble without a leader. The king's shot caught the man's arm near the shoulder as he leaped from his horse. He scrambled to the ground, ducked behind the carcass of a dead horse, and pulled the arrow from his flesh.

Meren drew his scimitar. Before he could speak, the king gave a war cry, vaulted over the wall, and ran at the dismounted raiders. Cursing, Meren, Karoya, and the war band hurtled after the boy, but a wave of raiders separated them from their royal charge. Karoya was at Meren's side, then past him, his longer legs eating the distance to pharaoh. Then the Nubian stumbled. His body jerked, and he hit the ground with a dagger in his shoulder. Karoya let out a piercing cry at Meren and pointed at the king.

"By the gods, I knew it!" Meren sprang across the wounded Karoya. This was what he'd feared. Desperate to prove himself a warrior, Tutankhamun had allowed the excitement of battle to overcome his reason.

Meren reached the king in time to hurl himself at the boy and block a blow from a spear. They rolled together, but they jumped up and countered the assault of two bandits. Meren saw the king counter a slice from a blade and stagger backward.

Tutankhamun's opponent was twice his weight. To Meren's relief, the king whipped out his dagger as the man charged him and jabbed it into the raider's unprotected stomach. Blood gushed onto the boy's hand and arm when he withdrew the dagger, but he ignored it and rolled to his feet.

It had never been an even match, skilled warriors against untrained outlaws who relied on surprise and superior weapons against unarmed peasants. The raiders fled in all directions, leaving weapons, horses, and stolen goods behind. Fighting their way to the king, Raweben, Hety, and Mose flanked their royal charge.

Meren saw the twins Seti and Hor pursue three bandits into the animal pen. Seti lifted a goat and threw it at a plump thief. The raider went down with the animal on his back. The goat bleated in outrage and nipped the man's buttock.

As the fighting ebbed, Meren followed the king to the pen. While they watched the spectacle, a flicker of movement caught Meren's eye. He turned, his scimitar raised, but three raiders were on them. Raweben engaged the first man. Hety went down under a blow from a staff, while Mose engaged the attacker. Meren leaped astride Hety's prostrate figure and swept his scimitar around in an arc. The raider ducked, feinted, and drew a dagger.

As the bandit cocked his arm back to throw, Meren heard the hiss of an arrow. The thief grunted as the missile pierced his gut. Three more arrows hit the man before he dropped. Then Tutankhamun was at his side, his bow still in his hands.

Mose still guarded the king with Meren, but the bandit leader and two of his men charged over a wall behind which they'd hidden. One thief swung a staff at the king's head. Tutankhamun dropped on top of the prone Hety. The bandit raised his weapon to bash the king's skull.

Even as Meren swung his scimitar, Tutankhamun raised an arm. His wrist flicked, and his dagger caught the raider in the throat. Meren's weapon sliced at the raider as he fell. Mose was busy dispatching the other man.

As Meren pulled his scimitar from the gut of the dead thief, a hand shot out and grabbed a fistful of hair at the back of his head. At the same time, his weapon was knocked out of his hand and a scimitar blade pressed against his side.

Meren saw Tutankhamun spring to his feet. Several of the war band rushed to the king, who thrust his arm out to prevent them from charging. They stood still while the raider moved away, using Meren as a shield. Quiet settled over the hamlet. The coppery smell of blood mixed with the odor of dung and straw. From beyond the settlement came sounds of pursuit and death. The twins, Horemheb, and a few others turned in their direction but made no sudden move toward the raider who held Meren.

From the corner of his eye Meren could see that the man was the leader the king had tried to kill earlier. He had a short, curled beard and long hair tied back with a gold ribbon. Blood oozed down his arm and the sleeve of his wool tunic. The raider's gaze darted from one opponent to another and settled on Tutankhamun. In accented, broken Egyptian, the man spoke to him.

"I kill this tall one you don't let Zababa free."

It took Meren a few moments to translate the mangled vowels and bad grammar. He caught the king's eye and gave his head an almost imperceptible shake.

Tutankhamun wiped sweat from his chin with the back of his arm. "Let him go."

Meren edged his hand toward the raider's blade. Zababa made a quick, light slash, and Meren gasped. The blade hadn't cut deep, and he pressed a hand against the wound.

Zababa held his blade over Meren's ribs. "Give chariot and promise no harm to Zababa."

The king's attention never left Zababa. Meren could see the boy's effort to hold the man's gaze. That meant that somewhere, a warrior was drawing back an arrow and waiting for the royal signal. Meren understood the king's dilemma. Tutankhamun dared not give the signal for fear Zababa would live long enough to kill him. Zababa's blade dug into Meren's flesh, and he clamped his teeth together to keep from making a sound.

"Promise now."

"Wait!"

Meren met the king's warning gaze and nodded, trying to make known his trust in the boy's judgment.

"You may have the chariot," Tutankhamun said, "but only if you free my man first."

"Give promise, little lord." Zababa jerked on his hair, but Meren set his jaw and refused to cry out.

"I promise," Tutankhamun said. "With Amun as witness, I, Tutankhamun, king of Egypt, promise you freedom if you release my servant."

Meren heard Zababa grunt and felt the scimitar slip a little as the thief called out, "King of Egypt? The little lord is king of Egypt?" A bark of laughter made Meren grit his teeth. "Give chariot, Egypt."

Meren could see Tutankhamun's strained features as he signaled for a chariot. When the vehicle arrived, Meren was dragged to it. He had almost decided to risk hitting Zababa when the king's young voice boomed into the night.

"Leave him. I gave you a promise, Zababa. The promise of a king. I give you another. If you take him, if you kill him, I'll hunt you down. I'll find you, and I will stake you out in the desert. With my own blade I'll peel the skin from your body and feed it to the jackals. But first I'll hack your cock off and roast it before your eyes. Before all the gods of Egypt, I swear I will do this."

Meren felt the thief's body tense. Millennia seemed to pass as the young king and the bandit engaged in a contest of wills.

"Pharaoh keeps his word," Meren said at last.

With a curse, Zababa gave him a sudden shove that sent Meren toppling out of the chariot. Stumbling, Meren almost fell, but arms caught him and lifted. Meren found himself leaning on the king as the thief barreled past them. Lord Uben-Ra, the youngest of the war band, followed Zababa with his bow. Tutankhamun shouted, and the youth lowered his weapon.

Horemheb came to Meren's side, lending an arm. He and the king lowered Meren beside the wounded Hety.

"Karoya?" Tutankhamun asked. Horemheb nodded in the bodyguard's direction. Across the village, Karoya's dagger wound was being dressed.

"His injury isn't bad, majesty."

Someone brought a lamp, water, and bandages, and Horemheb went to work on Meren.

"It's only a shallow cut, damn you."

Horemheb dabbed at the wound with a wet cloth. "Then this won't take long, so be quiet."

"Majesty, you should have let Uben-Ra kill that bastard Zababa," Meren said as he winced.

"My promise was given before Amun."

"A promise to a man who nearly killed me," Meren said.

Meren looked up to find the war band hovering about, waiting for the king to send them after Zababa. "Be it given to my ministers, or to that desert scum, my promise is the promise of pharaoh. I won't break it." He sank down beside Meren. "Of course, anyone who didn't hear me when I promised won't know to let Zababa go free. Will they?"

Meren noticed that Tutankhamun was careful not to lift his eyes until Uben-Ra, Seti, and Hor had drifted away in the direction of Zababa's flight. He also saw the strained look in the boy's eyes, the haunted air he remembered from his first encounters with death and blood. Meren's mouth twisted in a pained smile. "Such is the logic of princes. It circles and undulates like the crotch of a whore."

A warrior stumbled. Meren heard the war band's shocked silence, but the king was grinning at him. Laughter burst out of the boy as Meren had intended, dissipating the heart-tearing tension that was the legacy of battle.

"By the gods, Meren," the king said, "you're as irreverent as a Babylonian and as unpredictable as a desert storm."

After disposing of the thieves' bodies, the occupants of the hamlet were allowed to return. The royal party returned to their camp, which had been set up out of sight of the threatened villages but still near the desert's edge. The perimeter was formed by shields driven into the ground, so close together that they formed a wall. Two gaps had been left to allow movement in and out, but each was guarded. Within the square palisade, at the center of the camp, lay pharaoh's tent, surrounded by those of his officers. Tutankhamun's tent was more a pavilion. It was divided into curtain chambers and furnished with a portable throne, a folding camp bed of gilded cedar, and all the other luxuries with which a living god must travel. Before the royal tent stood tall poles bearing streamers and standards of battle.

Late though it was, however, the king wasn't in his tent. He and his war band were celebrating his first victory. Meren remained with his royal charge to see the downing of several cups of delta wine before retiring. He was resting on his own camp bed now after washing and having his cut seen to by the royal physician. Through the fabric of his tent torchlight danced, and he could hear the laughter of the war band. Finally, after the moon had set, even the young king tired. The war songs faded, and the camp was blanketed in silence. But Meren was still awake.

After what seemed like hours of trying to drift off, he sat up in frustration. Despite the wine, his body felt as taut as a bowstring. He told himself it was the aftermath of going into battle with pharaoh. In all the years he'd been a warrior, he'd never had to do that. He had never gone to war with Akhenaten, and the pharaoh Amunhotep had been too old to fight by the time Meren came of age. Having the responsibility of the boy's life during combat had been terrifying.

Meren tried to put the evening's events behind him, but then his thoughts drifted to the attempts to ruin his honor. Someone was frightened enough to risk exposure by concocting such incidents. The list of possible evildoers was obvious—Dilalu, Yamen, perhaps Prince Hunefer.

Sitting on the edge of his bed, Meren rubbed his eyes and muttered, "I think not Hunefer. He hasn't the wits."

He wasn't getting any sleepier. Sighing, Meren donned a cloak against the night chill and left his tent. Outside it was still dark, but the stars were fading. He walked through the phalanx of tents that surrounded the king's pavilion, past the open-air camps of the infantry escort and the lines of tethered horses. Meren paused to greet Wind and Star. Their nickering and the nuzzles of their soft noses calmed the whirlwind of his thoughts. He fed them handfuls of grain while he sought more peaceful thoughts, thoughts that would allow him the tranquillity of sleep.

But even with Wind and Star, peace seemed unattainable. Perhaps if he could be alone . . . Untying the horses, he took them with him out of the palisade. The sentries saluted him as he passed, and soon he had walked the animals out of sight of the outlying guard posts. He sometimes did this after a battle, when sleep proved impossible.

Going was slow; even his leather sandals provided little protection from rocks. As he tried to see in the dark, Meren realized that over the past weeks he'd felt as if he was moving in a black desert, with unseeable dangers and less power to protect himself than he had at this moment to keep himself from stumbling over rocks.

He hated feeling powerless and surrounded by invisible evil. He might gain control if he could remember something of those last days of Nefertiti's life. So far his attempts had failed. He'd buried his memories so effectively that they might as well have been sealed in the innermost vault of the great pyramid. Those days belonged to the time after Ay had persuaded Akhenaten not to kill him. Pharaoh had released Meren but kept him within reach by assigning him to Ay's service. Thus he'd remained in Horizon of the Aten while his young wife and family stayed in the country, away from danger.

His duties as Ay's aide often brought him to Nefertiti, and he'd spent a great deal of time in the queen's palace, bringing and receiving messages. Over the years he'd seen the queen mature, and from this vantage as an intimate of Ay, he became privy to the growing divergence of opinion between her and pharaoh. She had concealed this division from all but her father. Even Akhenaten hadn't guessed the extent of her reservations about the Aten. That much he remembered, but such recollections were only general ones. It was as if he were looking back at that time through a length of ash-covered funeral garment—his vision obscured by the gauze and cinders.

After a few attempts at remembrance, Meren found himself sleepy at last. He started back to camp, but was weary and decided to ride Wind. Riding bareback was a useful skill, one used by messengers and scouts. Every charioteer learned, for he might need to ride should his chariot be damaged in the midst of battle. There still wasn't much light, so Meren proceeded at a walk, but as he neared camp, he heard shouts and the blast of trumpets.

Kicking Wind into a trot and hauling Star behind him, Meren covered the remaining distance quickly. He approached the outlying post at a near canter. As he passed them, the guards shouted.

"There he is! He's here!"

Racing into camp, Meren hauled on Wind's harness as he was met by a phalanx of infantry, charioteers, and officers. In moments he was surrounded. Taken aback, Meren surveyed the men until he found Horemheb. The general was shoving his way through the crowd.

"General," Meren said, using his friend's title before others. "What passes here?"

As Ra brought forth the light of morning, Horemheb stalked over to him, his face wiped clean of emotion. He grabbed Wind's harness and spoke in a rough voice.

"Why?"

Meren's gaze cut from Horemheb to the men surrounding him, seeing wariness, astonishment, rage. "Where is pharaoh?"

"I'm here."

Men parted, and Tutankhamun limped toward him. He was bleeding from a cut on his temple. There was a gash on his left biceps, and he held a wad of cloth pressed to a wound on his right forearm. The boy came close, despite the protests of the physician who trailed behind him, pleading, and the attempts by Mose and his bodyguards to put themselves between him and Meren. Wiping a trail of blood from his eye, Tutankhamun braced his legs wide apart and fixed Meren with a gaze of bewildered horror. Horemheb started to say something, but a slash of the hand from pharaoh commanded silence. Stunned, Meren gaped at the king.

Tutankhamun took an unsteady step toward him and said, "By the god my father, why, Meren?" Those words held the anguish of a lost soul.

Shaking his head, Meren tried to speak, but the king snatched the hem of his kilt, twisting his bloodied fingers in the material and drawing close so that only Meren could hear his violent whisper.

"Tell me, damn you. What evil demon possessed you?"

Meren put his hand on Tutankhamun's, but the boy snatched it away.

"Majesty, I don't understand."

The king's harsh laugh sent an uneasy mutter through the men surrounding them. The physician scurried forward, but Tutankhamun motioned him away and kept his scimitar stare on Meren.

"What I don't understand is why you came back after you tried to kill me. Didn't you think I'd recognize your voice, even inside the blackest tent?"

Chapter II

Horizon of the Aten, the independent reign of the pharaoh Akhenaten

In the queen's palace Nefertiti was dressing for the morning devotion to the Aten. A maid held up a polished electrum mirror, and she regarded the paint that had been applied to her eyes. She waved the mirror away. Never had she expected to experience pain upon regarding her own reflection. After her last visit to Memphis, she could hardly look at herself, for the sight of her well-fed perfection only called up the memory of what she'd seen.

She'd gone to visit her former tutor, Tati, in a village near the capital. She had stopped at Memphis—White Wall, old capital of the Two Lands—and confronted the results of Akhenaten's new policies. Pharaoh was diverting to the Aten the entire endowments of the great gods of Egypt.

She had driven past the temple of Ptah on the way to the royal palace and found it closed. The dwelling of the artisan god who fashioned the world was deserted. Lay priests, god's servants, and lector priests no longer walked its columned courtyards. Where they had gone, she didn't know.

Vanished also were the officials of the god's granaries, his cattle herders and stonemasons, the makers of incense, and the painters who adorned the walls of the temple and lived in the city-within-a-city that surrounded the temple. So many depended on Ptah for their life and work.

Those who remained in the temple area were like spirits of the dead with none to attend their graves. They starved. Climbing down from her chariot, ignoring the protests of her bodyguards, she walked by children crouched in the dirt. Their distended bellies hung beneath ribs that threatened to press through their flesh. She saw their hope-dead eyes even now, back in her own palace. Every time she ate, she remembered the skeletal hands of a little girl who snatched at flies and shoved them into her mouth.

Closing her eyes, Nefertiti banished the vision of the starving girl. She went to the nursery first to kiss her little ones and listen to their chatter. The gods set each person upon the earth in his proper station. She possessed this palace with its terrace overlooking gardens and azure pools, its spacious rooms surrounded by more shaded gardens, courtyards, and vibrant frescoes. She lived with Akhenaten in the great riverside palace with its mighty battlements and countless rooms stuffed with furniture wrought of exotic wood and trimmed with gold. This was right, for she was queen of Egypt. But it wasn't right that those who had once worked and lived well should be reduced to misery.

Dawn found Nefertiti setting foot on the polished stone of the open-air temple within the palace, just as Thanuro arrived with the offerings he would present to the god. Thanuro was a third prophet of the Aten assigned to her service. At the same time he functioned as scribe of accounts of the house of the god. He oversaw the disbursement of revenues from the former estates and treasuries of Amun. Nefertiti's lip curled up, along with one eyebrow. Thanuro was an ex-priest of Amun who saw the wisdom of converting to Aten worship.

The man had been instrumental in ferreting out obscure endowments and revenues of the old god so that they could be transferred to the Aten. Thanuro had been one of those who invaded the archives of Amun, at pharaoh's order, to compile lists of the god's possessions. He thereby deprived Tati, among others, of the income the old scholar depended on for his daily sustenance and his funerary grant.

Nefertiti constantly had to find dispossessed priests new occupations. Sometimes a particularly rigid prophet or divine one would insult Thanuro, and the Aten priest would have the man bastinadoed. Then Nefertiti dared not interfere, for Thanuro had been appointed by pharaoh.

The priest came forward to stand before her. He bore a gold tray on which rested boxes of cedar containing frankincense, cassia, and myrrh. Behind Thanuro stood priests bearing offerings of food and wine. It was time for the adoration. Nefertiti took the tray from Thanuro and walked to the middle of the platform.

"Courage." Nefertiti tightened her lips, angry that the word had slipped out.

Thanuro was chanting and hadn't heard. She bit her lip and made her body go through the motions of worship. She needed courage to perform this adoration, for she prayed to her husband. Long ago Akhenaten made it clear that pharaoh was the only one in the world who could approach the Aten directly. Everyone else, including Nefertiti, prayed to the Aten through pharaoh as the incarnation of the sun disk. She never got over the feeling that the old gods watched her, for in truth, she'd never really believed in Akhenaten's god.

Oh, she lived as though she believed. No other course was possible, and for a while in the early years she had almost succeeded in convincing herself that Akhenaten's way was the truth. But Nefertiti found that her own nature fought against her. She was practical, as grounded in the black land of Egypt as any peasant. Her heart reasoned that the gods who had guided the Two Lands from the beginning of time, who had brought prosperity and empire, wouldn't go away simply because Akhenaten denied them. And now the Two Lands suffered. She suffered.

Perhaps her children's illnesses were a sign of the gods' wrath. The gods knew she worshiped the sun disk. Every time she approached the altar of the Aten, she expected to be struck down for her heresy.

Forcing the words out, Nefertiti begged her husband's intercession with the Aten so that her prayers would be heard. She raised the box of frankincense to the rising sun. Over the tops of the trees a band of pink light grew faint as the golden orb rose.

"Exquisite is thy dawn," Nefertiti chanted. "Thou living sun, beside whom there is no one else. Make thy son, the king Akhenaten, to live with thee for all time, to do what thy heart craves, and to witness what thou dost every day, for he rejoices when he beholds thy splendor."

Thanuro handed her another box. Nefertiti placed it on the altar as she recited the prayer for Akhenaten. "Give him all that thy heart wishes, as much as there is air in the sky, as grain in the fields, and as water in the sea, while may I continue in attendance upon him, until he assigns me the burial that he has granted."

When the ceremony was over, Nefertiti backed away from

the altar. It was an effort not to run down the steps, for she was impatient to get away from the priest.

"Majesty."

Thanuro sidled around to block her escape. He wasn't a man one could ignore. Possessed of a body that looked as if it were a block of wet clay that had been stretched sideways, Thanuro seemed to have grown horizontally rather than vertically. It wasn't that he was fat, just wide. He had thick bones, a square face, and protruding ears. Nefertiti thought he would have made a perfect gate for a temple.

"Yes, Thanuro." Nefertiti watched the prophet's face for telltale signs of eagerness. Thanuro took pleasure in giving her the details of his latest onslaughts against heresy.

"It has come to the ears of this servant that the great royal wife has visited the temple of Ptah in Memphis."

Nefertiti took a look at the aforementioned ears. "Your ears hear much that doesn't concern you."

"I beg forgiveness, majesty, but pharaoh has made me responsible for thy religious welfare. Thy ka must not be tainted through association with unbelievers. It is said that thy majesty has opened the royal granary at Memphis to beggars and heretics."

"Your ears don't look big enough to hear things said all the way from Memphis," Nefertiti said. "What is it you wish to say?"

Thanuro bowed low. "It grieves this servant that he might be forced to bring news of such disobedience to the notice of pharaoh. The king, may he live forever, will be most displeased. However . . ."

"Continue."

"It occurs to this servant that thy majesty might be in need of a better teacher in the way of the Aten. Perhaps if I were raised to a higher position in thy majesty's service, I might be of help."

Nefertiti studied Thanuro's dark rose lips and straight nose with its thin nostrils. The man was one of many she distrusted simply because of his willingness to abandon all principle for his own gain. Akhenaten seemed to have no interest in a servant's character as long as the servant groveled before him and his personal god.

"I've already written to pharaoh about the temple of Ptah," she said. "I shall consider your request."

She left Thanuro before her rage mastered her. Never had a servant tried to coerce her. Thanuro was getting greedy. It wasn't enough that he appropriated most of her offerings after the Aten had partaken of their essence. Nefertiti was sure that the valuable myrrh, frankincense, and cassia would find its way into the coffers of the priest or his relatives.

Charging out of the altar court, her women trailing behind, she passed a line of water jars waiting to be carried to the kitchen. She grabbed one, raised it over her head, and sent it crashing against a wall. The women backed up and gawked at her. Then they sank to the ground, faces in the dirt. Sebek and her bodyguards barreled into view. They halted and stared from the shards of the container to the servants.

Sebek was brave enough to speak. "Thy majesty forgot to wait for us."

"Serpents of the netherworld!" Nefertiti cast a look of longing at the remaining water jars. Shattering the clay vessel had been satisfying. No. She'd frightened the servants already. She set off for the stables again. "Slayer of the gods. Foul wretch. Thinks he'll force me to serve his corruption."

Sebek caught up with her. Nefertiti glanced at him and shut her mouth. Should the bodyguard learn that she loathed Thanuro, the priest was likely to end up impaled on a spear.

Nefertiti remembered the day Sebek's dutiful service had turned to absolute loyalty. The warrior had been assigned to her by Queen Tiye not long after she'd been chosen to marry Akhenaten. She hadn't paid much heed to him until she'd heard some gossip from her maids. Sebek had a young wife whom he adored. She was sick after a difficult childbirth, and Sebek was near madness with grief and fear.

It had cost her nothing to send her own physician to Sebek's house with orders to remain there as long as necessary. Unfortunately the young mother had died; yet when he returned to her service after burying his wife, Sebek had thrown himself at her feet and promised lifelong devotion, promised to die for her.

"Rise," Nefertiti said. "I regret that my physician couldn't save your wife, Sebek."

The guard got to his knees and kissed the hem of her robe. "Because of you, lady, I know that all that could be done for my wife was done. Never could I have afforded so fine a physician."

"But—"

"The lady is unaware, I see, of how many great ones pass their entire lives without performing such a kindness."

She hadn't argued with him. She hadn't said that perhaps her kindness derived from her less-than-great origins. She wasn't royal. She was the daughter of a noble, one without a speck of divine blood in her. And perhaps that was why Thanuro annoyed her so much. A woman of truly divine blood would know how to deal with the man.

Seeking to calm her agitated heart, Nefertiti indulged herself by going to the city docks on foot, with only Sebek and a couple of his men as escort. Before embarking on this adventure, she cleaned the eye paint from her face, discarded her jewels, and pulled off her wig. Without the trappings of her station, few would recognize her; they simply wouldn't expect to see the great royal wife on the docks.

Sebek protested that they should go by chariot. Nefertiti laughed at him and reminded the companion that ordinary citizens walked. She was supposed to be a commoner.

At the river the air was filled with the noise of dockworkers' chants, the hawking of vendors, and the frightened bellow of cattle on a freighter from the delta. The last of Nefertiti's rage at Thanuro faded. She reveled in the sights and smells of the quay. It wasn't often that she could wander about freely among the people as she had as a child. With her escort close behind, she walked down a row of stalls across from the ships. Each vendor sat behind trays, tables, or baskets laden with goods. She stopped beside an awning hung with belts and sandals. A toothless old man immediately began his chatter.

"The finest-quality sandals in Horizon of the Aten, good lady. I have pairs in reed or leather, and look at this belt. The best-quality faience beads. I have amulets for buckles, and they're charmed for health."

Nefertiti let the man drone on, fascinated by his rough voice, the accent that betrayed his origin near Elephantine in the far south, and the way the man looked her directly in the eyes. She took the belt from the vendor and ran her fingers over the glazed surface of the beads. They were brilliant Egyptian blue. She had no idea of the value of the garment. She'd never bargained for such a thing. The man wanted one-half copper shat, and she could tell from Sebek's expression that the price was too high. Letting the beaded length fall from her hand, she wandered away.

As she left, the vendor lowered his price. Nefertiti shook her head and wove through the crowded street to a booth where a woman sold beer to sailors. Several men squatted in the shade of an awning and sipped through long pipes fitted into clay jars. On the dock opposite this stall, a merchant from Byblos argued with an inspector of the palace about a bill of lading. Nefertiti's eye was caught by the lurid purple-and-red dress of a Syrian. She stared at the foreigner and wondered, not for the first time, how Asiatics could stand those long, tight sleeves and all that hair on their chins, faces, and heads. Linen and bare skin were much more comfortable.

Sebek moved to her side. "Majesty, we should be going. Pharaoh will be anxious if we aren't at the reception of the Babylonian emissaries."

"Just a little longer, Sebek."

The guard held out a sweet cake to her. He had a sack full of bread, onions, and dessert cakes. "You forgot to eat again, majesty."

Suddenly hungry, Nefertiti ate the cake in three bites and took the cup of beer Sebek offered. She heard a little girl's laughter, turned, and without warning beheld the cavernous eyes of the starving girl in Memphis. Sailors, dockworkers, and officials plowed past them while she stared at nothing. What could she do? Akhenaten wouldn't listen to her when she told him of the people's suffering. Her constant reminders of the consequences of his campaign against the gods already threatened to drive a wedge between them.

"Is something wrong, majesty?"

There were few men to whom she could speak freely. Sebek was one of them.

"Sebek, I swear that being a great royal wife is a burden heavier than a pylon gate, more confining than the bonds of a war captive. I can't rest from this burden if my guards won't let me. I ask you to help me by leaving aside courtly politeness and diplomacy, just once in a while." She waited for a reply, but Sebek appeared to have lost his tongue. Loneliness weighed on her ka with the heaviness of a thousand gold collars. She turned away.

She hadn't gone far when Sebek appeared at her side.

"Majesty, I promise not to object."

"Object? To what?"

"To thy majesty when she tries to drive her chariot down a near-vertical slope." Sebek glanced around the docks. "To visits to the dock vendors and the tomb makers' village."

Nefertiti began to smile for the first time since leaving Memphis.

"We'll follow thy majesty cheerfully. Even if it means spending hours in the House of Life reading from old, dust-infested books." Sebek hated reading. "Such duties are better than listening to the complaints of thy majesty's tenants."

"I hold audience but once a month," Nefertiti said.

Sebek bowed as he walked. "I am thankful, majesty."

"You don't sound like it. Are you weary of serving the great royal wife, Sebek?"

Sebek gave a hooting laugh. "Not when thy majesty insists upon roaming the streets of the city in common dress and without her attendants. My men and I are as agitated as scorpions in a basket."

Nefertiti smiled at the warrior. She'd grown to depend on his humor. As the years passed she had witnessed the results of her husband's religious intolerance and neglect of the empire. During that time pity for and loyalty to Akhenaten warred with her compassion for those who suffered under his rule.

"Thy majesty is troubled."

Nefertiti nodded but said nothing. Lately she had the feeling of foreboding. Akhenaten's intolerance was growing, and the more she tried to convince him of his error, the less he listened. He still loved her, but for how long?

In the distance she could see the river. A fishing boat rowed by two sun-browned boys and an old man glided toward the docks.

"If you fail," she muttered to herself as she watched the old man and the boys, "if you fail, who will speak for them?"

Chapter 12

Near Memphis, reign of Tutankhamun

There was an unreal quality to the light that burst over the horizon, or perhaps it was only his perception. Meren felt as if he were seeing everything through chilled honey. His thoughts were thick and slow. Surrounded by disbelieving and hostile men, he could only stare in confusion at the king.

"Well?" The king's voice was shaky but demanding.

When Meren didn't answer, Tutankhamun turned away and held out his hand. A bodyguard gave him a bloody dagger. The king thrust the sullied blade at Meren. Meren found himself staring at his own weapon, which he'd left in his tent. He knew it because it was one of a scarce few in Egypt made of iron. The flat of the blade shone dully—where it wasn't smeared with blood. Lifting his gaze to pharaoh's, Meren shook his head in silence, knowing that any words he spoke would be as feathers swept away in a Nile current.

"I gave it to you," Tutankhamun said in an unsteady voice, "and you tried to kill me with it!"

Meren found his voice at last. "No, majesty, I—"

The king's legs buckled under him. The crowd of soldiers made a sound of dismay as the royal bodyguards caught and lifted the boy. Horemheb shouted orders for the king to be returned to his tent. Then he whirled on Meren and pointed.

"Lord Meren, I arrest you for treason."

Horemheb reached up and clamped a hand on Meren's arm. Without thinking, Meren snatched the sword from his friend's hand and jabbed him in the chest with his foot. Horemheb flew back into the men behind him as Meren hauled on Wind's harness and let out a shrill whistle. At once Star reared, snorting and pawing the air. Infantry and charioteers alike scuttled out of the way.

While Star reared, Meren charged through the crowd. Men scattered, and he aimed for the pickets. Cantering directly at the line of horses, he leaned down and slashed the tethering ropes as he passed. As he cut the tethers, he gave another ear-piercing whistle and slapped several rumps with the flat of his blade. It was enough to stampede the animals, and in an instant horses were racing through camp and jumping the palisades. Arrows buzzed past Meren's head as he galloped after the frightened animals. He whistled to Star when a charioteer rushed at him, his scimitar ready. Swerving to avoid the man, he hugged Wind with his knees, and the stallion sailed over the palisade with Star close behind them.

With the fiery boat of Ra cresting the horizon, Meren raced down the desert road that ran north to the delta and the border of Egypt. He rode hard until he'd left the camp far behind and the sun was fully above the skyline. Then he slowed to a walk to allow Wind to cool down. There was no time to try to make sense of this disaster. Horemheb would come after him, and he had to decide where he was going. If he were an escaped slave or criminal, he would attempt to gain one of the oases to the west or cross the delta and perhaps join the crew of a merchant ship. There was another alternative. From the times of the great ones who had built the pyramids, rebellious subjects and defeated invaders had traversed the roads from the delta border to Palestine and beyond. Horemheb would expect Meren to do the same.

But he wasn't a slave, and he wasn't a criminal or traitor, and his life was here in Egypt. Meren stopped and jumped to the ground. Wind was lathered but still in good shape, and Star even better. The two stood by patiently while Meren walked away from the road to gather handfuls of desert grass. He brushed the ground as he returned, causing his faint footprints to vanish. Then he led the horses off the road, erasing all traces of their passage. The going was slow, but at last he was far enough from the road that he wouldn't be seen when riding his horses. By the time he turned back the way he'd come, heading for Memphis, the day was warm, and the white light of Ra seared his eyes.

The journey took him all day and most of the night, and he hoped never to repeat it. Sweat stung his eyes. He could feel the heat of the solar orb sucking the moisture from his body, and his heart was filled with weariness and confusion. But he dared not stop. The horses needed water, and he had no doubt that Horemheb would eventually realize he wasn't trying to flee Egypt.

When he could no longer delay returning to water, Meren turned east and headed for the Nile. He wouldn't have to go to the river, for it was Inundation, and the flood stretched far beyond the riverbanks. Near dawn, he reached water and rested beside a small, outlying canal. The respite was short, however. He couldn't afford to be seen by some peasant from a nearby village. Before light he headed west again and made for a line of cliffs in the distance.

The sun was high when he dragged the reluctant Wind and Star up steep, sand-covered slopes and jagged rock faces to duck inside a cave. Relief from the heat came immediately. Meren dropped the horses' leads, swaying on his feet at the difference in temperature. Bracing his legs apart to steady himself, he wiped his face on a length of cloak. Then he returned to the cave entrance to gaze across the vastness of the desert to the distant city. For the second time in his life, a pharaoh wanted to kill him, only this time he was a fugitive.

At least he was free, for the moment. But pharaoh's power was unlimited, his grasp long. Leaning against the side of the cave, Meren smiled bitterly. He was in a race now. A race with Horemheb. Could he prove himself innocent before his old friend captured him? And there was a third runner in the race—the one who had arranged this trap that had ruined him. If he lost the race to his hidden enemy, Meren was certain that the result would be his death.

Late that night Meren stood in the black emptiness of an alley in the foreign quarter of Memphis and surveyed the busy street, upon which lay a grand house. A trio of drunken Babylonian sailors swerved past. Meren shrank back into the alley, flattening his back to a wall. Raucous laughter and the sounds of a fight came from a tavern down the street. A vendor trudged past, his goods packed in wicker panniers on the back of a donkey. A cat stalked in their wake. Meren eyed it suspiciously, but it was far too lean to be Dilalu's pampered pet.

Finally the traffic ebbed. Meren walked swiftly to the gate of the enormous house and spoke to the porter.

"I bring a message for Othrys from my master, Nen."

The porter looked down his nose at Meren. He hadn't brought his horses or his weapon. Either would have marked him as someone of rank. Ordinary subjects of pharaoh had neither. Police, soldiers, and nobles bore weapons, and only wealthy charioteers and aristocrats had horses. The porter was staring at Meren's dirty, rumpled kilt and stained cloak.

"Give me the message."

Meren was prepared. "I am to repeat the message to no one but Othrys."

"The master is busy. Come back tomorrow."

For this, he was not prepared. Never in his life had he been discounted or dismissed. Blinking rapidly, he stood his ground.

"If I have to come back tomorrow, it will be too late, and your master will miss out on a matter of great profit. Will you take the blame for it? Say so, and I'll go. It matters not to me if you're thrown to the jackals."

Now he had the porter's attention. The man stepped aside and allowed Meren to enter the forecourt. In the light of torches affixed with wall sconces he could see a great house composed of several blocks rising three and four stories. Light wells brought air and sunlight to the various blocks, while stairs in each well served corridors leading to the various chambers on each level. The blocks were arranged around a central courtyard. Meren faced a colonnade of red wooden columns, and as he entered the forecourt, two sentries flanked him.

He was conducted through a labyrinth of corridors and linked rooms. The way was confusing and involved climbing and descending three separate staircases. By the time they stopped outside a door almost double his height, Meren was lost. No doubt that was the intent.

One of his guards went inside, returning in a few moments to hold the door open. Meren was shoved through the threshold, and he stumbled into a guarded antechamber. He went through several more rooms, each more secluded than the last, until the guards stopped him at another door. This one was as thick as those of the royal palace and had bronze fittings. It opened to reveal a silver-haired man in a long, tiered robe. Meren was given a final shove, and the door slammed behind him.

Without addressing him, Silver Hair spun on his heel and walked through the room. To Meren it seemed as if he'd plunged into the water. From floor to ceiling the chamber bore frescoes of the sea—dolphins frolicking in blue-green waters, surrounded by fish and octopi. In the light of fragile alabaster lamps he could see tables laden with gold and silver drinking vessels and wine flagons. An Egyptian-style bed rested on a dais inside a frame draped with sheers. Meren surveyed the room, which appeared deserted until Silver Hair went to an archway hung with more gauzelike curtains. He spoke in a whisper, and a shadow appeared on the curtains.

Through them stepped a man whose appearance marked him as a foreigner. The most foreign of his features were his eyes. Kysen had called them sky eyes, and they were indeed the color of the sky when the light of Ra has burned the deep blue of early morning to the white-blue of a summer afternoon. Othrys also had hair the color of aged honey streaked with the sun's rays, and a body laden with sailor's muscles. His skin was pale compared to Meren's and marked with scars that should have made him seem old. The tautness of his skin, however, revealed him to be a man of middle years, perhaps not much older than Meren.

Silver Hair oozed his way out of the room as Othrys crossed to a table and poured wine into a shallow gold cup engraved with a bull-leaping cycle. "What message from my friend Nen?" the pirate asked as he sipped his wine.

"Nen is Kysen, and Kysen is my son," Meren said quietly.

The gold cup paused halfway to the pirate's lips. Othrys swiveled on his heel; his stare could have pinned Meren to the wall.

"It's a mistake not to look at messengers, servants, and sentries," Meren said. "A stranger can winnow his way into the heart of your camp in such a humble capacity."

Othrys set the cup down and walked over to Meren. He stopped a couple of paces away and surveyed him from head to ankle.

"By the Earth Mother," he muttered. "Lord Meren, Friend of the King, Eyes and Ears of Pharaoh. What do you here, mighty lord?"

"You'll discover why anyway, so I'll tell you."

Meren told the pirate the story of the attack on the king and his flight. During the recounting Othrys didn't move. His gaze stabbed into Meren's, searching for the smallest deception or the least hint that Meren was withholding vital facts. When the tale was done, the pirate returned to the table, poured a second cup of wine, and handed it to Meren.

"And so you're a marked man, Egyptian. A traitor."

"Falsely accused," Meren said as he took the wine.

"Brought to your undoing by the malice of some evil power."

Meren said nothing. He was assessing Othrys. He'd taken a grave risk in coming to the pirate, who could easily kill him or hand him over to pharaoh. Behind those sky eyes Meren could see the rapid calculations of a man who existed on the edge of lawfulness, stepping over the boundary into transgression whenever it suited his purpose.

"My son has told me of your friendship," Meren said quietly. "Therefore I have come seeking refuge."

A breeze lifted the transparent sheers, and they brushed Othrys's leg. He swept them aside, revealing a balcony.

"Come. You've traveled far and must be weary."

They sat on the ledge of the balcony facing each other over the delicate golden wine cups.

Othrys gave Meren a casual glance. "It seems to me, Egyptian, that I could save myself a seaful of trouble by killing you and giving your body to pharaoh."

"That would anger pharaoh," Meren replied with smooth unconcern. "He wants me alive to question, and killing me would earn you the everlasting enmity of my son."

"I do not fear Kysen."

"And my charioteers."

"Ha!"

"And Ay."

"Ah, the vizier. I forgot about him." Othrys rubbed his smooth-shaven chin. "That would be most inconvenient, having the evil will of pharaoh's highest minister. It could interfere with . . . trade."

"At least."

"You're in evil plight, Egyptian, and you've brought it upon me by coming here."

"If you help me, you'll have the friendship and gratitude of the Eyes and Ears of Pharaoh."

"At the moment, it isn't worth much."

"It will be."

Othrys ran a finger around the lip of his cup and mused, "But if I get rid of you, I earn the gratitude of the one who planned your disgrace and wants you dead." Eyes the color of chilled water suddenly met Meren's. "I told Kysen not to interfere with Yamen, Dilalu, or Zulaya. Which of them plots your end?"

"I don't know. I've seen the merchant and Yamen, but not Zulaya."

"It matters not," Othrys said with a sigh. "If I kill you, news of it will come to the right ears."

Meren felt the chill of the embalming knife at his throat but smiled his most tranquil smile. "You're absolutely right, pirate."

For the first time he saw Othrys jolted from his airy confidence. Meren swirled the wine in his cup and continued to look amused.

"Of course, from the pattern of events so far, the most likely outcome of your killing me would be your own death."

"What?"

Setting his cup down on the balcony floor, Meren rose, folded his arms over his chest, and regarded Othrys. "The evil one will assume that you forced me to tell all I know of his transgressions before you killed me. Once he makes that conclusion, you'll join me in the netherworld."

"He can't reach me."

Meren held the pirate's gaze as his lips twisted into an ironic grimace. "If he can ruin me, he can catch you in his net." He didn't move as the pirate went still with contemplation. The breeze played with the curtains and danced in Meren's hair.

Suddenly Othrys grinned, slapped Meren's back, and said, "Welcome to my house, Egyptian. You're under my protection, and if you bring this evil one down on me, he won't have to kill you. I'll do it myself."

Chapter 13

Horizon of the Aten, the independent reign of the pharaoh Akhenaten

Nefertiti woke before sunrise. She turned onto her side and beheld a servant creeping about, lighting lamps. Her eye caught a scene from a wall mural of her and the children in a reed skiff. The boat floated in a marsh brimming with wildfowl. In the image heron and ducks fluttered above her head as she drew back a throw stick and took aim. Akhenaten had offered to have the scene repainted to omit Meketaten, but she'd refused. Her little girl was gone, and all she had left were things—clothing, toys, and paintings of the child like this one.

Meketaten had been her second-born, a little bundle of endearing glee who'd found gravity and decorum almost beyond her nature. After she died, Nefertiti hadn't wanted to live. Only the thought of leaving her five remaining daughters had kept her tethered to this world. Sometimes she went to the playroom in the queen's palace, where the girls were allowed to draw, and studied the dabs and streaks of red, yellow, and green that Meketaten had splashed on the floor and walls. No one had approved of her allowing the children such freedom. Royal princesses should be brought up mannered and well groomed and not given the freedom to spatter paint around an entire room. Nefertiti had ignored such advice, and Akhenaten, who had suffered from a royal upbringing, had sided with her.

This mural of the girls was her favorite. Nefertiti loved the cool blues, greens, and blue grays of the feathers and water. It was disappointing that the girls' bodies had been drawn with sagging middles like Akhenaten's. She wished everyone didn't have to look like a potter's discard simply because Akhenaten didn't have wide shoulders and a muscled torso.

Nefertiti rose from the bed and clapped her hands. Attendants appeared with toiletries. Even after so many months, it took all her considerable will to face a new day. There was a blackness about her heart that tinged the world with gloom. Desolation reigned her ka, and she knew she would never recover from losing that little being who had come from her body to bless her life with laughter. And even if she hadn't wanted to live for her children's sake, there was Egypt. Egypt was troubled, for pharaoh was troubled.

Akhenaten's hatred of the old order increased daily, fed by defiant priests and subjects. The people obeyed Akhenaten's edicts in form but believed as they always had in their hearts. And now pharaoh's frustration and hatred had impelled him to do violence against his enemies—but she didn't want to sail down that stream of thought.

Despite her desolation, Nefertiti dressed and proceeded with her morning activities. She ate the morning meal with her girls, settled their quarrels, and reviewed their lessons with their tutors. She had interviews with a few of the countless officials of the queen's household—her steward, the overseer of the cabinet, the chief of hairdressers, the queen's herald, the traders of the queen's household, the overseer of the seal.

She listened to complaints from the bearer of floral offerings for the queen, the chief of musicians of the queen's household, and the merchant who'd provided horses for her chariot. Of them all, only Sebek, captain of the troops of the queen, had no laments. Much of the routine was tedious, but it gave Nefertiti a sense of continuity and security she badly needed.

The sun was above the eastern cliffs by the time she finished and was ready to join Akhenaten in the morning worship. As was her custom of late, she was to meet her husband at the great Aten temple in the southern city. The drive down the main road that spanned the city from north to south was filled with the din of construction. They'd moved to Horizon of the Aten so quickly that many buildings were still being constructed. Akhenaten simply hadn't the patience to wait. Even the great Aten temple was constructed primarily of mud brick, so great had been pharaoh's haste.

She had discussed the plan of Horizon of the Aten with her husband, and they'd agreed that, if they were to have any privacy, the royal palaces should be placed away from the rest of the city. So the enormous riverside palace was far north of the city, with her smaller palace a little farther south. Below these lay the city itself, with its vast Aten temple, ceremonial palace, and the King's House, which they used when in the city. Interspersed among the government buildings and in enclaves to the north and south were the rest of the city's inhabitants—the ministers, officials, servants, and artisans. Horizon of the Aten was like no other city in Egypt. It had been planned. All of it was new. And no other god had a temple there. Akhenaten was confronted with no reminders of opposition, of the old ways, of the old king of the gods— Amun.

At the great Aten temple, when pharaoh shuffled into the colonnaded courtyard, Nefertiti and her attendants were waiting. She gave her youngest lady's wig a surreptitious jerk so that it sat straight on the girl's head and joined her husband for the adoration. In front of her and to either side stretched altar after altar. Not for Akhenaten the mysterious, secluded ritual of old. No, he worshiped in the heat of the sun, his god, offering simultaneously with his priests at hundreds of altars. Often, when she'd been standing in the sun too long, Nefertiti longed for the practical structure of the old temples. The thick stone walls and darkness of the sanctuaries meant shelter from the dangerous heat of the sun—a blessing from the old gods of which Akhenaten seemed oblivious.

After the ceremony Nefertiti accompanied pharaoh to the great audience hall of the ceremonial palace, where the king barely listened to reports from ministers and petitions from citizens, and received foreign delegations. Once she'd been proud that the ministers were carefully respectful of any advice she gave. When Akhenaten first allowed her to attend such governmental audiences, the ministers had assumed she knew little of the difficulties of expeditions to the gold mines of Nubia or the problems encountered in surveying crops for taxation. It hadn't taken long for them to learn otherwise. By contrast, Akhenaten seemed to think that any question would be solved by delegating it to a minister or by referring it to the divine wisdom of the Aten.

What was worse, pharaoh spent less than half the time his father had given to the task of governing. Long afternoons went by in the royal gardens, where Akhenaten would lounge under a tree watching his daughters play. Every day was a feast day, each night an occasion for dancing, juggling, love songs, and games. If Nefertiti hadn't taken an interest, government in the Two Lands would have floundered while pharaoh and his court diligently practiced sloth.

In the years since they'd come to Horizon of the Aten, Nefertiti had grown sick of afternoons spent prone on a couch with Akhenaten shoving food at her. She was fortunate that the solution to her problem had occurred to her. Invariably the heat, beer, and food lulled pharaoh into a nap each afternoon. She left as soon as Akhenaten fell asleep.

During these afternoons Nefertiti served as an unofficial vizier. What Akhenaten ignored and vizier Nakht mismanaged, she tried to salvage with her father's advice and help. Often Nefertiti joined Ay in the House of Correspondence of pharaoh, the office of works, or the police barracks.

One day she had discovered her father in the House of Correspondence, talking with the king's chamberlain, Tutu. The conversation centered around inventories of some kind, and Nefertiti grew tired of listening to them. She wandered through a hall where scribes sat in rows and scribbled notes on limestone flakes or wrote letters on expensive papyrus. She passed walls with shelves filled with docketed letters. Walking past five such archives, she finally reached a room where young apprentice scribes ground pigments for ink and burnished sheets of papyrus with smoothing stones. Remembering how cramped her fingers had become when she performed such tasks for Tati, Nefertiti watched several lads ply mortar and pestle. Across the room, through a door, she could see clerks taking delivery on a shipment of papyrus.

Drawing closer to the door, she watched slaves unloading bales from donkeys. She heard Ay calling to her and started back to the main hall. On her way she passed a room filled with clay tablets. The kingdoms of the Asiatics, Babylon, the cities of Palestine and Syria, all used the heavy cakes of earth as writing material instead of papyrus. A scribe would impress wedge-shaped symbols on moist clay and allow the inscription to dry. In Egypt, when the correspondence arrived, pharaoh's secretaries transcribed the clay tablets onto papyrus and then stored the clumsy originals.

Nefertiti picked up a sample. Someone had written the regnal year of Akhenaten and the date the letter was received on the side of the tablet. The edges of the brown cake were crumbling from being tossed about carelessly. Nefertiti ran her hand over the smooth surface of the tablet. Ay's voice came to her, and she hurried to join her father, the letter still in her hand.

She caught up with Ay and Tutu in the main hall. "I found one of the storage rooms. Imagine having to write on wet lumps like this all day."

"Cursed things," Tutu said. "There's a mountain of them in the courtyard out back. They took up so much room that the scribes shoveled them outside."

Ay took the tablet from Nefertiti. He held it to the light coming from a window.

"This is a letter from the prince of Gezer, majesty," Ay said to Nefertiti. "It was received three months ago."

Nefertiti turned slowly to face Tutu and asked quietly, "Why has pharaoh not been given a transcription of this?"

She watched Tutu peer at the tablet with a vague look on his face. The man waved his walking stick.

"Majesty, I'm sure someone probably already did that."

"You know very well the king entrusts all the correspondence from other lands to me," Nefertiti said. "My father and I summarize it for him each day, and neither of us have seen this letter. Come."

Her irritation growing, Nefertiti led the way to her find. Ay knelt beside a pile and held up one brick missive after another. In a few moments his hands were covered with dust, and his face looked as hard as the clay he handled. Nefertiti understood the look he gave her. She snapped at the chamberlain, "Who is chief transcriber?"

Tutu summoned the overseer of the House of Correspondence. The overseer summoned his assistant, who appeared after a slave was sent to find him. He scurried into the room with his mouth full of bread, wiping his hands on his kilt. At the sight of Nefertiti, the man started choking. The overseer pounded his back and thrust a cup of water at him. Nefertiti would have laughed if she hadn't been so furious.

"Speak," Ay said. He crossed his arms over his chest and glared at the scribe.

"Great lord, the only transcriber we had fell ill and died months ago. We sent for another, but since the temples were closed, it's been hard to find knowledgeable workers."

Nefertiti stared at the overseer of the House of Correspondence. "You only have one transcriber? For all of the writings that come from the monarchs of the Asiatics and across the waters of the Great Green, for all the vassals and petty princes, the tribal chiefs? *One?*"

"Actually they don't have even one," Ay said. "Haven't had for a long time, I'd say."

Nefertiti and Ay looked at Tutu. The chamberlain studied the carved tip of his walking stick while they waited. The scratch of reed pens on papyrus pierced the silence. Nefertiti could see the resentment in Tutu's eyes.

"The king complained of the amount of reading he had to do, even with thy majesty's help. Pharaoh was annoyed at the constant complaints and bickering of the vassals. His majesty spoke to me, and I suggested that we wait until many of the less important documents had collected. That way we could get rid of many at once instead of a few day after day. Pharaoh was pleased with my suggestion."

Trying to control her boiling temper, Nefertiti asked,

"How long were you going to wait before presenting this correspondence?"

"I await the request of pharaoh."

Ay almost shouted at the minister. "But the king probably thinks you'll come to him when you're ready!"

Tutu straightened his shoulders. He looked down his nose at Ay and sneered. "I understood the words of the good god perfectly. When the divine one wishes to see the writings of the wretched Asiatics, I will bring them before him."

"You'll bring them before me," Nefertiti said.

"But, majesty—"

"Do you question the word of the great royal wife?" Ay asked.

"No! Nonononoo."

Tutu bowed and bobbed and groveled before her. Disgusted, Nefertiti waved him out of the room.

As soon as the man was gone, Ay clasped her arm. "I know you were provoked, daughter, but tread carefully in your dealings with Tutu. He's a man who harbors resentments with the zeal of a miser."

"Don't worry, Father. I'll speak to Akhenaten. He'll be relieved that I've offered to take this burden from him completely. You know Tutu is right. His majesty barely tolerates listening to foreign delegations; he hates reading correspondence. And no matter what I do, Tutu will look upon my interest as an invasion. He's a petty little man." She gave her father a wry smile. "I wouldn't be surprised if he started throwing away tablets just to keep me from violating his boundaries."

"Things would be much easier if you succeed, daughter."

"Pray to the Aten that pharaoh allows me to speak." Nefertiti gave a small sigh. "He still thinks of me as a child. A day doesn't go by that he doesn't recall some embarrassing incident. Yesterday he told Merytaten about the times I used to run away from my lessons and go sailing in my skiff on the Nile."

"I remember, daughter. Queen Tiye was most grieved that you didn't show proper gravity at being trained to be queen of Egypt."

Ignoring her father's amusement, Nefertiti said, "I'll go to pharaoh now, before Tutu has a chance to think of throwing away the tablets."

That incident had taken place years ago. Since then she'd fought similar battles with other ministers and won them all. But with her little girl dead, fighting such battles took more strength of will than she feared she had. Nefertiti spoke the words of the Aten ritual without thinking, her gestures practiced and unhesitating after countless repetitions. She often indulged in reverie while performing the adoration. Since Akhenaten was the means by which the Aten communed with the world, her attention wasn't absolutely necessary anyway.

As the ceremony ended, Akhenaten gave her a kiss and looked into her eyes. "Beautiful one, you aren't sleeping. There are shadows beneath those magnificent eyes."

They stood together, bathed in sunlight. Hundreds of offering tables spread out before them in a consecrated field within the temple. Priests and courtiers alike kept their distance, for it was well known that Akhenaten tolerated no invasion upon his private conversations with the great royal wife. The rays of the Aten touched the cobra headdress of the king and made Nefertiti's electrum broad collar and bracelets gleam.

Akhenaten searched her eyes, his brow furrowed and his long, equine face troubled. "I must receive a delegation from the Assyrian king, my love, but I insist that you go home and try to sleep. It's nearly time for the girls to take a nap. If you rest with them, sleep will come."

"I don't think so."

"At least try, my love."

Sighing, Nefertiti consented and left the Aten temple. To her surprise, Akhenaten was right. Once the girls were asleep, she found that she could close her eyes and drift off to the sound of their breathing. Sometimes she forgot how perceptive her husband could be.

She woke late in the afternoon to find that the nurses had succeeded in getting the girls out of her chamber without waking her. Feeling almost at peace, Nefertiti decided to go to Akhenaten and thank him. She didn't understand how he could be so caring and kind to her and yet so blind to the suffering of those he'd displaced with his heresies.

Her guards formed a barrier between her and the people in the streets as Nefertiti drove to the ceremonial palace again. Her entourage passed a train of donkeys laden with vegetables, groups of scribes hurrying to various government offices, carrying chairs bearing court ladies, and a gaggle of Aten priests.

She reached the palace and couldn't find pharaoh in any of the usual spots where he sheltered from the heat. It wasn't time for worship, so Nefertiti inquired of the steward. She received the unexpected reply that pharaoh was at the police barracks.

She couldn't imagine why he was there. Military surroundings made Akhenaten nervous. Anyway, her husband preferred the tiled and gilded luxury of the palaces. Perplexed, Nefertiti set out with Sebek and an escort for the barracks, which were located to the rear and down the street from the ceremonial palace. The military sector of the central city lay beyond the records office and visitors' quarters.

She found Akhenaten by following the line of royal body-guards that stretched along the street and into the low, rectangular building that housed the city police. Inside, a sentry directed her through several offices, and outside again past stables and supply rooms to a small, windowless building. As she drew near the structure Nefertiti exchanged uneasy glances with Sebek. She was sure she wasn't going to like what she found inside.

A guard at the door saluted but failed to move aside. Nefertiti was about to send in a request for admittance when a man screamed. It was a mindless scream of agony such as she'd never heard. The sound penetrated to Nefertiti's bones and robbed her of speech. When the scream subsided into short, hoarse cries, Nefertiti shoved past the sentry, her guards at her back.

The blackness of the interior made her pause for her eyes to adjust. The building was split into two large rooms. The first, into which Nefertiti stepped, was lit by a lamp resting in a stand by an inner door. Against the walls she saw crouched bodies. As her vision cleared, Nefertiti saw that the bodies were three men whose arms were bound behind their necks. Five policemen stood near the outer door, armed with spears.

Near the lamp stood a man whose gold bracelets and short wig marked him as an officer.

"Pharaoh?" Nefertiti asked.

The man bowed and opened the door to the next room without comment. Nefertiti was through the entry and into the chamber before the reek of feces and sweat reached her. She heard Sebek gasp. Nefertiti swallowed her own nausea and stared at the scene before her.

The room had been bare until pharaoh came. It was a chamber of blank walls, a dirt floor, and no other openings except the door. The ceiling was low and added to the atmosphere of oppression and tightness. Toward the back of the room, suspended from ropes attached to beams in the roof, hung the naked body of a man, the man who screamed. More ropes stretched from his feet to a stake in the ground. Lit by alabaster lamps, the man's body glistened like a freshly butchered carcass. Hundreds of precise, thin cuts ran from his neck, down the man's chest, all the way to his thighs. Beside the victim a Nubian soldier wiped blood and flesh from a bronze razor much as a barber tends his instrument. Nearby on a stool was Mery-Re. In another corner a scribe sat with pen and papyrus.

To one side, ensconced in a cushioned chair of ebony and gold, sat pharaoh. The chair rested on a woven mat. Pharaoh's fan-bearer plied a fan over Akhenaten's head. Another courtier held a tray with wine flagon and goblet. Akhenaten held a vial of perfume to his nose. When Nefertiti entered, he turned and peered at her over the lip of the vessel. In a languid motion pharaoh held out his hand to Nefertiti. Nefertiti knelt before her husband and fixed her gaze on the gold roundels that decorated the king's robe. Fingers decked with heavy electrum rings lifted her chin. Nefertiti looked into the king's eyes. They questioned in a mild, distracted manner.

"My beautiful one has come. Have you rested well?"

"Yes, majesty."

"I am pleased. And it pleases me also that you've tired of dry bureaucrats and harvest taxation and come to see the more important work that takes my time."

Nefertiti kept her gaze on Akhenaten and away from the man on the ropes. "What work is this, majesty?" She signaled for Sebek and her guards to remain near the door.

"The work of my father the Aten." Pharaoh nodded his head toward the victim. "Lately it has been necessary to chastise those who seek to hide the wealth of the false gods from me."

Nefertiti understood immediately. Akhenaten had recently discovered that, under increasingly violent persecution, the Amun priests had hidden their valuables rather than have them sequestered for the use of the Aten. The man whose skin hung in thin, bloody strips was a priest.

Pharaoh sniffed at his perfume bottle and called for a stool for Nefertiti. From a dark corner stepped a man Nefertiti had never seen before. He was tall, as tall as the Nubian torturer, and as lean. Dressed in a kilt and pleated overrobe, he wore a broad collar of gold and turquoise beads and wide arm bands with insets of lapis lazuli. His rich trappings set off skin of a tone darker than Nefertiti's, yet lighter than the Nubian's. Pharaoh beckoned to the nobleman, calling him Kenro.

Kenro placed a stool beside Nefertiti and bowed. Nefertiti noticed his cool perfection. Every pleat in his robe hung straight. His linen gleamed white and spotless under the lamps. His feet in their red and gold sandals were free of dust. The flail in his hand was a work of art in black and gold enamel.

Even Kenro's face bore the flawless artistry of an expert at cosmetics, though the features were perfect to the point of almost feminine beauty. Long, slanting eyes regarded her steadily. They were deep-set, brown, and oddly calm.

A moan from the priest attracted pharaoh's attention. "Proceed, Kenro. No mere priest is going to keep me from finding the treasure of Amun."

Kenro moved with quiet grace to stand beside the Nubian. He whispered instructions, and the torturer applied his razor to the man's chest. He drew several horizontal incisions across the vertical cuts he'd already made. The victim screamed and jerked, but the ropes held him taut. His torso was soon a mass of oozing red checks. Kenro raised his hand. The Nubian withdrew his blade.

Kenro cocked his head to one side and looked at pharaoh. Nefertiti went sick at the dreamy expression on the man's face. She'd seen that look on Akhenaten's face when he made love to her.

"Well?" Akhenaten questioned impatiently. "Come, divine father, tell me where the treasure is. If you tell me, I'll have you killed quickly. Otherwise I'll have Kenro apply his more sophisticated instruments to you."

The priest was so weak his head had to be lifted. Through lips cracked and bleeding he whispered the name of a village in the Hare nome. "In the house of the doorkeeper of the chapel of the god Toth." The man's words ended on a sob.

Nefertiti stood up, steadying herself with a hand on pharaoh's chair. She could barely wait for Akhenaten to leave this room of horror with its blood and gilded furniture. The nobleman with the wine tray left, along with Mery-Re, Nefertiti's guards, and the fan-bearer. Nefertiti followed Akhenaten to the door while the scribe remained to finish his notes. She looked back to see that Kenro lingered beside the priest, his eyes sliding over what had once been the man's skin. Kenro wasn't going to kill his prisoner. Nefertiti knew it. She touched Akhenaten's arm.

"Majesty, the priest has defied you, yet he has suffered for it. Please, send him to the netherworld."

Akhenaten frowned at her. "You have sympathy for Amun and his followers?"

"I have sympathy for a man in pain, my husband. Is this wrong?"

"Yes. He deserves agony without end for defying me." Pharaoh suddenly ripped the dagger from his belt. "Kill him yourself. Show me your devotion, little warrior."

If she hesitated, Akhenaten would leave his victim with Kenro. Nefertiti took the dagger from pharaoh's hand—quickly, before she had time to contemplate what must be done. She sent Kenro and the Nubian backing away from the priest with a sharp command. She wasn't tall enough. She stood on a stool so she could aim at the priest's heart. Turning her back to pharaoh, she gripped the weapon and drew back her arm. The priest lifted his head. His eyes opened as he whispered words of thanks.

Nefertiti whispered, "May Hathor await you. May Osiris receive your ka." She dared not wait. She drove the blade between muscles and ribs into the heart of the priest as he smiled. Her hand met the scored mass that used to be a chest. She jerked the dagger out of the body and hopped back off the stool. The man's bowels released their contents, and the odor of feces and urine mingled with the smell of blood.

Nefertiti turned to Akhenaten, but Kenro was beside her. "If thy majesty will permit thy servant."

Gentle as the touch of a snake's tongue, Kenro's hands bathed hers with a clean, wet cloth. The dagger was wiped and given back to her. Wet fingers touched the back of her hand, and Nefertiti shivered. Not daring to think of what she'd just done, in an agony of spirit, she joined her husband.

"I didn't think you'd do it," Akhenaten said. Pharaoh studied Nefertiti as if she were a stranger. "You are indeed my little warrior."

"What is the name of the priest, majesty?"

"I've forgotten. It doesn't matter. He won't have a grave, and his name will be wiped out. This is one heretic whose ka will die permanently."

Nefertiti resisted when pharaoh attempted to guide her from the room. "I've never killed before."

"Do you want his hand?"

"I want no battle trophy, my pharaoh. That was no barbarian. If you will allow it, I would like to know the name of the first man you ever asked me to kill for you."

"Kenro knows."

Kenro spoke from somewhere behind Nefertiti. "His name was Montemhab, majesty. Superintendent of the god's treasury of Amun in Thebes."

Nefertiti thanked Kenro and Akhenaten. She followed the king out into the sun. The royal bodyguard formed around them. As she walked beside the king, Nefertiti made a great effort to listen to pharaoh's discussion of the hidden wealth he was determined to ferret from the temples. All the while another part of her heart vowed to find some way to help Montemhab's ka survive without a body. Pharaoh was going to have the corpse burned.

She managed to get herself through the next few hours without collapsing. Once she had regained the refuge of her own rooms, Nefertiti sank to the floor and lay there trembling and sobbing. She had killed. For mercy, it was true, but the act itself defiled her.

She lay on the floor for a long time, in darkness no blacker than the misery of her ka. As she lay there in desolation, at long last Nefertiti began to hate her husband. Behind the great vision of one shining god lay intolerance, ignorance, and cruelty. She had failed to banish them from her husband's character with her beauty and guidance. Such a thing had never been possible. Tiye and Amunhotep had been wrong to make her think it possible. Hope of moderation was dead, as dead as that poor priest.

It was a madness of the sun, like when he told you about the Aten coming to him in the desert. It was sun madness. May the gods help you if you ever provoke the demons that possess his ka.

That night, the evil dreams began.

Chapter 14

Memphis, reign of Tutankhamun

Disaster had come without warning. To Kysen it had been like reliving the nightmare of his childhood before Meren had bought him from his father—sudden violence without reason. In the middle of the night soldiers of the king had forced their way into the house, dragged him from his bed, and held him, Bener, and his men at spearpoint. They had searched every cubit from rooftop to cellar and carried away all correspondence, all records, anything written, even Bener's household accounts. Now Kysen realized why his father had instructed the scribes to get rid of any records relating to Queen Nefertiti. During the search a confused and disbelieving Maya came to tell them that Lord Meren had tried to kill pharaoh and had fled the country.

Kysen's protests had been useless. Royal sentries guarded the house, the stables, the charioteers' quarters, the cattle pens, service yard, servants' block, even the well and the gardens. The only place they hadn't invaded was the women's quarters. That was why Kysen had taken refuge in his sister's chamber after the invaders left. Kysen and Bener sat on a long cushion beneath a niche in which a statue of the god Bes rested and shared an evening meal, although neither was hungry. Fearful and enraged at the invasion of troops, Bener had turned on him, alternately cajoling and browbeating him for an explanation. He would never have told her the truth if it hadn't been for her last remark.

"You listen to me, Ky," Bener had said. "If I'm going to be killed, you at least owe it to me to tell me why."

She had voiced his greatest fear, and he'd confessed. Now that he'd finished telling her everything, he regretted his weakness. Father would be furious. If he was still alive. Even now Horemheb might be headed back to Memphis with Meren's body dragging behind his chariot. Kysen squeezed his eyes shut, trying to avoid the image.

"So," Bener said quietly. "What are we going to do?"

Kysen's eyes flew open. "Do? You're going to do nothing. If you haven't noticed, there are guards around every corner. There's even one in the chapel."

"I know that," Bener snapped.

"And I can't get word to Abu or Reia, because no one is allowed to leave, and anything I write is read before it's sent."

There was a tray of food between them, and Bener was spreading date paste on bread with an ivory knife. "I've been thinking about that."

"They'll read your letters too, want-wit."

Bener nibbled at her bread. "There are some things into which even royal guards dislike sticking their fingers."

"Oh?"

"Tell me, Ky. When you were married, did you inquire into the details of your wife's monthly time?"

His jaw unhinged as he stared at his sister. Bener returned his look of horror with a nasty little smile.

"Sometimes men are so stupid," she said.

"I—I don't see—"

"We can send messages through my laundry maid, concealed among bloodied cloths."

"But—"

"I'm not going to hear about your weak stomach, am I?"

Kysen licked his lips and shook his head.

"Good. Because I've already arranged things."

"Have you, by the gods?" he asked faintly.

"I had to," Bener said. "They're watching you too closely, and the only charioteers we have left are inexperienced." She made a little sound of disgust. "That Irzanen and the other one, Amenthu. We have to stop Abu and Reia from coming here."

"They won't. If they get as far as Memphis without being arrested, they'll hear of the trouble and avoid the house."

"But that means we won't know where to find them," Bener said.

"They'll go to Father."

Bener surveyed her date-covered bread. "Out of Egypt."

"Perhaps."

"Wherever they are, we're on our own," Bener said. "And we need help."

"No one at court can help us without being accused of treachery."

Bener brushed crumbs from her gown and said in a matter-of-fact tone, "Then we shall look for aid outside the court."

Kysen eyed her suspiciously, then shook his head rapidly. "Oh, no. That is madness."

"It is not. Ebana is perfect. Even Horemheb won't suspect."

Kysen rested his head in his hands and groaned. "I never should have told you."

"Nonsense," Bener said cheerfully. "Who better to help solve the mystery of a woman's death than another woman?"

He would have argued with his sister, but someone pounded at the door to Bener's chamber. His head shot up as a maid scurried in from another room on her way to open the door. Before she could reach it, the portal was bashed open to reveal a Nubian guard.

Kysen got to his feet as he recognized Mose, the counterpart of Karoya. The king's Nubian bodyguards intimidated not only because of their height and muscularity but also because they affected a severe, brooding silence. Kysen had never heard more than a few words pass Karoya's lips, and less from Mose. When the Nubian did speak, it was with an accent that belied the fact that he'd spent most of his life in Egypt. Behind him stood six more of his fellow bodyguards, their wrists and ankles encased in leather studded with gold, their belts of electrum, carnelian, and malachite, their spears tipped in gold.

Ignoring the maid, Mose stalked over to Kysen. "Pharaoh summons Lord Kysen." Without another word and with no acknowledgment of Bener's existence, the bodyguard turned on his heel and marched out of the room.

With a glance at Bener's alarmed face, Kysen followed him. As he reached the door, Bener called out to him.

"Kysen?"

He smiled at her. "I'll return soon."

It was a lie. He wasn't sure he'd return at all.

Meren threaded his way through the groups of laughing, chattering, and drunken patrons of the Divine Lotus. Two days ago, when he'd sought refuge with Othrys, he hadn't thought it possible for him to walk freely among men as he did. That was before Othrys persuaded him to allow the pirate to turn him into a Mycenaean Greek.

Meren had been handed over to the pirate's trusted aide and scribe, Naram-Sin, who summoned tailors and hairdressers and maids. With their help, the scribe accomplished the transformation with the ease of practice. To Meren's dismay, Naram-Sin made him wear a wig of curling locks that hung over his shoulders and down his back. It was of that strange hair color—a gleaming dark brown tinged with red. The scribe was pleased with the results, but by then Meren had had enough of him. Naram-Sin took entirely too much pleasure in his new duties as a body servant. He wore an expression of mocking humor that Meren suspected to be at his expense.

Meren's disguise was completed by a new wardrobe. He'd been furnished with tunics of foreign design cinched with braided belts and embroidered with geometric or leaf designs at the neck and short sleeves. Worst of all were the leggings. They were tight, and they itched.

While Meren was being disguised, Othrys sent men to rescue Wind and Star and take them to a safe hiding place. The stallions were too noticeable to be brought into the city. The pirate also sent agents in quest of Abu and Reia, but nothing had been heard from them. They did bring word that Meren's family was being guarded. He'd expected it, but the news that his children were imprisoned and watched still sent him into a fit of helpless rage.

Shouldering his way through the crowd around a couple of dancers spinning to the music of flute, cymbals, and drum, Meren stopped short when an Egyptian woman stepped into his path. She was dressed in the Greek fashion of flounced skirt and tight bodice cut to reveal the breasts, and was obviously one of the owner's servants.

"Greek," she said. "Do you miss your homeland? I can give you a taste of it."

Othrys had instructed Meren in a few words of the language. He responded with them, but the woman wasn't deterred. When he tried to go around her, she moved in his way again.

"All merchants and sailors speak my language, tall one." She came closer, took his hand, and put it on her hip and held it there.

He pulled his hand free and shook his head. Once more he tried to move away, but she blocked his escape, frowning.

"By the charms of Hathor, another one who likes not women. You have no interest in me, but I know a young man who's as pretty as he is talented, tall one."

Annoyed, Meren bent and whispered to her, "I have nothing to pay you, so be off."

"Ha! Now you speak." The woman whirled around, clamped her hand on the arm of a Babylonian merchant, and began her entreaties again as if Meren had never existed.

Resuming his search, Meren glanced around the main room of the tavern. There was a round central hearth with a blaze going to keep out the night chill. The air was hazy with smoke and thick with perfume and the odors of beer and wine. Cushions and mats were scattered around the great chamber for the customers, and there was a long table on which had been set tall wine jars and vats of beer. Wealthier clients sat at small tables, but those who wished to avoid expense or revealing light kept to the shadows along the walls. Customers came and went through the front door and up the stairs to rooms on the second level.

Still searching, Meren edged out of the crowd around the

dancers and finally saw what he wanted. He went to the serving table, where the attendant handed him a cup of beer. Othrys had an arrangement with Ese, the tavern owner, which afforded his men a share of her hospitality. Meren sought the shadows against the wall opposite the dancers. Walking slowly by clusters of Ese's less illustrious and law-abiding clientele, he reached the corner and lowered himself to a cushion between Abu and Reia.

"I wasn't sure you'd think to come here."

When they didn't answer, he glanced at them. They were staring at him.

"Lord?" Abu searched his face.

"It's a wig, you fool."

"Of course, lord, but you look like a—"

"A womanish Greek!" Reia exclaimed.

Meren glared at his charioteer. "Another word from you, and you'll be the one who's womanish."

"Sorry, lord."

"Follow me."

He left the main room through a guarded door in the back stairwell. It led to a courtyard that had been turned into a garden. Dark and deserted, it afforded a secluded place to talk. Meren found the blackest shadows under a spreading fig tree. Once they were alone, Abu and Reia pleaded for an explanation.

"They hunt you from Nubia to the delta, lord."

Meren told them all he knew, but when he was finished, it was obvious that he knew too little.

"Someone saw me leave camp, stole my weapons, and used them against the king," Meren said.

Abu asked, "One of the war band?"

"I don't think so," Meren said. "But anyone can be corrupted if offered something he dearly wants, or if he has a shameful secret. Everyone was celebrating that night. Vigilance was lax and drink plentiful at pharaoh's order. No doubt the guards at pharaoh's tent fell asleep from too much drink and afforded the traitor the opportunity to attack and escape while they were floundering in drunken confusion."

"And you say Karoya was wounded, so he wasn't with the king," Abu said.

"Pharaoh was generous and allowed all the men to celebrate at once. I should have objected."

Reia's soft voice came from a shadow. "Horemheb should have known better, too."

"Enough of this," Meren said. "I can't remain here much longer. What did you find?"

Abu came closer and lowered his voice. "The matter is grave, lord, for the plan was quite simple. Not long ago a traveling barber stopped in the village near Baht to ply his trade. Eventually the doorkeeper at Baht went to him, and after this barber trimmed his hair, the doorkeeper says he revealed himself as a secret messenger from you."

"From me," Meren repeated. "Why would I send messages to my doorkeeper through a barber?"

Abu and Reia exchanged glances.

"Forgive me, lord, but there have been times when I've traveled as a wood chopper, a faience maker, even a slave."

Reia cleared his throat. "And the Eyes and Ears of Pharaoh is well known for his use of indirection and concealment."

Meren waved his hand. "Go on."

"The barber said that you'd sent a parcel to be hidden at Baht until you came for it and gave the doorkeeper a sealed wooden box."

"The gold," Meren said.

"Aye, lord," said Abu. "The doorkeeper took the box and

put it among dozens of others in the kitchen storage room at Baht."

"Where it was discovered by the king's men," Meren said. He leaned against the trunk of the fig tree. "And the barber has vanished."

"We think he probably waited long enough to send an unsigned message about the gold to the mayor in Abydos," Abu replied.

"Have you learned nothing of where this cursed barber went?" Meren asked without much hope.

Reia stirred and said, "He has truly disappeared, lord. Which means that once his task was finished, he ceased to travel as a barber."

"Aye," Abu said. "I asked the doorkeeper to describe him. Unfortunately, his description is of little use—a man of middle height with a shaved head, of middle years. He had a few scars on his left arm, but other than that, there was little to set him apart from any commoner."

Meren said nothing and closed his eyes at this latest piece of ill luck.

Abu went on. "It's fortunate that I continued to question him, for then he began to complain of the barber's lack of skill. The doorkeeper said that he cut hair as if he was trying to do battle with it—grabbing hunks and slicing. His method of shaving was no better, and the doorkeeper swears the man was trying to cut his head off."

"A man better trained in violence than grooming," Meren breathed.

"A soldier," Reia added.

"From Yamen," Meren muttered.

Abu nodded. "Or a mercenary."

"Employed by Dilalu," Meren said on a sigh. "By the wrath of Amun, we must find this barber."

"He's disappeared, lord," said Abu.

Meren held up his hand. "What of this new steward of mine at the delta estate, Reia?"

"Your sister hired him by letter on the recommendation of a friend, lord. I talked to the steward, who is arrogant beyond his station and a fool. I think he's puffed up by having gained such an influential position with a great one. He assumed you conducted your affairs as did his last master, cheating where you could. He takes credit for obtaining necessary labor for you and faults the priests of Amun for objecting to a slight delay in getting the conscripts."

"So you're not certain whether the timing of this discovery is purposeful or just ill luck," Meren said.

"As you say, lord."

"Who was the friend of my sister who recommended this steward?"

Reia's smile was knowing. "Prince Hunefer's sister, my lord."

As if by signal, Meren and Abu cursed at the same time. Slowly Meren sank to the ground, crouching on the backs of his heels. He felt as if the tentacles of some hideous nether-world demon were closing around him, blocking his every escape attempt, squeezing him until his chest collapsed and he strangled. *Don't give in to the fear. Confusion of your wits is a greater danger than this unseen enemy.* He drew in a long breath and let it out. Lowering his head, he traced patterns in the dirt at the base of the tree trunk while he thought. Neither Abu nor Reia spoke. Both were accustomed to his long silences.

Finally Meren raised his head and stared at the patterns of light and dark shadow in the courtyard. "We will never catch these small fish who swim among the millions in the Nile. Like a good spear fisher, we ignore minnows and must stand still and wait for a giant to swim by."

"But, lord," Abu said. "We haven't much time. Pharaoh's troops are searching for you, and eventually——"

"Watch Dilalu and Yamen," Meren said. "This barber may return to one of them."

"Yes, lord."

"And don't try to send news of me to Kysen. My family mustn't be dragged into this any more than they already have been. I know they are worried about me, but they're safer in ignorance."

"Lord Kysen will try to help you."

"Curse it, Abu, he should do nothing. If I could risk it, I'd send a message ordering him to remain idle."

"But then he could be accused of concealing knowledge of a traitor if the messenger was discovered."

"Exactly," Meren said. "See if you can discover how my family does without endangering them." They lapsed into a morose silence.

Eventually Reia asked, "Shall we meet here again, my lord?"

"Not too soon, or we'll be noticed. Return in two days. Come."

Meren took them to a door in the wall that surrounded the courtyard and knocked on it. The portal swung back to reveal a muscled and looming doorkeeper.

Abu followed Reia through the doorway, then turned to Meren. "Are you certain you're safe with the pirate, lord?"

"As safe as anyone can be when hunted by the forces of the empire."

"And General Horemheb," Abu said.

"There is the danger." Meren shook his head wearily. "Horemheb knows me too well."

Reia appeared behind Abu. "Lord, flee the kingdom. Go to——"

"Where?" Meren asked. "It must be out of the empire and not to any ally of Egypt. Would you have me throw myself on the mercy of the Hittite king? Or shall I become a Greek pirate in earnest?"

Reia lowered his gaze, and Meren put his hand on the younger man's shoulder.

"I am grateful for your loyalty, Reia."

"You allowed me to become what I most wanted, lord. A charioteer. Even though I was a clumsy boy whom no one thought clever enough not to get trampled by his own stallion."

The sentry drew near, made curious by their prolonged leavetaking.

Meren stepped back into the courtyard. "May Amun protect you."

"And you." Abu glanced at the sentry and left off Meren's title.

The door swung shut, leaving Meren alone in the garden. Two days. He must wait two days, hiding and worrying and feeling helpless. As he turned his steps toward the Divine Lotus, Meren realized he'd go mad if he didn't do something. Yet he couldn't go out during the day. There was too great a risk that someone would recognize his face, even beneath this exotic wig.

By the time Meren had threaded his way through the groups of customers that packed the main chamber, he'd reached a decision. He would commit what he knew of Queen Nefertiti's murder to writing. He was in so much danger now that it wouldn't matter if the record was discovered. He could destroy it at any time, and the act of writing might quicken the memories he'd tried for so long to kill.

Meren spent a while in the crowd watching a pair of acrobats before going upstairs. He ascended the winding staircase to emerge on the roof. Crossing to the exterior stairway, he surveyed the surrounding buildings and streets before descending. Once on the ground, he avoided a pair of drunken sailors who had collapsed against the wall of the tavern, and slipped into the dark alley once more. He hated traveling in the dark, for it was almost impossible to avoid unspeakable puddles and noxious deposits of goat or donkey dung. Once he nearly landed flat on his back when his sandal skidded on a fresh pile.

As he stepped into the Street of the White Ibex, Meren stopped abruptly. Behind him he heard a footfall, and then nothing. Hardly breathing, he listened. He could hear the distant sound of laughter from the Divine Lotus. Calming the voice of his heart by slowing his breathing even further, Meren heard the slight breeze as it floated into the city from the north. Once he heard the hoot of an owl.

His senses stretched painfully, Meren waited. Sweat began to form on his brow. He hadn't been mistaken. He'd heard a footstep. The question was whether to go on, hoping to reach Othrys's house before he was attacked, or attempt to elude his pursuer before his hiding place was revealed. At last Meren moved, away from the pirate's house, back into the Caverns. If he was going to die, he would do it without endangering the man who saved his life by giving him refuge.

Chapter 15

Memphis, reign of Tutankhamun

When a nobleman went to the palace of pharaoh, he approached down an avenue designed to impress with its great length and the opulence of the ram-headed sphinxes—each larger than three men—that lined the way. The nobleman progressed with stateliness toward the soaring gate in the battlements and passed through massive doors whose thickness was enveloped in electrum. The myriad courtiers, officials, and hangers-on who filled the avenue, the gate, and the courtyard beyond all witnessed the great one's progress and noted that he was important enough to be allowed beyond the monumental barrier of the gate.

In such a manner had Kysen entered the palace previously. But on this night, he was driven by chariot away from the ceremonial avenue with its public facade of cloud-high carvings to a heavily guarded sally port. He caught only a glimpse of the interior of the battlements, and sensed a great weight of masonry over his head.

At that moment fear enveloped him. Rather than reveal it, he summoned the expressionless mask Meren had drilled into his heart long ago. Then he stumbled into the open and found himself behind a phalanx of service buildings in the narrow space between them and the defensive wall.

Overhead guards on their rounds paused to stare down at him in the light of torches carried by some of his guards. He glared back, but one of his escorts pushed him, and he tripped. Hands reached for him, but he shoved them away, rose, and hurried after Mose. He swung around the end of the service block, into an open area between two sets of barracks, and stopped.

Standing in the light of enormous lamps mounted on stands, shining like Ra from the reflected brilliance of electrum jewels that covered his head, neck, arms, and robes, pharaoh stood conversing with Ay and Maya. The king's war band formed a half circle to his right and left. Other than the two ministers, there were no other courtiers.

A hard shove propelled him into the half circle. Before he could be shoved again, Kysen went to the king and lowered himself to the ground. Touching his forehead to the packed earth, he remained as he was; he couldn't speak until pharaoh permitted it. Would he be allowed to defend himself, or would Mose simply impale him on that gold-tipped spear?

An officer stepped out of the ranks beside the king and boomed, "As pharaoh commands. Kysen, son of the traitor Meren."

Something inside Kysen broke; he remembered Meren's lifetime of devotion to Egypt, and boiling oil poured into his heart. "My father is no traitor!"

Mose poked him with the butt of his spear. Kysen swore, grabbed the haft, and jabbed the Nubian in the stomach. As guards rushed at him, Kysen released the haft and lifted his hands away from his body. He was surrounded by spear tips, but pharaoh raised a hand laden with gold rings. The spears snapped back, and Kysen found himself in a tight circle of Nubians.

Another signal from the king parted the circle. Breathing heavily, Kysen dared not move as the king came toward him, followed by Maya and Ay. At a wave of Tutankhamun's hand, he rose from the ground.

Pharaoh stopped three paces from Kysen. "Look at me."

Kysen had been avoiding just that, fearing his anger still showed. Slowly he lifted his chin. Meeting the gaze of a living god took courage. Meeting the gaze of this pharaoh took more than courage; it took a surrender of will.

Why this was so, Kysen couldn't tell. Perhaps his youth only magnified pharaoh's innate personal dignity. Perhaps the sadness that was never gone from the king's eyes for long evoked the feeling that Tutankhamun knew far more about the chaos in his soul than Kysen could bear to admit. At last pharaoh released Kysen from the prison of dark, heavy-lidded eyes.

"I will not ask you to tell me where your father has gone," the king said. "I know you well enough to imagine what I'd be forced to do to you to get the answer."

"My father is innocent, golden one."

"They found his dagger in my tent." Tutankhamun held up a bandaged arm. "My blood is still on it. Shall I show it to you?"

"Majesty, someone stole the dagger and pretended to be my father," Kysen insisted.

Tutankhamun shook his head. "I heard him. I'd put out the lamp because my head hurt from drink. The tent was black, and he awakened me. He said, 'Majesty, where are you?' and I called to him." The king rubbed the bandage on his arm. "If

I hadn't felt his movement as he sprang at me, his dagger would have found my heart instead of my arm."

What could he say against the word of the living god?

"Majesty, you know my father. He has come close to death countless times in thy service, to save thy life."

Fidgeting with his bandages, the king asked in a distracted voice, "Why did he do it, Kysen? It makes no sense—unless these charges against him are but the surface of a deep and secret poison."

"He is innocent, golden one."

"Is he possessed? My magician priests tell me that evil demons can occupy the ka of an upright man and drive him mad. Meren hasn't been himself of late. Is he possessed?"

"No, majesty."

Without warning the king grabbed Kysen's arm and jerked him. *"Then why did he try to kill me, damn you!"*

Feeling the hand of pharaoh on him banished Kysen's thoughts. His heart blank with shock, he could only stare at the hand on his arm. The fingers were long, and one bore a ring with a bezel carved with the royal cartouche. As Kysen blinked at the hand, Ay whispered to the king. Tutankhamun's hand dropped, and he stepped away from Kysen.

"My majesty is grieved beyond bearing at this treason," he said quietly.

As Kysen watched him warily, a change came over pharaoh. Grief faded, washed away by a tide of cool resolution and an aristocratic ruthlessness. The king clapped his hands. The war band parted to reveal two guards standing behind them, carrying a lidded basket between them. They brought it forward and set it in the middle of the war band.

The king walked over to it. "Bring him."

The Nubians hauled Kysen to the basket. At pharaoh's command Ay opened the container. Within lay hands. Right hands. Kysen counted eleven pale gray extremities, each with its dressing of blood and chopped veins.

Kysen had been in battle. He lifted his gaze to the king's and raised a brow. Tutankhamun clapped his hands again, and another basket was set beside the first.

"Lift the lid," pharaoh commanded.

His body numb, unable to refuse though he feared what he would find, Kysen fastened his hand on the wicker lid and opened it. A face stared up at him with parched eyes. Thin lips drew back over dry yellow teeth. Puckered skin covered the stalk of a neck that had no body to go with it.

Kysen almost smiled at the horror. "I know him not."

Pharaoh moved around the head sitting in its wicker nest in a cloud of sweet-smelling linen to stand close to him and speak as softly as a concubine in a private garden. "This is but a thief, the bandit leader we defeated before your father tried to kill me." The king leaned closer and whispered. "I cut off his head myself, Ky. I wanted to know what it felt like, to hack at flesh with an ax. Tell me where your father has gone and why he tried to kill me, or by the gods I'll do the same to you."

For a brief moment Kysen's eyes closed as revulsion claimed him. Then he opened his eyes, knelt, and exposed his neck.

"Thy majesty must deal with me as he has with the bandit, for I don't know where my father has gone."

A barrage of curses startled him. The king's air of viciousness disappeared in a fit of rage. Guards scuttled out of his way as Tutankhamun stalked back and forth, hurling epithets. Abruptly Kysen lowered his gaze to conceal his suspicion that the king had been engaged in a ruse that had failed. When the stream of curses ceased, pharaoh pointed at him.

"Meren told you I promised not to punish his family, didn't he?"

Confused, Kysen could only shake his head.

Tutankhamun stalked to him, halting but a pace away. "I am pharaoh, and pharaoh keeps his word. But I shouldn't have given such a promise. I see that now." Crossing his arms over the electrum-and-turquoise broad collar on his chest, Tutankhamun eyed him. "But I never promised not to question his family. Shall I question your sisters, Kysen? Ah, fear at last."

"Majesty." Kysen's voice shook, and he paused to control it. "I beg to speak to you privately."

Maya spoke for the first time. "Impossible."

"Go away, Maya." The king glared at his escort. "Stand at a distance, all of you."

When they were alone the king sighed and said, "Get up, Ky. I hope what you have to say will ease my grief. To lose Meren . . ." Tutankhamun looked away. "Speak."

"I swore to my father that I would never reveal what I know," Kysen said. "But his life is forfeit if I don't speak. Many weeks ago Lord Meren and I discovered an old and evil secret, one that will cause more grief to thy majesty."

Tutankhamun gave him a sharp glance. "Out with it."

"We discovered that Queen Nefertiti did not die of the plague but was poisoned."

To Kysen's admiration, pharaoh gave no hint of astonishment or outrage. The cloak of royal dignity remained, and the only indication of the king's distress was the great stillness that came over him. At the boy's slight nod, Kysen continued.

"Lord Meren has been trying ever since to discover the evil ones who were responsible, for he knew at least one still lived. We searched for the queen's favorite cook, but she and her husband were murdered before we could question them. Only a short time ago, we obtained the names of three men known to have the power and the opportunity to devise such evil. My father contacted two of them, and as he was about to summon the third, these evil rumors began. Then someone tried to destroy Lord Meren with this attack upon thy majesty."

The king had been watching Kysen closely. "You're lying to save your father. If this story was true, the evil one would have simply tried to kill Meren."

"No, majesty, for my father is hard to kill, and even if he was killed, I would still remain." Kysen smiled bitterly. "And if they killed my father, I would hunt the evil ones from here to the lakes of fire in the netherworld. And if I was killed, Abu would take up the task. No, disgrace is far more effective. Is thy majesty not separated from the one man who can tell the truth?"

Tutankhamun shook his head wearily. "The murder of a queen, a fantastic tale that seems conveniently designed to relieve Meren of his guilt. And if he wishes to tell me the truth, why is he not here? And why have most of his charioteers vanished?"

"Golden one, Meren has served loyally thy whole life—"

Kysen stopped because the king suddenly narrowed his eyes and drew a sharp breath.

"Yes," Tutankhamun said softly. "He has. When I was a child, he was appointed as one of my tutors and guided me faithfully—once Akhenaten and Nefertiti were dead."

Dread enveloped Kysen's heart. "Thy majesty doesn't suspect my father of murdering either."

"To be pharaoh, Ky, and stay alive is to suspect where one least wishes to. Your father taught me that."

The king eyed him silently for a moment. "Your father was with Queen Nefertiti a great deal in his capacity as Ay's aide, was he not?"

"Yes, majesty, but—"

"And if she'd lived, the queen would have been regent and

Lord Meren but one of many who served her father. She would have been first in my heart, and she would have had power until I came of age."

"If thy majesty would but send for the three men my father suspected—" Kysen began.

"Let your father give himself up to my majesty," the king said. "Convince Meren to surrender, and I will listen to this wild tale again." The king turned and signaled to Ay and Maya.

Kysen spoke rapidly before the two reached the king. "Golden one, I am a prisoner in my own house, and I don't know where Lord Meren is."

The two councillors joined them.

"Ay, withdraw the guards from Lord Meren's family."

Maya uttered an exclamation of dismay. "But, majesty—"

"My majesty is convinced that Lord Kysen is a loyal subject."

"But—" Maya closed his mouth when Ay put a hand on his arm.

Bowing, the vizier said, "Yes, majesty."

Kysen knew better than to trust such generosity. The fisherman might loosen the net; he didn't take it away altogether. "Golden one, I've told you the truth."

"Of course."

Kysen darted a glance at the king as he bowed. Gone was the hurt and distraught boy. In his place was Nebkheprure Tutankhamun, Lord of the Two Lands, Son of Ra, the young ruler who spoke of hacking the heads of criminals from their necks. Meren had taught the king well. Once his suspicions were aroused, the king would trust no one until this mystery was solved. And he no longer trusted Meren, in spite of the many times his councillor had almost died to protect him. For pharaoh, the risk of such trust was too great, no matter the impulse of his heart.

Kysen glanced at Maya, who seemed torn between his friendship for Meren and his love of the king. And Ay? No one could tell what Ay was thinking.

The king was watching him impassively. "Mose, escort Lord Kysen home."

"Please, majesty," Kysen said as Mose approached and clamped a hand on his arm.

"My majesty will hear no more."

Shrugging off Mose's hand, Kysen bowed and turned to follow the Nubian.

"Ky."

He looked back to find that the king had come after him. Kysen dropped to the ground. "Yes, majesty?"

"You may be assured, I'll never condemn your father unheard."

"Thy majesty is wise and merciful, but I fear Lord Meren won't be allowed to live long enough to be heard."

Chapter 16

Horizon of the Aten, the independent reign of the pharaoh Akhenaten

Nefertiti laid her reed pen down on the table and blew on the ink that covered the sheet of papyrus spread before her. She clenched her hands to keep them from trembling. Only her training at Queen Tiye's side kept her from plunging into a frenzy of useless action.

She looked up at her father and saw the same helpless fury that churned inside her. Ay sat nearby in the shelter of a kiosk in the garden of the royal palace. Nefertiti turned her attention back to the notes she'd taken on the translations of foreign letters from the House of Correspondence.

"It is the destruction of the empire if we don't do something," Nefertiti said. "I never thought pharaoh would allow Suppiluliumas to destroy the kingdom of Mitanni. Tushratta was once our friend."

Ay threw back his head, sighed, and contemplated the roof. "Once Akhenaten made that cursed treaty with the Hittite, you and I both knew what would happen. Mitanni is gone, and there's nothing we can do about it. Now, with the Asiatic vassals at each other's throats, Suppiluliumas merely has to see that no one forms a lasting alliance. The king of the Hittites pays Aziru of Amurru to stir dissension among the vassals, while Suppiluliumas writes sweet letters to pharaoh and sends presents."

"But all those loyal princes." Nefertiti searched through the stack of papyri. "Look, Akizzi of Qatna and Biryawaza of Upe plead for help. These are our regents, Father, and they're loyal. Nomads raid the cities of Palestine without fear of Egyptian troops. And today word came that rebels and nomads have destroyed two towns near Ugarit."

"I know, daughter."

Twisting a report in her hands, Nefertiti stared at a distant shrub without seeing it. "These rebels who want kingdoms for themselves, they use the nomads as a facade and a tool. Half the war we read about is contrived, but if we misread the situation and fail to send aid when it's truly required, we lose loyal vassals."

Ay was smiling at her. "Queen Tiye would be proud of you."

"Perhaps." Nefertiti tried not to show the doubt she felt that the queen would thank her for her many failures. Frustration cut off any more speculation about Queen Tiye. "If we fail to act, we could lose the vassals of Phoenicia, Palestine, Syria. The destruction will soak the ground with blood." Nefertiti rose and strode around the kiosk. A slave tending to their food skipped out of her way.

Ay was still smiling as he intercepted Nefertiti on her way around the shelter. Taking her hand, he said, "There has been much killing already, but you must realize that the Hittite king wants rich provinces, not burned earth."

"Did you read that letter from the regent of Gezer?"

Nefertiti shook off Ay's restraining hand. "Pharaoh's own commissioner is extorting silver from him. A man entrusted with the governing of vassals by pharaoh himself." Nefertiti snatched up a translation and shoved it at Ay. "Here. Look at that. Iankhamu seized the regent's wife and children and demanded two thousand pieces of silver for their return. If you hadn't sent a king's deputy to Gezer to inquire about administration, we'd never have discovered this in time. The corruption of pharaoh's officers is a disease that will kill the empire even if Suppiluliumas were to suddenly become Egypt's lover. Why aren't you angry?"

Ay pulled Nefertiti over to his chair and gently pushed her into it. He handed her a piece of spiced cake, and she bit into it as if it were the traitor Aziru.

"I've been angry for a long time," Ay said. "But pharaoh doesn't listen to me. He hears your voice. Quell the fiends that dance in your heart, daughter. I would discuss the problems we face and what you will say to pharaoh."

"It's taken us too long to decipher Tutu's mountain of correspondence. I'll see pharaoh as soon as we finish."

Nefertiti hadn't expected her conference with Ay to take the rest of the day. The sun set before she was able to request audience with her husband. Akhenaten was in his own apartments with the girls. Knowing better than to rush into a topic that annoyed her husband, Nefertiti allowed herself to relax with her family.

Merytaten sat on a pile of cushions and played a harp for her parents. The oldest of her daughters, Merytaten was an unfortunate child. The girl had never been clever of wit, and Nefertiti feared she would be as vapid a young woman as she was a child.

Little Ankhesenpaaten, now her next oldest, was Akhenaten's favorite. Pharaoh delighted in the little girl's open manner and chattering nonsense. They shared a love of music and nature. Only yesterday Nefertiti had come upon them while Akhenaten was reading his great hymn to the Aten. Young as she was, Ankhesenpaaten seemed to enjoy the beauty of the words. Nefertiti was about to send the girls to their apartments when Akhenaten rose from his couch and dismissed them himself.

Ankhesenpaaten's lower lip protruded in a pout that was becoming habitual. "But I don't want to go, Father."

Leading her by the hand, Akhenaten admonished the child with a mildness that only encouraged her. Nefertiti intervened, earning the girl's childish ire. Ignoring all protests, she directed the girl's attendants to remove her daughters.

When the children were gone, Akhenaten motioned for Nefertiti to take a cushion beside his couch and collapsed upon his own embroidered sheets as if dealing with the girls had exhausted him. He took up a silver bowl filled with dates. Biting a chunk from one of the candied pieces, he regarded Nefertiti happily.

"Tell me what you did today. Your adventures are always more interesting than listening to courtiers whine that they can't live without receiving more royal gifts."

"Husband, your patience is a gift from the Aten."

"As is your beauty, my dear." Akhenaten licked his sticky fingers before selecting another date. "I have missed you. What have you been doing this morning?"

His expectant look gave Nefertiti the chance for which she'd been waiting. Slowly, as if she were telling a story, she described the treachery and war that loomed beyond the borders of the Two Lands. She illustrated the destruction of cities and towns. Like an artist painting a relief, she dipped her words in brilliant colors so that they dripped with the red of life's blood, the sandy yellow of the dust that covered a nomad's skin, the black and gray of the burned brick of Jericho.

When she had finished, Akhenaten was quiet. Nefertiti's mouth was dry from talking. She held out her hand, and a servant placed a gold cup in it. Pharaoh was contemplating something beyond Nefertiti's left ear.

Finally Akhenaten spoke. "I can see I'll have to speak to the Aten about Aziru and these troublesome vassals."

Nefertiti nearly groaned with impatience. Why hadn't she expected such a response?

"Husband, we have to do more than just pray."

"Oh? I don't see what could be more powerful. I'll talk to my father the god."

Nefertiti slipped to the floor beside pharaoh's couch. She rested her arms on the cushions and met her husband's gaze. "We must do as your father did, as your ancestor Thutmose the Conqueror did. Pharaoh must go to Palestine and Syria at the head of his chariots and infantry. Take the Nubians and the archers. Go into the field and destroy the rebels. Cut off the heads of traitors like Aziru and protect your loyal princes. Nothing will instill fear of the god-king like rounding up a few traitors, impaling them, and displaying their carcasses on city walls."

Akhenaten was shaking his head, but Nefertiti rushed on. "Why do you think your father killed Aziru's father? The rulers of Amurru can't be trusted. You've scolded Aziru for years, and he still conspires with Suppiluliumas. Send a special force to kill Aziru before he gobbles up more cities for his Hittite master."

"Fierce little wife, I had no idea you craved the glory of conquest." Akhenaten patted Nefertiti's head. He leaned back on the couch and toyed with the golden pectoral necklace that hung from Nefertiti's neck. "I have no desire to leave Horizon of the Aten, and I'm certainly not going to go where I could be killed by a dirty, barbarian nomad in a fight to save some petty city-state."

"But we could lose the empire. Think of what might happen if Suppiluliumas controls all the lands from Mitanni to the frontier. Foreigners once ruled the Two Lands. They could again."

Nefertiti went still as Akhenaten sat up on the couch and glared at her. Obsidian black whirlwinds swirled in his eyes.

"Your words are blasphemy. I am the god of all on this earth. Even the Hittite dares not threaten me. The world is my empire."

Nefertiti made her voice steady in spite of the uneasiness she felt. "Even a god must use men to do his bidding. Aziru and the others are heretics. They worship foreign gods and defy you, the Son of the Sun. They offend Maat; they disturb the order and peace of the cosmos. Please, husband, allow Lord Ay—"

"No!"

"Yes!" Nefertiti jumped to her feet. Beneath her anger lurked the thought that she wasn't being at all diplomatic, but Akhenaten was so blind and stubborn that she wanted to tip his couch over and send him sliding across the floor.

"Then if you won't go, I'll go."

Akhenaten was off the couch before Nefertiti finished. Pharaoh caught her by the wrist. She'd forgotten what strength lay in Akhenaten's hands until they closed around her flesh.

"Do you seek to shame me, wife?"

"No," Nefertiti snapped. "I but seek to wake you." She stared into her husband's black-fire gaze without faltering. The moments went by, stretching out until she thought she would scream. Never had she confronted Akhenaten so openly. She thought of that priest of Amun hanging in that cell, bleeding. Then she started, for Akhenaten was chuckling.

"You're laughing at me!"

"I can't help it," the king said. "First you speak to me like a councillor, and then you almost insult me. I hadn't realized how bored I'd become. My beautiful one always brings excitement." Akhenaten patted her cheek. "Of course you're not going to war."

Rubbing her neck, Nefertiti berated herself for her failure. From talks with Horemheb, she knew the army chafed at being forced to stand by and watch the depredations of the Hittites. It was dangerous to lose the confidence of the military.

Tiye would be disappointed. If Pharaoh Amunhotep's ka was watching, he too would find her lacking. Nefertiti stared at a garland of blue lotus flowers draped along a food table.

"What can I do to take the sadness from your eyes?"

Akhenaten watched her with a gravity that surprised Nefertiti. "I don't know, majesty. I'm so worried about, about—"

"If I make Horemheb a king's deputy and send him north with a few squadrons to investigate, will you be content? Ah! Now you smile at me. The light of the sun is captured in that smile. Very well. You may arrange the whole thing with Ay. Don't bother me with details."

Nefertiti's smile spread into a full grin. "Thank you, husband."

Her grin faltered. Akhenaten leaned toward her and placed a hand on her shoulder. The hand slid down her arm and encircled her wrist. Nefertiti looked from the hand to her husband's face. Pharaoh's breathing quickened.

"Husband?"

She said nothing more, for Akhenaten kept silent. As

Nefertiti waited for him to speak, Akhenaten ran his hand back up her arm, across her shoulder, to rest at her neck. Akhenaten's thumb traced paths back and forth over the skin at her throat. Lowering her eyes, Nefertiti remained still, waiting for him to send the servants away. He didn't, for something stirred in his gaze, something that resembled a serpent on a blazing rock in the desert.

"Beautiful one, I've heard that you fail to worship the Aten in your palace as you did in the past."

Someone in her household had been telling tales again.

"Forgive me, my husband. I have been so anxious to relieve you of burdensome duties that I've been negligent."

"Better to neglect duties than the Aten."

"Are you angry with me?"

"No, no." Akhenaten stepped back from her. "But it disturbs me that you can so easily give up the path of truth. I like not what I hear, Nefertiti."

"What do you hear?"

"That your devotion to the Aten is of the surface only. That you seem sympathetic to those heretics who refuse to give up the old blasphemies. These are evil tidings I had not thought to hear of you, my love."

Nefertiti went to Akhenaten, placed her hand flat on his hollow chest, and looked into his eyes. "These are lies, husband."

"Are they?" he asked in a musing voice.

Lifting her gaze to him, Nefertiti said, "I make my vow in the presence of the one god, the Aten."

Once Akhenaten would have been satisfied with such a response. To her dismay, he didn't smile at her and accept the reassurance. Instead, Akhenaten watched her with judgmental gravity before waving her away.

"Leave me, beautiful one. I——I have to speak with the Aten.

There are things I don't understand. I must speak to my father, and I don't want you with me."

Protest would only provoke Akhenaten's temper, so Nefertiti returned to her own apartments. Uneasiness was her companion for the rest of the evening. Akhenaten was no longer so trusting of her as he had been. If she wasn't careful, he would guess how justified he was in his suspicions, and her influence would vanish. She had no choice but to continue on her chosen path. She was the only one who could make Akhenaten listen to reason. At least Horemheb was going north, but unless the army followed him, his mission would have little effect.

Late that night Akhenaten came to her. His attentions had a desperate quality, as if he sought escape from something he feared. As always when they were together, Nefertiti felt more caretaker than lover. There had been lessons from Queen Tiye in this as in all else, and Nefertiti had been a good student. But while they touched each other, she kept remembering that look in his eyes—that serpent writhing on a sun-blasted rock.

Its tortured twisting was an evil sign, one that had begun to appear in Akhenaten more and more frequently. She herself had never been its focus. But today for the first time, with his hand squeezing her wrist to numbness, she realized the serpent could turn on her, strike, and sink its fangs into her heart. If Akhenaten ever lost faith in her, there was no one, not even Ay, who could protect her from the wrath of this man who believed he was the incarnation of the one god in all the world.

Chapter 17

Memphis, reign of Tutankhamun

Kysen watched the royal troops leave while he stood beside Bener on the loggia. Their going was ostentatious, but of little consolation to him. Having dealt with criminals and traitors, he knew that the household would still be observed from afar all the hours of the day and night.

As the gate closed on the last guard, Bener nodded. "Good."

"The withdrawal means nothing," Kysen began.

"I'm not a fool." Bener led the way inside to the cool half-darkness of the reception hall and sank into her favorite chair, with its embroidered cushions. "The king's men can watch until they turn to dust. I care not."

"You weren't dragged before pharaoh. You didn't see the king's face."

"None of that matters, Ky. What matters is proving Father innocent."

Kysen gave his sister a skeptical glance before dropping to

a cushion on the floor. "And how will we do that when we can't set foot outside the house without being seen?"

"We'll have help."

"From whom?" Kysen growled. "Even Maya dares not visit us, and Horemheb is busy hunting Father. Who will aid us?"

Bener grinned at him and glanced over her shoulder. Someone came through the shadowed doorway that led to the family quarters. Kysen glimpsed a tall figure, hair the color of obsidian. When the newcomer move toward them with a leopard's hunting pace, Kysen caught his breath.

"Father?"

"I thank Amun daily that I'm not your father," Ebana said as he strolled over to them.

Scowling, Kysen rose and faced his father's cousin. No wonder he'd mistaken the man for Meren, for Ebana shared with his cousin the same wide-shouldered, long-legged physique, embodying the canon of proportions so dear to painters and sculptors. Each had long cords of muscle in the neck, shoulders, and arms, kept taut by hours of practicing war skills. Each had angular features and a strong nose softened somewhat by a wide mouth. Even their hair curled the same way, causing tendrils to trespass on their high foreheads.

Like Meren's, Ebana's hair had yet to show a trace of silver, but unlike Meren's, Ebana's face bore a scar. Kysen stared into eyes as black as his father's and spoke to his sister.

"What possessed you to bring him here?"

Bener rose and stood between them. "Do you know anyone else who would brave pharaoh's wrath to help us?"

Kysen broke his stare to give Bener an exasperated glance. "Do you know anyone who harbors more ill will toward Father?"

"Nonsense," Bener replied. "He saved Father's life not long ago. Ebana doesn't hate him as much as he says."

"How do you know that? I know what he's done. You don't."

Ebana forestalled Bener's retort with a raised hand. "Enough. I'll not be fought over like a carcass between two hyenas. Kysen, you forget that your father and I declared a truce."

"Only after he caught you—" Kysen shot a look at Bener and pressed his lips together.

Ebana gave him a smile that slithered through high grass and curled under rocks. "You speak the truth, but consider this, low-born cousin. If Meren is condemned, his whole family will suffer. As his cousin, who grew up with him, I'll share in the devastation. In proving your father's innocence, I merely assure my own well-being."

"Now I believe you," Kysen said.

Ebana turned and went to the master's dais, where he sank into Meren's chair with the grace of a prince. "Your faith is a comfort to my heart."

"Ass's dung."

Bener poked him with her elbow. "Hold your tongue. He's already been at work for us, ungrateful one."

"Ah, yes," Ebana said. "Allow me to add to your discomfort, baseborn cousin. I have sought out a friend among the king's war band and have an account of the attack on pharaoh."

Aghast, Kysen turned on his sister. "What have you been doing? And now that I think of it, how did he get here?"

"I sent a message in the laundry when the maids took it to the river to wash."

"But the laundry was searched."

Bener gave him a contemptuous look. "Not the women's blood cloths. Remember?"

Kysen opened his mouth, then shut it, then opened it again. "Oh, yes."

"And he got here by simply walking in the front gate."

"Oh." Kysen faced Ebana, his jaw rigid as he bowed in gratitude. "May Amun bless you for your aid. Please, tell us what you've discovered."

Ebana grinned at him. "Well done, for a commoner."

"Just tell the tale," Kysen snapped.

"Some of it you know. After the skirmish with the bandits, pharaoh decreed that everyone was to celebrate. Horemheb convinced the king that the guards at the palisade shouldn't drink, but those inside the camp did. Even the Nubian bodyguards downed jars full of wine. You know how it is after battle, the strain winds the muscles as tight as a wine press."

Ebana rose and left the master's dais to join them. "As the hours passed, some went to their tents or fires. Meren left early, but pharaoh remained to joke and compare experiences with his companions. It was still dark when the king retired, and soon the whole camp slept."

"I could have guessed all this," Kysen said.

Ebana lifted a brow, caused his scar to move. "Could you in your omnipotence guess that after Meren left, someone drugged the wine and beer, and that was why the attacker could slip past the sentries at pharaoh's tent?"

Kysen flushed and shook his head.

"I don't know if the king's wine was touched, for his supply is kept separate. But his body servant slept through the attack, and the sentries at the royal tent roused only slowly. By the time they reached the king, the evil one had slashed the back of the tent and fled. Once the alarm was sounded, it was discovered that Meren was the only one missing."

"All that means is the attacker remained in camp rather than fleeing."

Bener had been listening silently. She returned to her chair, shaking her head. "The plan is a simple one."

Kysen had learned not to scoff at his sister when she said things like this. "Yes?"

"Of course," Bener said. "One of those nearest the king is the attacker. A humble soldier might have been noticed approaching the royal tent, even if the king's companions were drunk. The evil one waited until he thought everyone was in a stupor, stole into the tent, and made certain to wake the king. The attack was never intended to kill pharaoh, only to incriminate Father. The intruder stayed only long enough to do that before slipping out of the tent and rejoining the rest in the confusion. He might have been quick enough to take his place among the sleepers and pretend to wake with them."

"Meren told me you were clever of heart," Ebana said.

"He did?"

Kysen glared at his suddenly pleased sister. "But pharaoh is adamant that he heard Father."

"He was half asleep, and his wits were clouded by wine," Ebana said. "And pharaoh's heart is grieved by Meren's betrayal. If he weren't so disturbed, he would have realized that if Meren had wanted to kill him, he could have done it without getting caught. Your sister is right."

Bener had been staring over Kysen's shoulder, her lower lip caught between her teeth. "Even with the sentries in a stupor, there could have been little time to act."

"I agree," Ebana said.

"Therefore it is most likely that the attacker was one of those closest to pharaoh's tent," Bener continued.

"Who had charge of it that night?" Kysen asked.

Ebana drew nearer Bener, his harsh features softened by conjecture. "Karoya was wounded and unable to attend pharaoh."

"Which means that Mose would have been on duty," Kysen said.

"Yes." Ebana glanced from Kysen to Bener. "Mose and one other. The Nubian called Turi."

The conversation subsided as all three of them engaged in contemplation. Finally Bener spoke in a musing tone.

"I wonder if either Mose or Turi have dealings with Dilalu, Yamen, or Zulaya."

Ebana's head swiveled in her direction. "By the gods, little cousin, your heart is as devious as your father's."

"Such a possibility is the result of following a reasonable path of thought," Bener replied.

"Indeed," Ebana said faintly as he glanced at Kysen.

"She has always been this way," Kysen said. "Only of late, she has insisted upon meddling in Father's affairs."

Ignoring him, Bener said, "You must find a way to question Mose and Turi."

"How simple." Kysen threw up his hands. "I'll trot into the palace and ask them to a feast, shall I?"

"Hmm."

Kysen scowled at his sister. "No, Bener."

"You're right," she said. "They wouldn't come."

Holding up a hand in protest, Ebana interrupted them. "Enough, both of you. There's no time for grand designs. I'll seek out the Nubians myself."

"And I'll make my own inquiries," Kysen said. "I can seek Othrys's help. The pirate might know something of Mose or Turi, if Bener will send a message for me in her . . . creative manner." He kept his mouth shut when Bener smirked at him.

"How fortunate for you, brother, that I don't hold your condescending attitude against you."

The patrons of the Divine Lotus were more drunk than usual. Their drunkenness had a wild and desperate air about it. Everyone from the maids who served the food to the most successful Canaanite smuggler jumped at sudden sounds and stared into dark corners with slit-eyed acuity. On the floor in one of those dark corners, Meren sat pretending to drink spiced beer. He was waiting for Abu as arranged, and he was as wary as anyone, for Horemheb had returned to Memphis. At the general's command, the city police had doubled their patrols. It had been one of these that he'd barely escaped three nights ago.

When he arrived at the tavern this evening, the Lotus's owner, Ese, told him she'd had visits from three different patrols. Since Ese disliked men intensely and noblemen in particular, Meren was uneasy using her tavern as a meeting place now that she felt threatened. However, Othrys, who had accompanied him, assured him that Ese was more afraid of him than the city police and wouldn't reveal Meren's presence. Othrys was entertaining his allies in piracy at the moment—sailors, ship captains, port officials, Asiatic merchants, and the corrupt Egyptian traders who bought goods for temples, nobles, and government offices. The Divine Lotus was more packed than usual.

The crowding suited Meren, for it meant that he was ignored in favor of the abundant drink and roast ox Othrys had provided. He took a sip of beer, trying to ignore the stale taste. He was feeling lost and powerless, as he had when Akhenaten killed his father for refusing to renounce Amun. After he'd avoided being killed himself, Meren had spent his life trying to make certain he'd never be powerless again—and he'd failed. His impotence was a rat gnawing at his gut, and every action he took reminded him of how lost he was.

He'd never realized how much he'd taken for granted until he'd been forced from his position and his home. Although in the past he'd taken various guises in the service of pharaoh, he'd always chosen to play the part of men of whom he'd had adequate experience—rich merchants, soldiers, foreign nobles. Such disguises were too dangerous now.

Thus continual vigilance was essential, for his must give no orders—something he did as naturally as he breathed. He must walk differently, not stride as was his habit and expect others to get out of his way. He couldn't look at people in his own manner, for a great man stared over the heads of most and looked directly at anyone he wished. He had to amend his manners; they were those of an aristocrat. He had to fetch his own food and clothing and empty the bowl of sand under the toilet in his room.

Every moment he had to guard his speech and roughen his accent to that of a Greek commoner. But what had almost given him away several times was his habit of resting his hand on the dagger thrust into his belt—that dagger he could no longer wear without revealing himself. Greek sailors didn't go about wearing weapons any more than did ordinary Egyptians.

Meren tensed as a foreign merchant stumbled in his direction. It was Dilalu, who was known to frequent the Divine Lotus. Asiatics like him were recognizable by their multicolored and fringed wool robes. The merchant's clothing danced with embroidery and gold appliqués. He had a wide face, but the lower half was obscured by a beard and curling mustache. Meren drew in his legs as the man zigzagged toward him and into a pool of lamplight. If Dilalu got a look at his face, he might be recognized.

Drawing his legs close to his chest, Meren tried to melt into the corner, but Dilalu's foot hit his ankle. The merchant tripped and would have plummeted to the floor in front of Meren had someone not caught him. Abu hoisted the man upright, twirled him around, and aimed him at one of Ese's prettiest dancers. The girl caught him, laughed, and began whispering in his ear. Soon Dilalu was giggling, his near accident forgotten.

Abu lowered himself beside Meren, who sighed and whispered, "My thanks."

"It was nothing, lor—it was nothing. What is Dilalu doing here?"

"Getting drunk on wine and pleasure, from what I can see. The Divine Lotus attracts most foreigners. You know that. I have to get away from this drunken offal before he runs into me again. Follow me to the courtyard."

Meren threaded his way through Othrys's numerous acquaintances and into Ese's courtyard. There amorous couples groped each other among the shrubs and flowers. Once Meren had found an isolated refuge in the shadows behind a tamarisk tree, Abu began to whisper to Meren.

"I have news—"

Meren shook his head. "That can wait. How does my family?"

"Lord Kysen was taken to the palace three days ago."

Meren felt the world spin for a moment. "He came back?"

Abu nodded. "Pharaoh spoke to him, but he was taken home." Abu frowned and rubbed his chin. "Afterward the men guarding your household were removed."

"It's a trap. Pharaoh has been an excellent student, Abu."

"Aye, but that's not what disturbs me. I was able to view the house for a brief time from the roof of another building."

"You should be careful," Meren said. "They're looking for you as well as me."

"I'm careful. I saw Lady Bener talking to her personal maid in the kitchen yard."

"She's well?"

"Too well. You remember how she used to look as a child

when she'd devised some plan of devilment that had succeeded? She wore that same look while she was talking to the maid."

Meren covered his face with his hands. "Oh no. She has involved herself."

"I think so, because today Reia saw Lord Ebana enter the house."

Startled, Meren gaped at Abu. "How long has he been there?"

"I know not, lord."

Meren groaned. "Bener was always his favorite niece. She would tell him her plots and plans, and he'd keep her secrets. She remembers him as he was before pharaoh murdered his family, and I'd wager a chariot that it was she who sent for him."

"Perhaps, but there's nothing that can be done about your children at the moment, lord."

Whispering a stream of curses, Meren began to pace back and forth in front of the tamarisk tree. "Very well, but when I'm free again, I'll take a chariot whip to that girl." He saw Abu's grin. "This time I mean it."

"Of course." Abu's tone was skeptical.

Eyeing his aide, Meren asked, "How long have you been with me?"

"The lord was but a youth when I came to train him."

"But how long?"

"Over twenty years."

"Too long, Abu. You know me too well."

"You suffer much, lord, for it isn't like you to complain and lament."

Meren stopped in front of his aide and clasped his shoulder. "Forgive me, these leggings itch and I haven't been able to go about in daylight for what seems like years. Without the feel of Ra's light on my skin, my ka shrivels like grapes left in a tomb. What have you to tell me?"

"Reia and I did as you instructed, lord. We've been watching Dilalu and Yamen as much as possible. Neither has done anything suspicious. However, Dilalu is making preparations to go back to Byblos, and Yamen will soon depart for Megiddo as king's herald to assess tribute."

"Damnation, if they leave—"

"Fear not, lord. I was trying to tell you, I think I've seen the barber."

Meren drew closer to his aide. "Where?"

"This morning a soldier reported for duty with the squadron under Yamen's command at General Nakhtmin's barracks near the palace. This soldier has a shaved head, but he's growing his hair again, so it looks as if he stopped shaving it quite recently. And, lord, he is left-handed. I saw him with Yamen drawing a bow in a practice yard. There are scars on his inner arm from blade strikes."

"By the gods, Abu."

"Yes, lord."

"We must arrange a meeting with Yamen."

"In what manner?"

"What are his habits?" Meren asked. "Does he frequent any tavern or other place at night?"

"He visits the daughter of an incense maker in the Street of Perfumers." Abu glanced up at the moon. "He crosses the city almost every night to see her. Soon he'll be on his way."

"Good. You and I are going to pay Yamen a visit while he's indulging himself. It's always best to take an enemy in a vulnerable position, and I can't think of one more vulnerable than a man lying with a woman."

"Aye, lord."

"We've been here too long. Leave as you did last time and meet me behind the carpenter's workshop down the street."

"Yes, lord."

"Well done, Abu."

"I but followed your commands," Abu said. He almost saluted, but stopped himself and left by the back courtyard door.

Meren went back inside the tavern, his ka much lighter. At last the battlements of secrecy that protected Nefertiti's murderer were crumbling. Yamen was responsible for the plot to destroy his name. The question was why. Was it because Yamen himself had orchestrated the queen's death? If so, there was yet another above him who had issued the command, for Yamen hadn't been high enough at court to manage the deed by himself. And how had Yamen known that Meren suspected him?

Ever since he'd begun to inquire into Nefertiti's murder, he had run into one obstruction after another. He'd sought the queen's favorite cook, whom he suspected of administering the poison, to no avail. Her sister's wits were scattered, leaving him with no way to discover whether his suspicions were correct. The queen's steward had got himself killed before Meren could question him. And he'd barely embarked upon his quest to investigate Othrys's three candidates for murderer when he was snared in this evil trap and accused of attempted regicide.

Like Dilalu, Yamen had been at Horizon of the Aten when Nefertiti died. He'd had the men and the power to get rid of the cook and ruin Meren, but so did Dilalu. Only the barber linked Yamen to the plot to destroy him. If this half-bald soldier wasn't the barber, Meren was left drowning in ignorance again. And then there was Zulaya, whom he'd been on the verge of contacting when he was forced to flee. Zulaya was still a mystery to him.

Keeping to the shadows and obscure corners, Meren left the Divine Lotus and met Abu behind the carpenter's workshop. The space behind the house was littered with wood shavings, discarded lumber, and broken tools. Meren stepped over the remains of an adze handle and joined his aide, and they set off for the Street of Perfumers. It was a dangerous journey, for they had to cross the palace district and dodge police and military patrols. They skirted the area as much as they could, going completely around Horemheb's headquarters and ending up on the north side of the palace. There they entered a neighborhood of artisans—goldworkers, joiners, chariot makers, and perfumers.

The house of the perfumer was wedged between two larger structures, the agglomerated workshops of two extended families. The expansion of families into new quarters had left but a sliver of a passageway between each dwelling. As Meren approached the perfumer's, he heard the slapping footfalls of a patrol. Darting into the passageway with Abu behind him, he slipped around an exterior stairway and waited. He glimpsed a three-man patrol, spears used as walking sticks, as it tramped past.

When the patrol was gone, Abu snorted and said quietly, "They'll never catch anyone, lumbering about like drunken hippos."

"I doubt if they want to catch anyone," Meren replied. "Most city police I've met take care to avoid places where they're likely to find someone to arrest."

"True, lord."

Meren rested his back against the bulk of the staircase, hoping that his dark clothing would make him invisible. While he waited, he reviewed what had been discovered about Queen Nefertiti and her household.

Before Meren's own troubles intervened, his scribes had been examining government records and bringing back verbal reports. As with any great royal wife, Nefertiti's household had extended over countless estates and possessions throughout the empire. Her immediate servants were numerous as well. There had been waiting ladies—the daughters of princes and nobles—three personal maids, five dressers, several physicians, her steward, the chief scribe and his staff, her captain of troops and his men, her traders, and her overseer of the cabinet, who dealt with the queen's wardrobe. He'd reconstructed this list from his scribe's reports, not from his patchy memory.

Royal accounts had yielded payments to hairdressers, cosmetics attendants, a keeper of the queen's jewels and his assistant, a bearer of floral offerings, the queen's Aten priest, her musicians, singers, porters, and sandal-bearers. He'd found a sealer of the storehouse of gifts of the queen, three personal heralds, and a vast array of kitchen and garden staff, along with the woman who was overseer of the queen's bath. Rations had been dispensed to the queen's cup-bearer, her chariot driver, her grooms, and the keeper of the queen's pets. Nefertiti had left bequests to many of her servants, including the mistress of the queen's oils and unguents.

Unfortunately, the documents failed to list many of these servants by name. He could trace only the highest, many of whom had left royal service completely or had died. Two of the queen's physicians who had attended her during her last illness had died, and that worried Meren. The third, a woman, still attended Queen Ankhesenamun. Would a woman so highly regarded by the royal family have poisoned her mistress? Of that he had great doubt.

Another high servant had been Thanuro, the Aten priest appointed to serve the queen by Akhenaten. Once the queen had taken ill, the priest had conducted sacrifices to beg the gods to save Nefertiti, but he hadn't visited the sick woman. After the king and queen were both dead, the priest had retired. Meren remembered hearing that he'd died on a journey to a foreign estate he'd been given by Akhenaten. The steward, of course, had been in charge of the household and had access to the favored cook. But someone had directed his actions. Someone high enough to impose his will upon a royal servant; there were few such men.

An evil possibility had occurred to him while making the interminable list of queen's servants. He—Meren—had been a constant visitor to the palace in his capacity as Ay's aide. Being in the palace so frequently during the queen's final days made him vulnerable to the same suspicions he had against her servants. He'd been justified in his secrecy. Should pharaoh discover his inquiry into the queen's death, his cautious heart would conclude that Meren's recent mad actions resulted from a murderer's guilt and fear of exposure.

Shifting his weight from one foot to the other, Meren surveyed the dark streets at either end of the passageway. Few were abroad this late, and he was beginning to think Yamen wasn't coming. Resolving to give his quarry a little longer, Meren resumed his contemplation.

Records from the days at Horizon of the Aten were incomplete. Only those of immediate use had been taken when the court had moved back to Memphis. These were scattered among various government departments. Many had been left in the nearly abandoned city, which now was the residence only of the mortuary priests who attended the royal tombs. These pharaoh had not yet transferred, even though the graves they tended were empty. Tutankhamun was reluctant to remove them, for such an action would signal to the whole kingdom that the bodies of Akhenaten and his family had been taken away. The king was fearful of a repetition of the desecration that had been wrought upon his dead brother's body.

A stealthy and thus limited examination of accounts from the royal treasury had revealed some important news, however. In Nefertiti's final months, there had been payments of grain and small amounts of gold to Dilalu by the queen's steward. He had also found ration disbursement records that disclosed that Yamen had been assigned to the queen's household guard for a brief time. Of Zulaya there was no record at all, and Meren was beginning to think that the man had been somewhere else, possibly in one of the cities in which he owned property—Byblos, Aleppo, or Damascus.

Meren shoved away from the stairway and rotated his shoulders, which had grown stiff with prolonged inactivity. Motioning for Abu to remain where he was, he slithered down the passageway to the Street of Perfumers and looked at the sky. The moon was gone. Yamen wasn't coming.

Returning to the staircase, he whispered to Abu, "He's not coming. We'll try again tomorrow night."

He slipped out of the passage with Abu at his heels. Traveling as a wanted man meant skulking down foul alleys and over the rooftops of buildings when he could be sure a family wasn't sleeping outdoors. He couldn't hop and clamber over roofs in this crowded district, however. With reluctance, Meren picked his way through side streets and alleys, trying not to step in dog and goat dung or pools of muddy piss. He made it through several noxious passages before his sandal landed in muck that oozed between his toes. It was as black as night in the netherworld, but Meren recognized that unpleasant, slimy texture. Abu stopped beside him and made a noise of commiseration.

Cursing, Meren lifted his foot and sniffed. He sniffed again. No acid odor. He smelled dirt mixed with a coppery scent he knew from the battlefield and practice yard. Forgetting his foot, he squatted and reached out. His fingers touched skin slick with blood, and then he heard a whimper.

Chapter 18

Memphis, reign of Tutankhamun

Meren slid his hand along an arm, up a shoulder, to a neck damp with blood. Abu reached past him, searching, and found a dagger beneath the victim.

A faint voice made harsh with effort sounded loud in the blackness. "Finish it, and may the gods damn you."

"Yamen?" Meren's searching hands encountered others clamped over Yamen's belly.

"Who is—" Yamen broke off to laugh, and the laughter turned to wet coughing. "My lord Meren, by the light of Ra. You're not dead yet?"

"Rest yourself," Meren said. "I'll send for help."

"No!"

With a bloody hand Yamen grabbed Meren's and dragged it to rest on a gaping hole in his gut. There was no need for argument. The wound was deep, and of the kind for which there was no remedy. Meren freed himself and placed Yamen's hands over the wound.

"I haven't long," Yamen said, his words growing more and more indistinct. "What a fool I was to trust——"

Meren squeezed Yamen's arm to keep him alert. "Trust whom?"

The soldier began to laugh again. "I was so pleased to come to your notice. Then he came and warned me. Should have known then. Too confident."

Hearing a cough, Meren lifted Yamen against his leg, and the gasping eased.

"Who did this? Who killed the queen? Yamen, there's no time. Tell me before it's too late, and I'll avenge you."

There was a weak chuckle. "Queen? Should have known he wasn't helping me out of friendship. Stupid . . ."

Meren felt Yamen's body go slack. Desperate, he slapped the man's face. "Yamen!"

He heard a cough and felt blood splatter on his wrist. Blood from the mouth. There was no time.

"Yamen!"

Abu had been keeping watch. "Lower your voice, lord."

Meren bent close to Yamen and hissed, "Speak, you sodding whoreson."

Yamen gave a choking cough and garbled his words. "Avenge me? No, sacrifice me. He learned that when he . . . He'll sacrifice you as he does all who know him."

Uncontrolled laughter bubbled from wet lips. Meren started when Yamen grasped his wrist with a bloody hand and pulled him close to hear a harsh whisper.

"He is in my heart. There is no other who knows him." This time the weak laughter was mocking, malevolent.

A wet hand fastened on Meren's neck and pulled him to

within a finger's width of Yamen's lips. If he hadn't been so close, he couldn't have heard the man's last words.

"All perish who threaten him."

"Damn you, Yamen, tell me his name!"

Meren felt the gory hands slip from him and heard the final hiss of escaping breath. Behind him Abu muttered prayers and spells against evil. Meren crouched beside the body, head bowed, frustration and rage rising in his heart. Because of this man he was an accused traitor and his family in danger. Kysen, Bener, Tefnut, Isis, all could lose their lives. He wanted to chase Yamen into the netherworld, wrap his hands around the man's neck, and wring it until he got the answer he wanted. Months of apprehension, of looking over his shoulder, of fearing for the king, for Kysen, and all the others rushed upon him, and Meren's long-held temper snapped.

"Come away, lord. He has become *mut*, one of the dangerous dead. His spirit is evil."

Meren grabbed Yamen's body and shook it. "Tell me his name, you mother-cursed ass!"

He kept shaking Yamen until he was jerked away from the body and shoved against a wall. His head hit the mud brick. The pain jolted Meren from his rage, and he lapsed into silence, breathing rapidly.

After a while Meren said, "You can release me, Abu."

Stepping back from Meren, Abu turned his head. "Listen."

"A patrol?" Meren shoved away from the wall. "We can't be caught here."

Without a thought for the body or ka of Yamen, Meren darted down the passageway and swerved around a corner into a crooked path between houses and the city wall. Walking rapidly, he headed toward the Caverns. They hadn't gone far when they heard cries of alarm from a city patrol.

"They found him," Meren said. "Hurry."

He sped up, stepped into a street of beer houses and taverns, and almost collided with someone. Meren shrank against a wall, trying to become one with the shadows cast by a torch set in a sconce beside a door. He glimpsed a cloaked man and caught a dizzying whiff of wine fumes.

"Miserable peasant," the cloaked man muttered as he wove his way down the street.

Abu, who was holding Yamen's dagger at ready, relaxed and came over to Meren. "Allow me to go first, lord. This night's deeds have upset you."

"I'm not upset, I'm furious."

"Indeed, lord." Abu set off without further discussion.

They reached the Divine Lotus with no other encounters and approached the rear entrance. The guard stared at them briefly but allowed them to enter the courtyard. Othrys's celebrations were still going on and had reached a gleeful loudness that irritated Meren. He drew his aide to a corner of the courtyard beside an ornamental pavilion.

"What should we do now, lord?"

"Listen to me carefully, Abu," Meren whispered. "The danger is even greater than we supposed. All who know the identity of this murderer perish, even warriors like Yamen. The only way to guard against such power is not to work alone. You and Reia will have to contact Ebana."

"But Ebana hates you."

"Perhaps. But we were brothers once, and I know him as I know myself. He loves me, though he has tried to cast me from his heart. He wouldn't have gone to my house if he weren't trying to help me. Go to him. Tell him what has passed, and tell him this from me. The guilty one who attacked the king must have met with Yamen immediately before we left on the raid. He probably has been known to have dealings with Yamen before. Tell Ebana he must find this man, quickly, before the hidden one who killed Yamen finds me."

"Yes, lord."

"And Abu——" Meren hesitated. "If you should hear that I'm captured or killed, you must decide whether it is safe for Kysen and the girls to remain in Egypt."

Abu grasped Meren's forearm in a warrior's clasp, which Meren returned.

"It shall be done, lord. There will be no need to leave Egypt."

"I pray to Amun you're right," Meren said wearily. "Take great care when you leave this place. I'll get Ese to give me a room for the night. I must cleanse myself, and it's too dangerous to leave with the patrols aroused by Yamen's death."

"Blessings of the gods be with you, lord."

"They haven't been of late," Meren said.

Once more keeping to the shadows, Meren gained the door to the tavern and stepped inside. The stairwell was empty, so he ascended to the second-floor landing, where he waited while several patrons passed by with Egyptian women dressed in Greek clothing. When they vanished into a bedroom, he continued to the third floor and eased open one of a pair of doors made of the finest cedar. Looking through the crack, he found the room beyond empty and went inside. As he shut the door, a woman came into the antechamber through an archway. It was Ese, the owner of the Divine Lotus. A woman of middle years and a youthful body, she had luxuriant, curling brown hair and an air of promised pleasures. When greeting customers, she exuded the mysterious attraction of Hathor, goddess of love. When she was not on duty, however, her dark, heavy-lashed eyes lost their light and became the flat, pitiless orbs of a serpent. As far as Meren could discern, her distinguishing characteristic was an abiding resentment toward all men.

Ese saw him, gasped, and nearly dropped the eggshell-thin ceramic cup she was holding. "Ass's dung. What are you doing here, Tros?" She addressed him by the Greek name Othrys had given him.

"My thanks for your concern for my welfare, Ese, but no, I'm not wounded, just drenched with someone else's blood."

"Get out. You'll ruin my fine floor mats and furniture."

"I need a room, Ese."

"I said get out. Out of my tavern."

"Don't you want to know whose blood this is?"

"I don't care." Ese whisked past him and opened the door. "Leave, or I'll call some of my men to throw you out."

"Will you do that before or after you explain to Othrys why you've denied me the help you promised?"

He waited while Ese debated whether his presence posed a greater danger than the pirate's wrath. Again, her fear of Othrys won.

"Follow me."

She led him to the chamber beyond the archway. Tired as he was, Meren paused in astonishment to survey delicate, hazy curtains billowing in a breeze. They were draped across a long balcony that overlooked the courtyard. The room itself was painted with a pastel blue over which had been drawn frescoes of the sea and its creatures. Placed about the room were caskets and chests worked in ebony, ivory, and cedar. He caught a glimpse of tables bearing embossed silver cups, goblets and flagons trimmed in gold, and an open jewelry casket. A necklace trailed over the rim, its beads in the shape of sun disks with spiral rays. Ese pointed impatiently to another door.

"Bathing chamber," she snapped. "Be clean by the time I return. I'll find something for you to wear. You'll frighten my patrons if you go about in that bloody tunic."

When she was gone, Meren looked down at himself. His tunic, his leggings, and one foot were smeared with blood and dirt. His arms were no better. He screwed his face up in distaste, then stripped and entered the bathing chamber. He stepped into the plastered stall, picked up a jug, and began pouring water over himself from the tall vat that stood nearby.

As the cool water hit him, Meren began to feel the tightness in his body loosen. Weariness followed this release, and he dumped water over his head to keep alert. It was then that he remembered the wig. Pulling it from his head, he tossed the wet mass to the floor. He scooped up soap paste from a dish and rubbed his entire body.

Whoever sees Nefertiti's killer dies. The words chased themselves around and around in his heart. Those who might know something would die; even those who knew nothing of the queen's death were killed if they posed a threat. Othrys had been right. Whoever was responsible was one who fed on evil, enjoyed seeing others trapped, helpless, desperate. Meren paused in rinsing the soap paste from his body. At least part of the reason for his disgrace must lie in the nature of this unseen enemy. Could Dilalu be such a man? He seemed too foolish, but the foolishness might be a guise. Or had he been chasing phantoms? Was the killer much closer—among his friends and enemies at court? Most had been at Horizon of the Aten when the queen died.

Yamen's last words must hold a key to the identity of the enemy. What were they? Ah, yes. *He'll sacrifice you as he does all who know him.* What else? Meren grabbed a bathing cloth from a pile in an open chest. What had so amused Yamen that he'd laughed even as he died? It had been strangely familiar. *He is in my heart. There is no other who knows him.* The feeling of familiarity teased him, then vanished. Meren uttered an oath and stepped out of the bathing stall.

"You're in a foul temper, lord."

Meren whirled around to find Naram-Sin leaning against the door, smiling. Without thought Meren's hand had gone to his side, where a dagger should have been. He noticed the direction of the intruder's gaze. Scowling, Meren reached for a dry bathing cloth and wrapped it around his waist.

"What do you want?"

Laughter like the gentle lapping of water against a riverbank made Meren want to hurl the water jug at Othrys's scribe. Naram-Sin vanished for a moment and returned with a pile of clothing. Shutting the door, he placed his burden on top of a chest and picked up a tunic of dark green. Before Meren could protest, Naram-Sin gathered the fabric in both hands and dropped it over his head. Meren had no choice but to drop his towel and thrust his arms through the sleeves. Dragging the tunic down, Meren emerged in a fury, only to find that Naram-Sin had turned way to pluck a braided cloth belt from the chest.

Before his self-appointed body servant could touch him, Meren grabbed the belt and pulled it around his waist. "Go away."

Naram-Sin picked up a pair of leather sandals.

"What happened, lord?"

"My affairs are not yours."

"Ese complained to Othrys that you were in her chamber, getting blood all over her valuable possessions. You're in danger, lord, and the master has made me your guardian."

Meren looked up from tying his belt. "I need no guard."

"The master disagrees. This evening he has had reports of

many soldiers in the city, and there are rumors that pharaoh will reward the man who finds you."

Meren stared at Naram-Sin, who smiled his intimate smile. He knelt with the sandals and reached for Meren's foot. Meren stepped back, bent, and snatched the sandals from his unwanted servant.

Sliding into the footwear, he said, "Othrys wants to be rid of me because he fears for his own head. That's why he's so anxious to help."

"He considered giving you to pharaoh," Naram-Sin said softly.

Meren paused in running his fingers through his wet hair. "Oh?"

"But I convinced him that in doing so he would invite inconvenient royal attention. I said that pharaoh is wise beyond his years and might ask himself why you sought the protection of a man who is supposed to be but a Greek ship captain and trader."

Meren didn't reply at once. He studied Naram-Sin, trying to divine the man's motives. Was his obvious interest that of one who preferred men, or was it but a ruse?

"What do you want, Naram-Sin?"

"Only for the lord to allow me to aid him."

"And in return?"

Meren stiffened as Naram-Sin came closer, but the scribe stopped when he was within a pace of him.

"In return," Naram-Sin whispered, "I want . . . friendship."

Turning, Meren walked to the door and opened it. "I can't be the friend of a man whose very name is a lie."

"Kysen told you my name is that of an ancient king," Naram-Sin said.

"Yes."

"But that doesn't mean that the spirit of the name is a lie."

"I have no time for or interest in this game," Meren said. He pushed the door open wider. "Wait outside while I finish dressing."

With Naram-Sin out of the bathing chamber, Meren put on a new wig that the scribe had provided, along with a clean loincloth. Meren would have traded either for a dagger or scimitar. Outside, Naram-Sin was draped across Ese's sleeping couch. He got up as Meren entered and spoke before they reached the antechamber.

"If you live . . ."

Meren glanced at him and lifted a brow. "Yes?"

"If you live, perhaps I'll tell you my real name. If that will bring your friendship."

"I don't care what your real name is. I'm going to find Ese and arrange to sleep here tonight."

Naram-Sin shook his head. "Othrys commands that you return to his house. You can be better concealed there. I know a safe route that runs through the houses of friends."

"As long as I don't have to step in any more dung piles."

Meren followed Naram-Sin downstairs and into the main tavern room. They were passing the great circular fireplace when someone crossed their path. Flame light touched a robe of crimson sewn with roundels of gold. A hand burdened with rings of amethyst, green jasper, and chalcedony flashed out and caught Naram-Sin by the shoulder. Meren was forced to stop behind his escort.

"Naram-Sin," said the owner of the hand. "May Baal and Ishtar bless you."

The scribe bowed with the ease of the finest courtier. "Zulaya. Good fortune to you. We thought you'd gone to Byblos."

"I'm honored that Othrys speculates upon my whereabouts."

"Only in passing," Naram-Sin replied with another bow. "Your pardon, but I'm on an errand for the master."

The scribe moved, but Zulaya stepped into his path and waved at Meren with the cup of wine he was holding. "Othrys has a new servant?"

Meren kept his mouth shut. He didn't trust his ability to play a common Greek sailor before this well-traveled merchant. Naram-Sin glanced over his shoulder at Meren as if he'd forgotten him.

"New servant? Oh, no. This is Tros, a friend." Before he could react, Naram-Sin wrapped a hand around his arm and pulled Meren against him. "Tros is from Mycenae. His family is high in the favor of the prince."

"Ah," Zulaya said as he bowed to Meren. "I have many dealings with other Greek cities, but not Mycenae. Perhaps we could share wine and speak of trade?"

Meren opened his mouth, but Naram-Sin spoke first.

"A most tempting invitation, but we have promised to be elsewhere, and it's getting late. Perhaps another time?"

Zulaya inclined his head and stepped aside. As Meren passed, he said, "It's a dark night, Tros. Be careful."

Meren nodded and hurried after Naram-Sin. He caught up with the scribe as he stepped outside. One of Othrys's guards was waiting. Meren kept silent until the guard led them into a deserted house. Then he stopped Naram-Sin.

"Where did Zulaya come from? How long was he in the Divine Lotus tonight?"

Naram-Sin gave an impatient sigh. "By the earth mother, you demand the impossible, lord. I cannot know everything, even for you."

The guard suddenly became interested in the plaster on the wall in the next room as Meren stalked closer to the scribe.

"I've practiced the patience of Isis with you, Naram-Sin.

Give me an untwisted answer before I tie your legs around your neck."

Holding up his hands, Naram-Sin chuckled and said, "I obey, great lord, but you won't like my answer. No one knows when Zulaya arrives or when he leaves, not even Othrys."

"So he could have just arrived. He could have been in the streets earlier in the evening."

"He could have been in the netherworld," Naram-Sin replied, "and neither you nor I would know it." The scribe lowered his voice. "It is said that Zulaya's power comes from demons of that place."

"Power comes from wealth ordained by the gods, Naram-Sin."

"And birth, lord."

"Do you know a well-born man without wealth?" Meren made a slashing motion with his hand. "I've no time for useless speculation. You've ruined my plans for this Zulaya. He's seen me, and now I can't make his acquaintance as Lord Meren."

"In truth, lord, you're more likely to gain Zulaya's trust as a Greek. He leaves the trading matters here to his underlings and has few dealings with Egyptians."

"When will he come to the Divine Lotus again?"

Naram-Sin shook his head and gave Meren a smile that irritated its recipient with its familiarity. "His visits to the city are brief and rare. A merchant prince must travel ceaselessly, for he trades in countless places. As for finding him again—"

"I must find him again," Meren said.

The scribe hesitated, his brow furrowing as if he struggled with some elusive thought. "Lord, Zulaya is like the desert storm-winds; he appears from nothing and vanishes into nothing."

"Nevertheless—"

Meren went silent and raised a warning hand to Naram-Sin. They had been standing in a narrow room, the roof of which was supported by a single column. The house itself had no second story, and the roof served as a living area. He'd heard a distant thump on the roof, as if someone had landed on it from the second story of the building next door. Meren signaled to their guard. The man hurried through the house to the rear door, but as he disappeared Meren heard scurrying from above. Launching himself after the guard, he burst past Naram-Sin.

"Come, quickly!"

He ran through the house to the rear door, which stood open. Throwing himself beside the portal, he grabbed Naram-Sin before the other man could run outside. The guard reappeared, beckoning. Meren slipped out of the house, followed by Naram-Sin. Keeping their backs to the house walls, they hurried for the shelter of an alley shrouded in blackness. As they gained concealment, Meren glanced back and saw movement on the roof of the house they'd just left. Then a shout cut through the quiet.

"They've gone out the back!"

Naram-Sin grabbed Meren's arm and whispered furiously, "Follow the guard. I'll go separately, and they'll have to chase us both."

"It's too dangerous," Meren said as Naram-Sin began to push him toward the guard. "If they catch you—"

"If they catch *you*, Othrys will kill me. Now go!"

Naram-Sin whirled and ran back the way they'd come. At the same time, the guard grabbed Meren's arm and hauled him down the alley into another passageway. As they ran, Meren heard more shouting, then the sound of running, closer and closer. The guard stopped and shoved Meren ahead of him into a doorway.

"Stay still," the man hissed. "Not a move until they pass."

The guard stepped into the middle of the alley, turned his back, and looked over his shoulder as their pursuers came into view. Then he fled. Meren pressed himself against dry old wood and held his breath as five men with knives and scimitars hurtled toward him.

Chapter 19

Thebes, the independent reign of the pharaoh Akhenaten

A year, an entire year—Inundation, Emergence, Harvest—and she still lived. Nefertiti sat in a small audience chamber and stared blankly at one of the frescoes in the Theban royal palace. Her little girls were gone, one by one. All but Merytaten and Ankhesenpaaten. Gone. First Meketaten had caught an ague that worsened until she could no longer breathe. Then a plague had swept out of the northern empire to strike Egypt, taking her youngest ones, even the littlest, Setepenre.

That plague had scourged Nefertiti's heart and left her empty and writhing in agony. All her prayers, those of the priests and physicians, had come to naught. The gods had abandoned her.

Ay had convinced Akhenaten that she needed to get away from the palace and the city where she had lost her children, and so her father had brought her to visit her sister. Nefertiti cared not where she was. The pain was the same. Ay fussed at her, urging her to eat, to go out, to sail in the royal barge. These things she could not do. There was no reason to do them.

Her father had taken on many of her duties, as had Merytaten. Akhenaten sent an endless stream of letters full of worry, full of comfort, all useless. His grief did not touch her, and for that she felt guilty. He had loved the girls as much as she, and without her, he had no one with whom he could share his torment. But she was empty and exhausted. If she had to endure his clinging sorrow, she would go mad.

The gods had abandoned her. What other explanation was there for the loss of so many innocents in so short a time? She had prayed to them all—Amun, Mut, Osiris, Ra, but especially to Isis, the mother of all the gods. Her babies had died anyway. And only now, months past that time of destruction, was she beginning to understand the reason the gods had abandoned her. She and her husband had rejected the origin of all existence, the power from which all creation issued— Amun, the hidden power of life, the unknowable source. Without the king of the gods, she was doomed, as were her remaining children. All was blackness and chaos.

She heard a noise and glanced up to find her father walking toward her. She hadn't noticed his arrival, although her attendants must have announced him. Forcing herself to pay attention to him, she even managed a partial smile of greeting. Ay didn't smile back. He marched over to her.

Mooring himself in front of her chair, he said, "Daughter, I love you too much to allow you to commit self-annihilation." When she merely sighed, he continued. "You're still a mother, and more important, you're still queen of Egypt. Like you, Akhenaten is submerged in his grief, but unlike you he has sought refuge with the Aten. His withdrawal grows with the days, and Egypt suffers." Bending down, Ay put his hand on hers. "You're stronger than this, stronger than pharaoh."

Nefertiti shook off her father's hand. "There's nothing inside me. My ka is empty." She scowled at Ay. "Besides, I've had enough of standing between pharaoh and the world. Why must I be the shield and bear the burdens, take all the blows?"

"Because you are the great royal wife, and pharaoh will heed no other in all of Egypt." Ay crouched before Nefertiti and bent on her an intense, urgent look. "Your lot has been hard, your grief as immense as the desert, but you must accept what has happened and continue with the tasks we've set for ourselves."

Nefertiti closed her eyes. "I can't."

"Remember that priest, the one you mercifully dispatched? I know you had his name secretly carved on a wall in Amun's temple. Because of you, his ka won't perish." Ay put a hand on her cheek. "Without you Egypt will suffer; children like your own will suffer. Something must be done to bring order before the kingdom drowns in chaos. Remember those who suffer because the temples have been closed."

She looked away. "Yes. I remember, Father. But I have no strength inside me."

"Shall I bring a few hungry children to the palace?" Ay asked. "Perhaps the sight of their protruding ribs and great, dull eyes will give you strength."

"The gods have abandoned me. They've abandoned Egypt."

Abruptly, her father stood and shouted at her, "Then what will you do about it?"

Nefertiti started and blinked at him. It had been many years since anyone had dared yell at her.

"Do about it?"

Ay didn't answer.

"*Do* something about it," she repeated. Her fingers drummed on the arm of her chair, and an almost imperceptible glimmer of light entered her ka. She fixed Ay with a sharp stare. "You know what you're saying?"

He nodded.

"Then arrange it. It must be done now, while I'm in Thebes and away from pharaoh."

Three days after the confrontation with her father, Nefertiti feigned illness from lack of food and took to her bed. That night Ay's most trusted guards were ordered to duty at the palace, with Sebek in command. When the moon set, Nefertiti rose and dressed, donning a cloak and a short wig that made her look like one of her personal maids. Sebek and another guard were waiting outside her quarters. Her head bowed, she followed them through the quiet palace, into the pleasure gardens, and out of the royal precinct.

They went to the river, where a yacht awaited them. Nefertiti led the way across the gangplank, and as she stepped on board, her father came out of the deckhouse to meet her.

"You weren't followed?" he asked.

Nefertiti glanced back at Sebek, who shook his head.

"Come," Ay said.

They entered the deckhouse, and Nefertiti was visited by memories of her childhood. The chamber was furnished much as it had been then, with intricately woven mats on the floor, wall hangings embroidered in the city of Babylon, and an abundance of floor cushions. Ay's chair stood beside a table, and there was the little folding stool she'd used. Its seat was crafted of ebony and ivory to resemble a leopard skin. Nefertiti contemplated the spots while her finger traced the slick ivory.

Ay left her in the deckhouse, alone except for a slave, one

who had been with her family since before Nefertiti had been born, to fan her and serve food. The slave held out a tray laden with beef, mutton, and spiced duck. Nefertiti shook her head and dismissed the woman.

She wished she could sit on the folding stool, but her place was in Ay's chair. Throwing her cloak over her shoulders, Nefertiti sat and arranged her gown around her legs. With the ease of many years' practice, she assumed the posture of a queen, arms draped along the chair arms, chin high, expression distant.

The door opened, and her father came in with a man dressed in a kilt and frayed overrobe, the pleats of which had long ago lost their fine edge. The visitor's head was devoid of hair except for wispy strands of silver that stood up from his scalp and fringed the side and back of his skull. His eyes were small, and his nose jutted forward. It dominated the receding mouth and chin. Small ears hugged close to his head. The rest of him was thin and frail.

Nefertiti felt a sting of pity, for the man was quivering like jostled yogurt. "You may speak."

"Great queen, I am from the Hidden One." The man shrank back and trembled more violently.

"Fear not," she said. "We're safe here."

The priest seemed to try to melt into the deck. "Danger is never far from servants of the Hidden One." He licked his lips. "I am Shedamun."

Shedamun was chief lector priest to Amun. Nefertiti glanced at her father; she hadn't recognized the man, he had changed so in appearance. He'd lost hair, flesh, and much of his old assurance. She had thought Shedamun was hiding or dead.

One of the holiest of the god's servants, Shedamun was known throughout the Two Lands for his powerful magic. To him went the privilege of reading from the sacred texts of the god. From the reading of the words came power of the gods hidden in deep antiquity. Shedamun's reading was imbued with sanctity.

Nefertiti could remember Akhenaten's father saying that no royal endeavor would succeed without a favorable reading from Shedamun. When Amunhotep had been ill, the lector priest's voice brought ease from suffering. Shedamun was one of the few who knew the secret words by which Amun was invoked.

"There was a rebellion in Nubia once," Nefertiti said. "The pharaoh Amunhotep said your words brought the magic of Amun to bear upon the rebel tribes."

"What? Oh, yes, majesty. Are you sure we're safe?" Shedamun's gaze searched the cabin for listeners. "Great royal wife, I come from the high priest. There are so few of us left that he had to send me."

The man must be woefully short of priests if he sent this quaking, unworldly scholar. Of course priests of Amun were scarce now.

Nefertiti nodded to give the old man courage.

"I memorized the message," Shedamun said after a final look around the cabin for spies. He pitched his voice in a singsong manner that almost made Nefertiti smile.

"The high priest of Amun to the great royal wife, mistress of the Two Lands, Nefertiti, may you live in prosperity, health, and in favor of Amun, king of the gods. I say to Amun, keep the queen in health." Shedamun cleared his throat. "Thus says the high priest. Great royal wife, the priests die. Those who live dare not shave their heads nor perform lustrations, nor make any worship of the Hidden One. In the Two Lands the thief becomes a lord, and the sinful man rules the temple. Wretched Asiatics and Nubians threaten from north and south. The land is not fruitful.

"Thus says the high priest. For many years I have watched the sickness grow within the body of Egypt, and I have great sorrow. For many years I have heard of thy piety. Thy mercy has come to me on the tongues of priests and workmen."

"Stop," Nefertiti said. "The pharaoh Amunhotep always said the high priest used five words where one would do. Can you omit some of them?"

Shedamun grinned. His eyes became distant as he mentally thumbed through the pages of the letter. "Let me see." Shedamun cleared his throat again. "The House of Amun suffers. We have no more tribute from the vassal towns of Syria. Our herds are confiscated. We no longer own fields and gardens. This year alone we lost ten thousand slaves. All of our storehouses have been seized: the treasure of the god—gold, silver, lapis lazuli, malachite. In one treasury, three hundred twenty-seven vessels of electrum, gold, and obsidian. We have no galleys or barques, no black bronze, no woven robes, incense, or honey, no precious wood." Shedamun paused and wet his lips. "The list goes on, majesty, but you understand the point."

"Of course." Did the priests think she'd been asleep since becoming queen?

"Lo, the farmers of the god, the vintners and herdsmen, the scribes and gardeners, cooks, painters, and doorkeepers, they suffer from hunger, for we can give them no bread or beer."

"Shedamun, I'm well aware of the suffering of pharaoh's people. You'd better come to the point, for we cannot risk a long meeting."

"Yes, majesty. The high priest begs thy mercy. He pleads with thee to intercede with pharaoh on behalf of Amun."

Nefertiti rose and nodded at her father, who helped the old man to his feet.

"I understand your message," she said. Walking away from the priest, Nefertiti hesitated, but she'd already endangered her life and her father's. Not to go forward was to have risked all for naught. She turned and gave Shedamun a regal inclination of her head. "Thus says Nefertiti, great royal wife, mistress of the Two Lands, to the high priest of Amun. Indeed, the land of Egypt suffers. Chaos reigns, and my majesty believes that order must be restored. Maat—the truth, harmony and order of existence—must govern Egypt again."

Nefertiti paused as she noticed that old Shedamun had tears in his eyes and was bowing repeatedly in gratitude.

"The path to . . . restoration is fraught with peril," she said gently. "My majesty will labor to clear the path, but this work will take time. Meanwhile, converse between us must be as secret as the passage through the netherworld. Lord Ay will make the arrangements. It is my command that you send an unknown man to Horizon of the Aten to act as messenger. Thus says the great royal wife."

"Thy wisdom and mercy are unequaled, O mistress of the Two Lands," Shedamun said. He pressed the hem of his robe to his damp eyes. "It's not easy to be brought so low, especially for the high priest."

"Blessings of the gods be with you," Nefertiti said.

She inclined her head. At her gesture, Ay took the priest's arm and urged him to the cabin door. With each step Shedamun turned his head this way and that, a frightened sparrow in search of hidden falcons.

While awaiting her father's return, she paced. When the messenger arrived, she would send him to Thutmose the sculptor and keep him out of pharaoh's sight.

Nefertiti wandered back to her chair with her thoughts flying. The high priest of Amun, once the most powerful man in the kingdom next to pharaoh, begged her help in restoring Amun. She recalled Shedamun's list of the god's holdings. The temple of Amun had been richer by far than any other. Amun's dependents were countless. His slaves numbered several hundred thousand. Once, his gold would have filled the pyramid of Khufu.

"Perhaps the temple was a little too rich," she murmured. Tracing the carving on the chair back, she continued talking to herself in a whisper. "All that wealth. Does the mighty Amun really want that much? I know the high priest does; is that the same thing?" She pounded the chair with her fist. "Restoration must bring back the favor of the gods."

Sinking into the chair again, Nefertiti rested her chin in her palm and pondered the danger of questioning the gifts her husband's ancestors gave to Amun. For many years they'd endowed the god with riches beyond any other deity. After all, it had been Amun who gave victory to Pharaoh Ahmose when he defeated the Hyksos invaders. It had been Amun who gave Thutmose the Conqueror the power to create the empire.

"When pharaoh withdrew his devotion, Amun took back the empire and opened the way for invaders again. Amun visits his wrath upon Egypt. And upon me."

On the floor of the cabin a beetle, sacred creature of the god Khepera, waddled across the mat. It was said that a great beetle rolled the sun before it from east to west. Akhenaten called such beliefs nonsense. The sun was the sun, the Aten, the fount of all life. The Aten needed no help getting across the sky. "Little scarab," she said to the insect, "will you ask Amun if he will accept me as his servant again? I'm not sure I'm worthy to join the company of Ahmose and the Conqueror."

At the sound of the door creaking open she looked up. Ay came toward her.

"Shedamun is gone."

"You know what will happen should Akhenaten find out we've but spoken to a priest of Amun," Nefertiti said.

"Daughter, we've discussed the peril already."

"I could have done this without you, and you wouldn't have been involved in the danger."

Ay came to stand with the chair between them. "I've been speaking to Shedamun for months."

A sudden chill overtook Nefertiti, and she shook her head. "You've seen what he does to traitors."

"I've seen what his heresy has done to you, to your children, to Egypt." Taking her arm, Ay led her onto the deck.

The Nile was as black as the sky, and the only sound heard above the water hitting the side of the yacht was the cry of a heron. The only light came from a lamp near the gangplank. Ay's attendants, soldiers all, stood guard with Sebek.

As she listened to the heron, Nefertiti's heart jumped in her chest. For almost the space of an hour, she had forgotten her babes. She closed her eyes, willing tears away. Pain wrapped its cloak of torment around her once more, and the course ahead seemed beyond her strength. Yet for a brief time her pain had receded; she hadn't believed it possible. Her father had been right. She had work to do if her remaining children were to live in the favor of the gods. And she must think of young Smenkhare and Tutankhaten now that Tiye was gone.

Smenkhare was heir, was he not? The youth had grown up torn between his mother's traditional beliefs and Akhenaten's heresy, and the older he grew, the more restive he became. Yet Smenkhare was wise beyond his years and might prove an ally. She would talk to her father about seeking the boy's collaboration, but she was reluctant to risk his life. Egypt needed an heir, for the only other male of Amunhotep's body was the child Tutankhaten.

Someone must try to put things right, someone expendable. Nefertiti smiled grimly. Who better to risk the wrath of pharaoh than a grieving woman who held her life cheap? For she was willing to conduct her treasons in the very house of the king. The gods might protect her if she labored to restore their temples. And if Akhenaten discovered her betrayal before she had convinced him to allow the restoration?

She didn't think she'd mind dying. It was the path to her lost children.

Chapter 20

Memphis, reign of Tutankhamun

Meren's eyes flew open as he thrust himself upright, his hand already grasping a dagger. Spinning from his sitting position, he dropped to the floor, crouched, and slashed at the air with the blade. When it hit nothing, he waited, his gaze darting from shadow to shadow. The only sound he heard was his own hard breathing.

Finally he realized where he was—the house of the pirate Othrys. Was it morning already? Feeling foolish, he rose, his shoulders sagging with weariness. Last night he'd barely escaped the men who hunted him. They'd followed the guard only a little way before two of them retraced their steps and ran into him.

It had been a bloody fight. If his attackers had been royal troops, he might not have survived. But they hadn't been, and he'd killed them instead and made his way back here. Neither his guard nor Naram-Sin had returned, and Othrys had sent men looking for them. Meren had fallen asleep waiting for them, wondering who had tried to kill him and how his attackers had known where to find him.

Sleep would be impossible now that his heart was ramming itself against his ribs, so Meren washed and dressed. As he finished, Othrys slammed his chamber door open without asking permission to enter.

Meren scowled at him. "Did you find them?"

"Who? Oh, Naram-Sin. Don't be deceived by his manner. He's a trained warrior. He came back shortly after I sent men looking for him. The guard is dead."

Sighing, Meren shoved the Greek wig on his head and said, "I'm sorry."

"I'll find out who did this, but that's not why I'm here." The pirate stepped into the doorway and said, "Come."

An old woman followed him into the room. Her head hung between her shoulders because her back was bent with age. This crooked posture caused her ash-white hair to swing forward, covering her face. She wore a stained, wrinkled long-sleeved garment that hung about her thin body. The old woman carried a basket of wet laundry in her arms and shuffled with tiny steps. Meren stared at her in surprise, for at home no laundress would ever have business with him. She minced to a halt before him, and Meren surveyed her from gray head to small feet. Small feet. He knew those little feet, and he was certain they didn't belong to an aged laundress.

"Bener!"

His daughter's head snapped up, and he beheld a grinning, self-satisfied young woman. She dropped her basket and flung herself into his arms. Meren forgot his astonishment and squeezed her hard, burying his face in the rough wig that surrounded her head.

"Father," she whispered. "I've been so frightened for you."

Her voice jolted him from the luxury of relief. He straightened and held her at arms' length.

"Damnation. What are you doing here?"

"Abu got word to us that you were here. He sent a message through my laundress, as I was using her to get messages to Cousin Ebana."

Meren was staring at his daughter in disbelief. "The laundress would be questioned and her basket searched."

"She was questioned, but they didn't search. Not this particular kind of laundry."

Meren glanced into the basket at the clean, wet bundles. His eyes widened as he recognized them, and he looked at Bener with renewed astonishment. Then he scowled again.

"You must have avoided Kysen as well as the king's spies, for I know he wouldn't allow you to come here."

"Father, there's no time for arguing. I've important news."

Othrys came to stand beside Bener. "She's right. Listen to her, and scold later."

Wavering between fear for Bener and the knowledge that she and the pirate were right, Meren nodded. Bener smiled with pride as she recounted her successful ruse for passing messages and told what she, Kysen, and Ebana had discovered.

"So Ebana sought help from an old friend in the office of records and tithes," she said. "This man owes Cousin Ebana many favors, and he has arranged to meet both Turi and Mose."

"How?" Meren asked.

"Ebana's friend is overseer of records and royal gifts, and he has sent word to each separately that there has arisen a question of title to the lands awarded them by pharaoh. Each thinks a rival claimant has appeared and that the overseer wishes to speak with him and take his part in the dispute."

"And the meetings?"

"Ebana instructed his friend to tell both Turi and Mose to meet him on his way home, as his days are full of tasks at the moment. They are to meet at that old shrine behind the grain magazines of Ptah. You remember the place."

"Yes. It hasn't been used since the days of Amunhotep the Magnificent's grandfather, and it was old then. It's still standing?"

Bener nodded. "Each man thinks the overseer is meeting him to get an account of his case to present to the vizier's judges. Kysen and Ebana will be waiting instead, and they want you to be there to question the Nubians."

"I see," Meren said. He closed his eyes and pinched the bridge of his nose. "How will Kysen leave the house undetected?"

Bener was grinning again. "I've offered him the use of my disguise."

It was Meren's turn to smile. He could imagine Kysen's disgust at having to dress like a woman, much less an aged laundress.

"Father," Bener said. "Cousin Ebana says you'll be able to discover the guilty one once you confront him, but I don't see how he can be so confident."

Meren gazed over his daughter's head at nothing, his thoughts traveling years into the past. "I'd forgotten how much my cousin and I think alike."

"But how will you discover the criminal?" Bener repeated.

"The less you know, the better." Meren remembered to be irate with his daughter. "And you're never to come here again. Stay home, where you belong. No following Kysen to the shrine this evening."

"Fear not, Father. Kysen and I made a bargain. He let me come to you, and I promised not to go to the shrine."

"Good," Meren snapped.

Othrys clapped his hands together. "Excellent. I'll be rid of you soon, and all will be well."

Meren glared a warning at the pirate, who caught his look and changed the subject.

"Now, lady, before you set off on your long journey across the city, allow me to give you a morning meal. Food, drink, and time with you will improve your father's foul humor."

One of the hardest things Meren had ever done was allow his daughter to shuffle out of Othrys's house alone with that basket of laundry. He worried about her the rest of the day. Even struggling with the mystery of Nefertiti's death proved but a temporary distraction. So far, he'd managed to knock a few chips from the stone barrier that encased his memories of that time and protected him from the pain they evoked. Keeping out of sight in his chamber until dusk, Meren took out the papyrus upon which he was writing his recollections of Horizon of the Aten.

Nefertiti had taken ill about a week before she died and had gradually grown worse, as had her younger children a few years earlier. Everyone had taken her symptoms for those of a plague that appeared periodically in Egypt, usually from the vassal lands of the Asiatics or from Nubia. Ten days of illness, gradual worsening, then death.

Now that he knew the signs of poisoning by the *tekau* plant from his physician, he could see that the queen had exhibited them shortly before he'd arrived at the palace with foreign correspondence Ay wanted her to see. Upon entering the small audience hall where Nefertiti usually received him, he'd been told that the queen had taken ill with a fever. Later she had received him despite her suffering; the ague had made her skin hot to the touch, red, and dry. So great had the fever been that she'd become disoriented during the interview.

Upon reflection all these years later, Meren realized that it had been that first attack of fever that had misled the physicians and everyone else. A virulent fever was the first sign of the plague. The queen's disorientation, her eventual delusions and blurred vision, had been attributed to the fever, as had that rapid and loud voice of the heart. Although the physicians had noted that the queen had not broken out in red marks—another sign of the plague—before she died, the significance of this had been lost in the shock of her death and the grief that had followed.

Indeed, even in the intrigue-ridden imperial court, where poison was always an unspoken menace, no suspicions had been voiced. The queen's illness had extended over a long period of time. Meren, and certainly everyone else at court, was accustomed to suspecting poison when a death was sudden and the cause unknown.

In the days that followed Nefertiti's first attack of fever, Meren had seldom left the queen's apartments except to go to Ay with reports of his daughter's health. As she worsened, he sent for his mentor, and after that, Ay rarely left her. Meren remained as well, but he kept himself hidden when pharaoh appeared to grieve over his wife and exhort her to rally. In the end, not even pharaoh's pleading helped. Nefertiti suffered fits in which her body contorted violently. Then she became senseless, and on the tenth day after her illness, she died.

Meren knew who had put the *tekau* poison in the queen's drink and food—her favorite cook, at the instigation of her steward. But the steward had been an obsequious place seeker and a coward. He would never have acted alone. If only he could remember more, especially of the daily routine at the palace. Then he might find some sign of the queen's killer.

Until he could recall more, he would continue to review the lists of those who had been Nefertiti's enemies. The more he explored the events surrounding the queen's death, the longer the list of enemies grew. Of these, the greatest had been the Hittite emissary to the royal court, Yazilikaya. In the last years of Akhenaten's reign the Hittite had found his attempts to allay pharaoh's suspicions and keep him inactive against his king's maneuvers thwarted by the queen.

And at the last, when the kingdom and Akhenaten had both deteriorated almost beyond recall, pharaoh turned to Nefertiti for help in a way that had shocked all of Egypt. As with many events deemed great transgressions against the right order of things, the whole kingdom now ignored them. It was as if these events had never happened. Akhenaten's actions during the last few years of his reign were never mentioned. Even Tutankhamun dared not speak of what his brother had done. And, unwilling though Nefertiti had been, her acceptance of Akhenaten's plans had plunged her into the swirling void of chaos that pharaoh created.

All public record of it had been expunged; such a thing had never been done, at least, not within the memory of anyone living. It was unnatural. There weren't words for it, and the gods had rebelled against it. Perhaps their displeasure at the transgression had been the real cause of Nefertiti's death, and Akhenaten's.

Meren's rush pen faltered as he tried to write the next line. The habit of secrecy was too great. He couldn't yet bring himself to write of Akhenaten's last offense. Laying down the pen, he folded the papyri and stuck them beneath his tunic so that they were held in place by his belt. He couldn't leave the record in Othrys's house. His only alternative was to carry it with him, and it was time to meet Kysen and Ebana.

Othrys and several of his men accompanied Meren as far

as the magazines of Ptah. The pirate vowed that Meren would be less noticeable walking in their midst than he would be alone. In late afternoon, in the hour or two before darkness, the streets of Memphis teemed with pedestrians, subjects of pharaoh from every station in life returning home from a day's labor.

Temples emptied of priests, students, artisans, and suppli-cants. Government offices disgorged their workers—scribes of accounts, tithes, granaries, storehouses, and treasures. Port offi-cials went home, as did maids, women market vendors, gold-workers, overseers of cattle, outline draftsmen, carpenters, and fishermen. Meren kept his head down and made way for the chariots of grand noblemen returning from court or from the temple of Ptah. Like Othrys and other more ordinary citizens, he stumbled over boy students who hurtled through the crowds with their scribe's kits dangling from grubby fingers.

The crowds thinned as they made their way to the rear of the enormous grain magazines of the temple of Ptah. The high, arched vaults would overflow with grain after next har-vest. When they reached the rear of the buildings, only a few stragglers passed them. Othrys stopped at the corner of the last magazine and peered around the corner. Meren came to stand beside his host and looked into the uneven and ne-glected lane that came to a dead end at the shrine. A dog trot-ted out from between two buildings, but it saw them and retreated. Nothing else moved.

Othrys backed away from the corner and turned to Meren. "I leave you here. If you don't come back to my house, I'm not going to look for you."

"Your concern for me is touching," Meren said.

"By the earth mother, I've done more than any of your pre-cious Egyptian friends."

Meren smiled and bowed slightly. "Forgive my foul temper.

254 LYNDA S. ROBINSON

It comes from being forced to wear this cursed wig. It itches worse than these leggings."

"But no one would recognize you in it," Othrys replied.

"You have my gratitude and my friendship," Meren said. He offered his hand, and they exchanged a warrior's grip. "If I live, you will receive proof of my thankfulness."

"Farewell, Egyptian. I'll go home and pronounce curses on those who plot your destruction. May fate be with you."

In moments, Meren was alone. The carnelian orb of Ra was sinking behind the city's tall buildings when Meren stepped into the lane. Elongated shadows cut across his path, and the air seemed to turn gold with the sun's passage. He could smell water from the submerged fields of Inundation, along with the odor of cooking fires. Ahead of him stood the shrine. It had been built as a part of a temple complex hundreds of years ago, when the city was much smaller. Memphis had encroached upon its perimeter walls, and finally the little temple had been abandoned, its buildings quarried for their stone.

All that remained was this little square structure, a processional kiosk that everyone referred to as a shrine. Its columns were square, and it had a central staircase leading up to a threshold from which the doors and shutters had vanished long ago. The doorway was flanked by two tall windows, and the whole of the outer surface was carved. Meren had visited the place as a youth and remembered seeing raised reliefs of a pharaoh, Sesostris, presenting offerings to a god.

Meren reached the shrine. Avoiding the stairs, he went to one of the windows and surveyed the interior. Devoid of furnishings, it was littered with trash blown from the lane— scraps of a papyrus sandal, dead palm leaves, a few feathers, and sand. Meren walked around to the back. A storehouse

had been built so close that he had to enter the space between the two buildings sideways. He hadn't been there long
when four men appeared in the lane. As they approached the
shrine and stepped out of a long shadow, Meren breathed
more easily. Abu and Reia walked ahead of his son and
Ebana. All of them were armed. Slipping from his hiding
place, Meren waited beside the shrine. Abu saw him first
and saluted. At his movement, Kysen grinned, called to
Meren, and ran to him.

"Father!" Kysen halted abruptly and studied his father.

"I'm well, Ky." Meren dragged his son into his arms for a
brief, rough embrace and released him.

"What happened?" Kysen said as the others drew near. He
held out a dagger, which Meren took and slid beneath his
belt. "How could pharaoh believe you would—"

Meren held up his hand. "Later." He grasped Ebana's arm.
"Cousin."

There was no need for words. One glance at those features
that were so like his own wiped away years, and they were back
at his father's estate in the country, daring each other to spend
the night in the ghost-infested desert. They smiled at each
other, and for once bitterness and accusations of betrayal
failed to divide them.

Ebana put his fists on his hips and grinned at Meren. "If
you keep getting yourself into such peril, I'll have to give up
being a priest of Amun and become your bodyguard."

"I've missed you," Meren said.

Ebana's smile faded. "Our estrangement wasn't my fault."

"Ebana, don't."

"I know. This isn't the time. With your permission, cousin.
Your men should find cover in the darkness of the shrine, as
should we."

The kiosk had a central chamber flanked by a smaller room

on each side, formed by rectangular pillars. It was gloomy in the larger room in spite of the gaping doorway, and dark in the smaller rooms except near the windows. Abu and Reia melted into the shadows of the two western pillars inside a flanking chamber while Meren and Kysen took a pillar on the east and Ebana the remaining one.

They'd just taken their places when an obsidian figure walked into view from the direction of the magazines. It was Mose. Long strides brought him to the foot of the stairs. As he mounted them Turi hurried around the corner of the storehouse and to the front of the shrine. The two guards stared at each other in the fading light, then exchanged queries in their native language. In confusion they continued their exchange as they ascended the staircase and entered the shrine.

Meren waited until they were well inside before moving. In silence he slipped around the pillar and put himself between the two men and the doorway.

"Greetings," he said, causing the Nubians to whirl around and reach for their daggers.

As they moved, Kysen, Ebana, and the rest appeared, their weapons drawn. The Nubians froze in the act of drawing their blades.

"Hands away from your daggers," Meren commanded.

Abu relieved them of their weapons as Kysen joined Meren.

Ebana took a position at the doorway, leaning against the doorjamb, and watched the lane. "Whatever you're going to do, do it quickly, cousin."

"Aye, Father," Kysen said. "We can't stay long. And we can't drag them through the streets. I told Ebana we should have abducted them from their homes and secreted them somewhere."

Meren shook his head. "There's no need. A few words with these two should suffice to prove me innocent."

"A few words?" Kysen gave him a startled look.

Walking over to the silent Nubians, Meren looked up at them, for they were almost a foot taller than he. "Repeat these words. Majesty, life, health, prosperity."

Turi and Mose exchanged blank looks. Then Turi spoke.

"Majesty, life, health, prosperity."

Kysen gave Meren an inquiring look. "This makes no sense."

"It would if your heart wasn't weighted down with ignorance from being of common blood," Ebana said from his post by the doorway.

Kysen flashed a disgusted look at Ebana but said nothing.

Meren signaled to Reia. "Take him out and release him."

Reia escorted Turi from the shrine, and Meren faced the remaining Nubian.

"Royal bodyguards are like slaves at court, like furniture. Are they not, Mose?"

The Nubian said nothing. His features seemed as expressionless as those of a lizard.

"And furniture does not make noise," Meren continued. "Certainly a noisy guard is a worthless one. And chatter isn't the way of a Nubian warrior. Is it, Mose?"

Kysen drew nearer and breathed his words. "By the wrath of Montu, Father."

Meren nodded to his son, then whipped out his dagger without warning and touched the point to the ebony skin over Mose's throat.

"Say the words, or by the gods I'll make you scream them."

All he got in response was the same impassive regard he'd come to expect from any Nubian royal guard.

Drawing close to the man, Meren spoke softly. "Remember

the time I captured the leader of the miserable Asiatics who murdered everyone at the fortress called Might of Horus? Remember how long it took him to die out in the desert?" Meren withdrew his dagger and tapped his fingers on the blade. "It's so easy to attract the creatures of the desert to a bleeding body—snakes, scorpions, ants . . . vultures."

Mose stared into his eyes and shook his head.

Meren smiled at him. "You have family, don't you, Mose?"

This time Mose blinked. Meren darted at him, placing the blade at his throat again. "Speak. In the voice you used in the tent that night, not with your usual accent."

"Too late," Ebana said.

Meren withdrew the dagger and joined his cousin in looking out the doorway. Soldiers with scimitars and shields approached down the lane. Dozens of bows pointed at the shrine from the corners of the grain magazines. Above all the others, Meren recognized the black head of Karoya.

"Curse it, how did Horemheb know? Abu, Kysen, bring the Nubian."

Meren stepped into the half-light at the top of the stairs. The approaching soldiers stopped. Motionless, Meren waited without surprise as the troops parted, revealing pharaoh. He was almost jolted from his composure when he saw who was behind pharaoh. Bener stood beside a guard, who was holding her arm. Once again she was dressed as an aged laundress.

Horemheb appeared at pharaoh's side. "Take them."

"No!" Tutankhamun said. Horemheb whispered to the king, but Tutankhamun shook his head and silenced the general with a slice of his hand.

The king walked toward the shrine, and Meren descended the stairs. They met in the empty space between the troops and the shrine.

"Golden one, you shouldn't have come."

Tutankhamun's smile was bitter. "I had to. I have to know the truth. Why did you do it? Have you been a traitor all this time?"

"No, majesty. I am as I always was, thy servant. I would give my life—"

"Don't. I'll hear no protests of loyalty. I'll commit you to trial in secret to save your family the disgrace, but I'll hear no protests of loyalty from you."

"Then will thy majesty hear proof of his servant's innocence?"

"What can you say that will excuse what you did?"

"I can say nothing, but there is one whose words will end this deceit."

Horemheb marched to them. "Forgive me, majesty, but it's growing dark."

Tutankhamun waved the general into silence. "I will listen."

Meren summoned Kysen, and Mose was brought out of the shrine between him and Abu. Ebana followed. Tutankhamun frowned as he recognized his guard, and he turned to Meren.

"Command Mose to speak the words I instructed him to speak before you came, majesty."

"What confusion is this?" Horemheb asked.

Raising his hand, pharaoh continued to stare at Meren without responding. Meren met the king's gaze directly. He hoped that some small remnant of faith in him still existed within this youth for whom he felt both the love of a father and the reverence of a subject. Tutankhamun still hesitated.

"Majesty," Meren whispered. "You hold my life. I beg you, don't crush it beneath your sandal."

For the briefest moment the boy closed his eyes, and his face contorted with pain. The spasm passed, and the king met his gaze once more.

"Mose, speak."

Mose's lips pressed together. At the silence, Tutankhamun's eyes widened. Meren gave the Nubian a nasty smile.

"Pharaoh is quite unaccustomed to disobedience, Mose."

Horemheb suddenly stalked over to the guard and said, "Yes. I suggest you do as the divine one commanded before I make you."

When the Nubian remained silent, Meren sighed and said, "I see I must remind you of our conversation in the shrine, Mose. The desert, your family? Speak."

His gaze darting from Horemheb to Meren, Mose opened his mouth. Ebana's dagger prodded him in the ribs from behind, and the words came out at last.

"Majesty, life, health, prosperity."

At first there was silence. Then the king took several steps that brought him closer to Mose, and Meren joined him.

"Say it again—no—say this. Say, 'Majesty, where are you?' "

As if the words were dragged from him like pyramid blocks on a sledge, Mose complied. "Majesty, where are you?"

Slowly the king turned to face Meren, his face pale. "Like you. His voice sounds like yours. There isn't even an accent."

"Yes, majesty. And now we must ask who bribed him to pretend to be me and feign that attack on you, and why. I think you'll find, Horemheb, that Mose has suddenly acquired much wealth."

"Mose," the king said. "I command you to respond."

But Mose wasn't attending to pharaoh. As Meren watched the Nubian, alarm writhed like a cold snake in his belly, for Mose's gaze was directed over the pharaoh's head, over the heads of the men surrounding them, at the rooftops. When the guard's eyes widened in terror, Meren moved. At the same time, Mose lunged at them. His hands fastened on the king, and the Nubian dragged the boy against his chest like a shield. Instantly Meren tore the king from Mose's grip and felt a stinging jolt in his side. Ignoring the pain, he twisted and plunged to the ground with the king beneath him.

Above him all was confusion and noise.

Horemheb shouted, "Not the one on the roof, the Nubian! Get the Nubian Mose!"

Dust flew into Meren's face as men ran by. He heard arrows whistling and blades clashing, but he was more concerned with lifting himself so that he could assess the danger to the king, who was swearing and spitting dirt underneath him.

Planting his hands on the ground beside pharaoh's head, Meren lifted his upper body. Pain arced through him, and his left arm collapsed. The chaos above him descended and wrought havoc with his senses. He seemed to be living just outside his body.

With vague surprise he looked on as Horemheb pulled him off the king and laid him on his back. Tutankhamun rolled over, crouched beside him. Pharaoh's mouth moved, but the sound of his words seemed delayed. Meren was even more astonished when the king bent and gripped something sticking out of the ground close to Meren.

When Tutankhamun broke the end of an arrow, the agony that resulted told Meren that the missile was buried in his side, not the ground. Meren searched for the wound and clamped his hand over the point of entry. Horemheb was still beside him while the king propped Meren's head on one leg.

"What are you doing here?" Meren snapped at the general. "Find the bowman."

"Every man I have is chasing him and Mose, including your son and your cousin and your charioteers. Don't tell me how to hunt criminals, Meren. I found you, didn't I?"

"You let Mose get away?"

"Damn you, Meren. The men closest to the king were trying to protect him from the bowman, and the ones farther away didn't know Mose was a criminal."

"My apologies, old friend," Meren said.

Grimacing, he looked around at the wall of men surrounding pharaoh, then up at the king. Tutankhamun was regarding him with a mixture of anxiety and relief.

"It wasn't necessary to prove your innocence in so dramatic a manner," the king said. He placed his hand over Meren's bloody one. "I already believed you."

Meren smiled, but his lips contorted with pain. "My heart exults in thy majesty's safekeeping."

Pharaoh said something in reply, but to Meren the king seemed to recede into the distance. He blinked, which was a mistake, because he found he couldn't lift his eyelids. The noise and confusion returned, grew louder, and then faded into a whirlpool of blackness.

Chapter 21

Horizon of the Aten, the independent reign of the pharaoh Akhenaten

Nefertiti watched Akhenaten stalk along the edge of the reflection pool at the riverside palace. In spite of the heat, he wore a cloak over his robe and paused often to lift his face to the sun. His gold leather sandals sent pebbles flying into the water as he scuffed along. Finally he returned to the shade of the acacia tree beneath which Nefertiti's chair rested and stood before her.

"I no longer remember how many times we've argued about this, beautiful one. I'm weary beyond enduring, and your discontent grieves me."

"I've always told you the truth, husband. The army grows restless with the Hittite jackal prowling the borders of the empire."

"And I repeat—the Asiatics live in chaos. It is their normal state. Once Mitanni held sway; now the Hittites dominate. One day the Assyrians may claim that right. Such internecine squabbling means little to Egypt, as long as our trade routes remain safe."

Nefertiti rose and put her hand on Akhenaten's arm. "And how long will they remain safe, husband, if the Hittites come to think Egypt is soft?"

"Fighting unnecessary battles wastes the blood of my people and displeases the Aten," Akhenaten said as he patted her hand.

Moving closer, Nefertiti looked into her husband's obsidian eyes and made her voice low and rough. "My love, is it not better to fight a few small battles to warn the Hittites than to allow them to mistake Egypt's resolve? If they become stronger and thus overconfident, it's certain that we'll have to spill much more blood later than if we push them back now."

"Hmm. Perhaps, beautiful one, perhaps."

Nefertiti watched her husband's interest fade. It was becoming more and more difficult to get him to attend to foreign business. He was engaged in some inner struggle having to do with the Aten. That much she knew. But the nature of the struggle and what it meant for Egypt was still a mystery to her.

Akhenaten was smiling at her. Drawing her along with him, he strolled beside the reflection pool. Slaves scurried up to ply fans above their heads.

"I'm so fortunate to have my beautiful one as great royal wife," Akhenaten said. "You relieve me of many burdens, my love, and free me for more important work with my father the Aten. Because of your help, I'm beginning to receive complete Maat—divine truth—from the sun disk. Soon all of Egypt will live in truth."

Nefertiti stopped and turned to look at him. "But the— the difficulties with some continue."

The black fire of his convictions flared in Akhenaten's eyes and then vanished with frightening abruptness.

"Fear not, my love. All will be resolved in time." He smiled and began walking again. "Let us not speak of such unpleasant things. You're going to your sister again. I don't like it, these visits to the city of the false king of the gods."

Akhenaten directed a sideways glance at her, but Nefertiti only gave him a smile of amusement.

"The temple is closed, the priests dispersed or dead, and Amun is gone. Otherwise I wouldn't go to Thebes, even to visit my dear sister."

Kissing her cheek, Akhenaten said, "It is a great comfort to know that you live in truth as I do, my beautiful one. I don't know what I would do if that weren't so."

Court business delayed Nefertiti's journey to Thebes for a few days. As the stubble in the fields shriveled under the heat of the Aten, so her ka withered in ever-present grief for her children. While she struggled in silence, the court adapted itself to Akhenaten's growing preoccupation with the Aten's revelations. An easy task, for all that the living god desired instantly came to be.

She sent Ay to the hidden messenger chosen by Shedamun with instructions and embarked at last for Thebes. The days sailing upstream should have been peaceful. They would have been if not for the nightmare. Always the dream began by the river's edge.

Clad in a shift, she scooped mud from the river bottom and mixed it with straw. When she had a mound of the ooze prepared, she picked up a bucket and poured the mud into wooden molds to make bricks that would dry in the sun on the bank. She worked in the heat until she had seven rows of bricks that stretched along the bank as far as she could see.

She was kneeling over her latest effort when Akhenaten appeared from the sky. Pharaoh landed in the middle of her bricks, squashing them to shapelessness, and strode toward her. As her husband trampled the neat squares, she protested, but Akhenaten only smiled and kept walking until he stood over Nefertiti.

Wearing his double crown, Akhenaten was naked and carried his golden crook and flail. Pharaoh planted his feet apart, right in the middle of two of Nefertiti's best bricks.

"Beautiful one, this work isn't important. Pleasing me is important."

While Nefertiti crouched before him, Akhenaten laughed. The king discarded his scepters and began to grow. His body stretched until it was the size of one of his colossi, and then it started to grow breasts in imitation of the stone image. The hips widened, and Nefertiti stared in horror. Akhenaten bent down from his great height, picked her up, and tore her shift.

Fortunately, her favorite maid slept in her cabin on the royal yacht. When Nefertiti woke sweating and disturbed, she had company. The next evening at sunset she was on deck, craning her neck for the first sight of the temples of Amun. For as long as she could remember, the gold-tipped flagstaffs with their scarlet banners meant homecoming. Impatient, she dragged a stool to the railing. She stood on it to watch the setting sun illuminate the stone and bricks of the houses and temples of Thebes. One of her ladies came to stand beside her.

Nefertiti pointed in the direction of the Amun temple and its surrounding structures. "We're almost there." As they sailed closer, she nearly betrayed herself with an exclamation. Even from the river she could see that only one flagstaff remained, its banner shredded and limp.

Although it had been closed, the temple hadn't deteriorated to this state the last time she visited the city. The house of the god was dark. Gashes cut through the paint on the massive pylons, and the great doors—stripped of their gold—hung open. She blinked. Was she mad? Did she see a peasant leading donkeys through the sacred precinct? Tents. She saw tents, and goats.

Mighty Amun, forgive us. There were weeds growing inside the temple courtyards. No wonder the gods had abandoned her. But she couldn't do anything to prevent this rapid deterioration. If she did, word would speed to Akhenaten. Her actions were watched by great ones and commoners alike, including those in her household. Some, like Tutu, kept their ears pricked for any transgression that might be used to lessen pharaoh's affection for her.

Walking along the railing, Nefertiti let the desecrated temples go by. Silence governed the normally talkative crew of the royal ship, but she paid no heed to the apprehensive glances the sailors cast at her. She would pray to the Hidden One for forgiveness.

Until she arrived at the palace, Nefertiti avoided looking in the direction of the temple. It only reminded her of the god's anger and how her children had suffered because of it. While her household prepared for residence, she tried to take comfort in the familiarity of her old rooms. The jewel-blue of the water scene on the floor had been the girl's delight. In a spot near the bed, her favorite painted fish gleamed, all black, blue, and yellow scales.

When she could stand no more of the bustle of unpacking, she dismissed her attendants. A stroll around the bedchamber convinced her that no one lingered nearby. From a casket she removed a pen holder. A tubular case made for rush pens, it was another of Akhenaten's myriad gifts. The container was modeled in the shape of a palm-tree column and consisted of wood overlaid with gold foil and inlaid with precious stones.

Nefertiti ran her fingers over the bright green-and-blue hieroglyphs that spelled her name before she removed the stopper and pens. With a last glance around the room she worked a finger into the tube and withdrew a roll of papyrus. The pen holder was discarded. Sitting cross-legged on the bed, she unrolled the papyrus by the light of an alabaster lamp.

Her own handwriting scrawled across three pages in what she liked to think of as a plan to restore the Two Lands to Maat. It had taken her and Ay many days of plotting and planning to come up with these few scraps of paper. The most difficulty was caused by trying to balance the needs of the Two Lands against the prejudice of Akhenaten and the cries for revenge from the priests of Amun. Add to that the dissatisfaction in the army, and achieving harmony and balance became more difficult than making friends with a jackal.

Her fingers let the papyrus snap back into a tight roll. Never had she felt so desolate and alone. Ay's plans to return the army to its old efficiency, her strategy to round up those who embezzled imposts and dues intended for pharaoh, all depended on their ability to invoke obedience from the powerful priesthood and army. It was she who must command the loyalty to the throne despite the hatred Akhenaten deliberately courted.

With a sigh Nefertiti twisted the papyrus and slipped it back into the pen holder. She blew out the lamp, discarded her robe, and lay down. She said a brief prayer to Amun, asking for a peaceful sleep.

"Husband, why can't I hate you? Then my heart would find balance."

It wasn't within her ka to despise Akhenaten completely. No one had ever told her that love was a hard thing to destroy. For every time Akhenaten indulged in an excess of fanaticism, there was an unexpected kindness to match it. And Akhenaten was good to her as well. She remembered the day on which she'd become his wife. He'd given the largest feast she'd ever seen. And in the years that followed he had confided in her, trusted her, and become openly proud of her governing skills. When Nefertiti sequestered herself with Ay and a pile of foreign letters, Akhenaten would forbid the court to disturb her.

If only he was totally evil; but he's not. He's kind to the people of his city. He cares for those who are in trouble, once he can be brought to pay attention to them. He even keeps that drunken steward Ahmose, and I wouldn't have that idiot in my household for a week.

Nefertiti rubbed her temples and tried to ease the tension in the muscles across her forehead. She would try to forget Akhenaten for a little while. She needed rest, and she craved respite from this eternal battle between love and hate.

Three nights of solitude brought some peace to her ka. She spent this time cultivating the appearance of inactivity. She gossiped with her sister and ladies. She sailed on the river and chose new pleated gowns of the sheerest linen. Then word came from Shedamun that the priests of Amun would be in Thebes in nine days. By the end of those nine days, Nefertiti was sick of fittings and holdings feasts for local nobility. She was even more tired of the rituals of the Aten carried on by the ubiquitous Thanuro.

"The man is irritating," Nefertiti said to her father. "When he isn't performing rituals, he's busy ferreting out more of Amun's hidden treasures or trying to get me to give him yet another lucrative post."

It was the day of the meeting with the priests. She, Sebek, and Ay stood beside the Nile, watching fishermen cast their nets. Ay waded out among the water plants, spear in hand. His voice subdued, he stared into the river. "Thanuro knows that there are two paths to the king's favor—absolute devotion to the Aten, and service to you. Perhaps you haven't given the man enough to do." He stabbed downward, but missed.

Nefertiti chuckled. "He could give you fishing lessons."

Ay rolled his eyes and splashed drops of water at her.

Nefertiti returned the splash, then grew serious. "About our plans for this evening. Did you not say that famous dancer from Tyre was in the city?"

"Yes," Ay said.

"Is she good?"

Ay shrugged, but Sebek answered.

"Majesty, she and her troupe could hold the attention of an army."

"Bring her to the palace tonight and see that she distracts my household. Say that I've given permission for a banquet for my hardworking servants."

Sebek and Ay grinned at her.

That night Nefertiti set out for the meeting with an easy heart. Ay came with her into a poor district where the meeting was to take place, but she refused to take any guards other than Sebek. Thus it was a small party that stepped into the narrow front room of a deserted fisherman's house. Sebek remained outside.

In the uncertain light of clay bowls filled with oil, Nefertiti could barely make out three men in plain, cheap kilts. One carried an old walking stick, and none had the shaved head of a priest.

Nefertiti stepped from behind Ay and drew back the hood of the cloak she'd worn to conceal her face. Lamplight cast a dull gleam on the gold at her wrists. As the cloak fell away from her face, she heard a gasp quickly stifled. The three men knelt. The fact that they didn't touch their heads to the floor wasn't lost on Nefertiti. She gave permission for the men to rise and took the only chair in the room. Ay took up a stance at her right hand.

From a black corner Shedamun edged forward to stand between the priests and Nefertiti. "I—I told you the queen would come. I told you. Th—they didn't believe me, majesty."

Nefertiti made a slow, economical gesture with one hand. Shedamun quieted. She had to establish dominance at once. Already the man with the walking stick was eyeing her with satisfaction. She could almost hear the man's thoughts. He probably expected an awed and frightened woman.

"Father, you may give me the names of these men."

"Great queen of the Two Lands, beloved of the good god, here stand before you the second prophet of Amun, the divine father Iny, and the lector priest Bekenamun."

The second prophet of Amun stepped forward. With a bow, he leaned on his walking stick and addressed Nefertiti. "Mighty queen, I am Unnefer of Thebes." Unnefer curled bony fingers around his staff and leaned in Nefertiti's direction. "I have come to hear thy answer to the message sent by the revered high priest."

The words were subservient, and Unnefer said them in a deprecating tone. Nefertiti rested her hands on the arms of the chair and looked at the priest.

"Maat has been banished from the Two Lands. The gods punish Egypt and will continue to do so until the divine order is restored."

She received four grateful bows for these words.

"I would know how the high priest of Amun proposes to help me restore Maat," she said.

Unnefer needed no further encouragement. He drew himself up to his full height. "Evil cannot be banished from the Two Lands until the King of the Gods reigns once more in Thebes. Amun demands his house and his possessions. Egypt must worship the Hidden One, beg his forgiveness, supplicate him with gifts. The rage of Amun is great. Witness the lawlessness and plagues that threaten our cities. If we were to offer all the gold in Nubia to the Hidden One, it wouldn't be enough. The god cries out for vengeance, majesty. Without it, chaos will destroy Egypt."

During this tirade Nefertiti kept her gaze on the second prophet. She'd expected anger and demands for restoration. She'd expected the hunger for lost riches and power. All these she perceived. And something more. She saw Akhenaten's intolerance. Unnefer looked nothing like her husband. The priest was short and built like a small crane with narrow bones and legs much too long in proportion to his torso. Age lines made rivulets perpendicular to his lips, and his lower face had that sunken look that went with the loss of teeth. But regardless of his age or god, Unnefer spoke with the same fury she'd heard so often from pharaoh.

Whatever the cost, these two infernos must not meet. Nefertiti held out her hand. Ay placed a cup of wine in it. She let the men wait while she took a sip. The two junior priests exchanged uneasy glances.

"I agree," she said.

Unnefer smiled and took on the air of a basking crocodile.

"The house of the god must be put in order. The old ways must be brought back." Peering at Unnefer over the rim of her cup, Nefertiti paused before she went on. "I'll have to approach pharaoh, and this is a most difficult task. I don't have to speak of pharaoh's attitude. It will take much time, I fear." She saw the three begin to relax. "In the meantime there is much to be done in the service of Maat. I expect the priesthood to labor hard, since I too will be working."

"Labor, majesty?" Unnefer sounded as if the word was one he didn't associate with himself.

"Yes. I know that the servants of Amun have been dispersed from Thebes, but I also know that they remain in the

towns and villages of the Two Lands." Nefertiti crossed her
ankles and took another drink. "There are pure ones and
hour priests scattered from Bubastis to Elephantine, and they
all owe allegiance to Amun and the high priest." Without
warning she raised her voice. "They will stop preaching
against pharaoh."

"The king is possessed by evil demons," Unnefer said.

"Your priests will cease to encourage disobedience and rebellion. You'll agree, or this meeting is at an end." Nefertiti
felt Ay stir beside her. She hadn't told her father she was planning to make this threat, but it was her sacred duty to protect
Akhenaten. Her husband didn't have the sense to do it himself.

Watching Unnefer's round eyes squeeze shut, she thought
the man would dare to curse her. Admiration for the man's
discipline came to her as the priest set his mouth in a thin line
and muttered an obedient response.

"It's well that you agree." Nefertiti gave them a bright smile
and soft laugh. The priests jumped, and Unnefer gave her a
long, guarded look. "You see, I don't know where I'd find
other knowledgeable priests to staff the newly restored temple if I became displeased with you. Of course there are
plenty of courtiers who'd want the positions." Standing,
Nefertiti handed Ay her cup. She let the cloak slip to the floor
and walked across the room to Unnefer. "Yes, I'd waste a lot
of time if I had to recruit priests with the proper devotion to
pharaoh." She glanced back at Unnefer with another smile. "I
knew the servants of Amun wouldn't fail me."

There was an odd sound. It was the grinding of Unnefer's
few teeth.

"Great royal wife," Unnefer said. "Thy will shall be done."

"Yes, it will. But I'm not finished, Unnefer. The priests will
also help me in other matters. Food must be distributed from

the royal estates. Corrupt tax officers and soldiers must be discovered and punished. The peasants have to be protected against thieves, noble or otherwise. I'll send you lists of tasks, and soon I'll send my own representative to you in Elephantine. Amun's followers are countless; they will be my eyes and ears in this restoration."

"Highness, we are priests," Unnefer said.

"You're going to be much more. You will succor the poor and ferret out corruption. You'll aid the police and army so that peace will reign." She stopped; Unnefer's face had taken on a stunned look. "I'll provide Amun with supplies and slaves from my own estates once pharaoh has been persuaded to agree to the restoration."

She was gratified when the three priests bowed in response to her words. Nefertiti went to her father, and Ay settled her cloak on her shoulders. Unnefer scuttled over to her, bowed, and whispered so that only she could hear.

"I've been remiss, most divine queen."

"Oh?"

"The high priest most adamantly instructed me to pray for the health of pharaoh, may he live—forever."

Nefertiti's hands stilled their smoothing of the cloak. She lifted her gaze to Unnefer and gave an almost imperceptible nod.

"The high priest is concerned about pharaoh's frequent illnesses. The wind Shu carries such news to all parts of Egypt. It is well known that pharaoh is not as he should be." Unnefer lowered his voice. "Many fear that one day soon the hawk will fly to the sun."

She let the priest wait for her reply. She gazed at one of the clay lamps while her fingers continued their slow dance across the fabric of the cloak. When she finally spoke, Unnefer started.

"Pharaoh is in excellent health. The wind distorts sound, Unnefer. Pay no attention to the howling it creates. Those foolish enough to do so imperil their own lives by rushing toward noises that don't exist. They sometimes run off cliffs and get themselves killed."

She got out of the house without doing violence to the priest. Her departure was abrupt, but it was better than murder. When the door shut, she stood with her back to it. Taking deep breaths, she waited for her wrath to ebb.

Ay touched her arm. "What did he say to you?"

Nefertiti heard her voice quiver as she whispered, "The whole purpose of that meeting, it wasn't restoration. It was to see how I would react to pharaoh's death."

Nefertiti stepped into the deserted and dark street. Sebek drifted ahead through the blackness.

"We could have them killed."

"No. We need them as much as they need us. Besides, if there's one thing being a queen has taught me, it's that knowing who your enemies are is an advantage beyond the riches of Punt."

"At least now we know," Ay said. "Pharaoh would kill the Amun priests, and they would kill him."

"By the netherworld, Father, how am I to bring the two together?"

"An excellent question, my child."

Nefertiti sighed, slipped her hand through her father's arm, and glanced back at the fisherman's house. "If I fail, I'll be the one who dies."

Chapter 22

Memphis, reign of Tutankhamun

Meren was dreaming in a foreign land. He could see himself, for his ka had left his body and floated above the sunlit chamber in which he lay. The room was painted like the sea—swirling waters of blue and green, cresting white waves—and his golden couch floated in the middle of it all. Around him swam the voices of those he knew—Kysen, Bener, Ebana, even Ay. They were talking about him. He wanted to join in the talk, but no one saw fit to wake him. He tried to wake himself without success. His eyelids were fastened together as if with carpenter's glue. His ka drifted from one person to another and tried to make each listen to no avail.

Then he heard a voice that shouldn't have been there—he heard the voice of pharaoh. At the sound of Tutankhamun's voice, Meren's ka plummeted back to his body, and his eyes fluttered open. His gaze fastened on the person nearest him, his physician, Nebamun, who nodded at him with satisfaction. Next he found Kysen staring down at him with a tense look of apprehension, and beside him hovered Bener, whose clasped hands showed white knuckles. Near the foot of his bed stood his cousin, arms folded over his chest. Ebana smiled slightly and nodded at him.

On the other side of the bed Ay waited, leaning on his staff of office and shaking his head. A movement beside him attracted Meren's attention. He turned his head and was jolted fully awake at the sight of pharaoh in blood-stained kilt, wrist guards of leather and gold, and uraeus diadem. Meren shoved himself upright and cried out at the stab of pain in his side. The king, Nebamun, and Kysen grabbed his arms and helped him lie down slowly.

Ebana merely lifted a brow. "You know better than to move like that with an arrow hole in your side."

Meren looked down at himself and found his torso crisscrossed with bandages. Nebamun inspected the padding over the wound and determined that it was still in place while Meren discovered he was in his room in his own home.

"The fresh meat poultice will remain until tomorrow," the physician said to Kysen and Bener. "Then I'll replace it with oil and honey. There will be a fever, but it should pass in a few days if he rests."

"Well done," Bener said to the physician. Nebamun bowed and began gathering his instruments.

"I trust Nebamun," the king said, "but I'll send one of my physicians so that I may have a report of his condition daily."

Kysen and Bener bowed.

"Thy majesty is the embodiment of kindness," Kysen said.

Bener nodded. "I'll watch over him day and night, golden one."

"I'm not dying," Meren said, knowing he sounded like a

querulous babe. "I'm grateful to thy majesty—" He flicked a glance from the king to Ebana to Kysen.

"Where is Mose?"

"Horemheb is still looking for him," Ebana said. "I'll see if there's word." Meren, furious to be trapped in his bed, watched his cousin leave.

Bener was talking to Nebamun, and Kysen joined them. Shifting his weight, Meren found Ay's staff sailing over him to lay across his legs.

"You're not getting out of that bed."

Meren scowled at him. "I've had worse wounds than this. The arrow went clean through."

Sighing, Ay removed his staff and turned to the king. "I leave him to you, majesty."

"Yes," Tutankhamun said. He waved his hand in an economical gesture that sent everyone retreating from the chamber.

Once they were alone, pharaoh drew a chair over to the bed and sat. After a small hesitation, he put his hand on Meren's arm.

"I must beg your forgiveness. I should never have believed—but I heard your voice, and there was your dagger." Tutankhamun shook his head and fixed a sorrowful look on Meren's bandages.

"Majesty."

"Hmm."

"The divine incarnation of the god does not beg forgiveness."

"Goats' dung!" The divine incarnation bit his lip. "Perhaps not, but the mortal in him does. I hunted you like an escaped slave."

"Does thy majesty beg forgiveness often?"

"Fear not. Ay is the only other of whom I've asked it."

"My heart is glad."

The king jumped to his feet, shoved the chair aside, and stalked up and down the length of the bed. "This isn't the time to lecture me on royal dignity and divinity." He stopped at the head of the bed and stared down at Meren. "I know it all. When I sent for Kysen, he told me about Nefertiti."

If he hadn't been in pain and weary from the ordeal of being a hunted criminal, Meren wouldn't have burst into a blasphemous tirade of curses before pharaoh. As it was, he mastered himself only when too violent a movement made him gasp.

"You can't blame Kysen," Tutankhamun said. "He was trying to save your life."

A curt nod was all Meren could manage through the pain.

The king smiled ruefully. "You must have come close to your quarry. Whoever commands Mose must be the murderer of—" He glanced around the room but didn't finish. "I haven't told anyone. Not even Ay. Especially not Ay."

"I'm glad, majesty." Meren shifted his weight so that it didn't press on his wound. "The evil one must have had Mose followed with orders to kill him when the opportunity occurred. Majesty, thus far, almost everyone I've suspected, or about whom I've inquired, has died."

"Then you must keep this safe," pharaoh replied. He held out the packet Meren had slipped beneath his tunic—the record of his inquiries and memories.

Meren took it from the king. It was stained with blood and crumpled, but still intact. "I suppose there is good in Kysen's blunder. It will be a great deal easier to pursue my inquiries now that I don't have to conceal them from thy majesty."

"You shouldn't have—no, I understand why you kept this secret." Tutankhamun closed his eyes for a moment before continuing. "But you can't protect me from the truth. I was there, too. I may have been a child, but I remember some things."

Meren waited for the king to continue, but he could see that Tutankhamun had retreated into a silent realm of unhappiness, where dwelt many of his memories of Akhenaten and Nefertiti. Then the grieving boy vanished, to be replaced by the young king.

"You must end this soon, Meren. Find the demon responsible. Do it quickly, but secretly. I want no public airing of this crime. It will give the priests of Amun an opportunity to renew their campaign to vilify my family."

"Aye, majesty, but—"

The chamber door burst open. Horemheb stalked into the room, followed by Kysen.

Bowing quickly to the king, he said, "Majesty, we chased Mose across the city. He was trying to reach the docks, but someone killed him before we could recapture him."

"How?" the king asked.

Horemheb nodded at Meren. "Another arrow from above, through the back. Several, that is. Someone wanted to make certain the Nubian wouldn't live to be captured." The general wiped sweat from his brow. "With the golden one's permission, I must direct the search for this murderous bowman."

When Horemheb was gone, Tutankhamun pulled the chair back to the bed and sat again. Kysen stood on the other side of the bed. All of them contemplated Horemheb's report. Finally the king spoke.

"You weren't surprised that Mose is dead."

"No, majesty," Meren said. "Remember what I said of the evil one. And I've had time to think since I've been a fugitive. As the Eyes of Pharaoh, I've dealt with many evildoers, both petty and great. But in all my experience, this killer is the most demonic. He spares no one; he trusts no one. And because he butchers all who can identify him, he remains safe, untouched, unknown. I wonder how long he's been preying upon the unsuspecting among us."

Kysen knelt beside Meren, and his glance rested on his father's wound. "Indeed. He has no remorse, no allegiance to anyone but himself. He is a drinker of blood."

Meren rested the back of his arm on his forehead and sighed. "Majesty, you were a child when the queen was killed, but you were in her household. Do you recall what happened to any of her servants?"

"No." The king leaned forward in his chair. "Wait. I think I remember. . . . After Akhenaten, Nefertiti, and Smenkhare died and I became king, Ay mentioned the disposition of servants from the royal households. He was talking to one of his underlings. I remember that many retired with estates granted by me, and Ay said it was for the best. I suppose he meant that some of them were stained by their fanatic service to my brother and that to keep them would create strife and factions at court when we needed desperately to heal and forget."

Tutankhamun's brow furrowed with the effort to recall more. "Many of the highest in Nefertiti's household retired—the steward, of course, the captain of the queen's guards, her overseer of vineyards, her priests, the overseer of horses, her personal maids." The king spread his hands wide. "I can't remember anything else."

"I've had to be most clandestine in my inquiries regarding them," Meren said.

"Aye, Father, but we still leave a trail of bodies wherever we search."

"Mother of the gods," Tutankhamun whispered.

Meren and Kysen looked at the king. He turned an incredulous stare on them.

"The guard,"

"Mose, golden one?"

"No—Bakht. The one whose death you kept forgetting to investigate. Remember, I favored him because he would tell me wonderful stories of times past." Tutankhamun wet his dry lips. "And the ones I loved best were those from the years of my childhood, when he served as a guard in the household of Queen Nefertiti."

Meren turned to Kysen. "Where is Abu?"

Kysen left in search of the charioteer. The king made only one remark while they waited.

"I liked his stories because he never mentioned the heresy or the strife. He talked of our adventures sailing skiffs on the Nile, of the festivals, of the kindness of Nefertiti. And I remember trying to see the queen when she fell ill. I insisted on dragging my nurse to the queen's chambers, even though she told me I couldn't visit. Bakht was on guard that day, and he wouldn't let me in her apartments. He was most kind and promised to pass on my prayers for her health."

Abu arrived, out of breath and disheveled. He prostrated himself before the king, but rose on Tutankhamun's command.

With great care Meren propped himself up on his elbows. "Abu, before I was forced to flee, I had you inquire into the death of that royal guard."

"Bakht, lord."

"Yes. What have you discovered?"

Abu glanced at the king.

"You may speak freely," Tutankhamun said. "Lord Meren and I are completely reconciled."

"Did you not speak to the overseer of the royal menagerie?" Kysen asked.

"Aye, lord. He insists that the baboons wouldn't have attacked a man who fell into their enclosure. The males would scream and bare their teeth and make a great noise, but he is most adamant that they wouldn't try to kill him."

"But he's dead," Meren said.

The king threw up his hands. "And the report said he had many wounds."

"Did you progress no further?" Kysen asked.

"Many perilous days have passed since the lord gave the command about the royal guard." Abu rubbed his chin. "I think I may have asked Nebamun to look at the body." He paused, then nodded. "Yes, I did ask him, because I remember that we weren't sure if it was too late and Bakht had already gone into the natron in the place of Anubis."

Nebamun was summoned, and he remembered his journey to the place of Anubis.

"I was able to see the body, majesty, but before I could write a report for Lord Meren—" The physician stopped with his mouth open.

"Continue, man. I know what intervened."

"The wounds that killed the royal guard were from a knife. An extremely sharp knife, not the ragged tears that one sees in animal attacks. Certainly the bite of a baboon would never make a wound so deep as to hit the spine."

Meren thanked the physician, dismissed him, and lay down on his back again.

"Bakht was knifed and then pushed into the animal pen," he said.

Kysen went to a table, poured a cup of water, and brought it to Meren. "Surely there would have been blood where he was attacked."

"There may have been," Meren replied, "but I was too distracted to examine the menagerie. Majesty, I have failed thee."

Pharaoh took the cup from Meren and helped him drink. "Only a god wouldn't have been distracted by the burden you've been concealing. And you must remember, the evil one made certain you had little opportunity to do anything but flee for your life."

"Thy majesty is certain it was Bakht who was on duty when the queen was ill?" Kysen asked.

"Yes. I liked his stories and used to pester him for a tale almost every day."

"By the gods," Kysen said suddenly.

Meren propped himself up again, and he and pharaoh regarded Kysen with inquiring looks. Kysen looked from one to the other.

"Mose," he said, turning to Abu. "Was Mose on duty the night Bakht was killed?"

Abu shook his head. "No, lord. He wasn't among—wait." Abu narrowed his eyes. "There was a youth, barely out of training. He was most disturbed by Bakht's death but had little to contribute that would help solve the mystery of his death. I remember him lamenting that he hadn't heard Bakht cry out for help, so of course that means the killer didn't strike until the boy was gone. But the boy said he had to return to the menagerie for his sandals, which he'd left near the gate. As he was leaving, he noticed Mose approaching from the palace."

Meren dismissed Abu. Still propped up on the bed, he searched for something to say to the king. He'd tried so hard to keep the danger away from pharaoh, and it had slithered into the palace through the menagerie gates. No, the danger had been closer than that all along.

All at once his arms lost their strength, and he fell back on the linen-covered mattress. Kysen rushed to him with a damp cloth, but Meren shoved it away. He was already clammy. The king stood over him, threatening to summon Nebamun.

"I beg thy majesty not to," Meren said faintly. "I'll rest. All I need is rest."

"It's unreasonable to be so furious with yourself," Tutankhamun said. "How could you know the extent of the power of this drinker of blood, as Kysen calls him?"

"Thy majesty should set me to solving petty thefts. It's all I'm good for."

"All you're good for is rest at the moment, and I'm not going to listen to such absurdities. Kysen, set a guard around Lord Meren. It's reasonable to expect an attempt on his life now."

Meren opened his mouth, but the king was gone before he could protest the order. Kysen followed, leaving Meren to fume by himself. He must have drifted into sleep soon after, for he woke to find Bener and Kysen engaged in a whispered quarrel over his bed.

"I wouldn't have been discovered if it weren't for that stupid Lord Irzanen," Bener hissed. "I vow he has the wits of a mollusk."

Kysen poked a finger at his sister. "You promised not to stir from the house!"

"I was doing well until that fool Irzanen saw me in the street. Can I help it if he gawped at me as if I were a three-headed hippo? He stopped me and demanded what I was doing, and by the time I made him go away, one of the king's spies must have seen us."

"And followed you and summoned the king," Kysen said with brotherly contempt.

"I concealed myself well," Bener protested. "None of you saw me."

"None except pharaoh!"

"You two are squalling like cats in the night," Meren said.

Bener's face appeared before him as she bent over the bed. "Father, are you well?"

"I'll deal with you tomorrow."

"But my leading pharaoh to you was a most fortunate occurrence," his daughter said brightly. "You were able to reconcile by saving his life."

Kysen groaned, but Meren didn't feel well enough to argue.

"Go away, both of you. You're making me feel worse."

When they were gone, Meren allowed himself to smile. Bener was by far the cleverest of his daughters—at least when it came to matters of reasoning. In this she reminded him of Nefertiti. Nefertiti. She had been a great queen, and had she lived, Egypt would have benefited from her regency during Tutankhamun's childhood. She might even have quelled the wrath of the priests of Amun, so great had been her power to charm and compel obedience.

Memories of her were becoming clearer now, especially those in which Akhenaten had no part. He recalled one day in particular at the queen's palace in Horizon of the Aten. He had brought correspondence to her from Ay, and she received him in one of the pleasure gardens. Nefertiti was seated beneath an embroidered canopy beside a reflection pool filled with glittering fish. As he knelt before the queen, she was finishing an interview with Prince Smenkhare.

The prince left, and Meren was discussing with the queen a message from the Egyptian garrison at Qatna regarding the recent machinations of the Hittite king. Their discussion was interrupted by the arrival of Tutankhaten, who had plagued his governor until he was allowed to seek out Nefertiti. Meren had grown used to the royal family's informality—the constant presence of children, the freely expressed affection. It was yet another of Akhenaten's innovations, one that scandalized traditional Egyptians used to the divine dignity from their living gods.

Tut made his obeisance to the queen. Meren was astonished that a child of six could adopt so formal a demeanor.

The child said his greeting perfectly, and he moved with a grace that spoke of Nefertiti's influence. After managing the greeting, however, all courtliness disappeared under the weight of a happy smile.

"Nefer!" Tut crowed. He laughed and threw himself at the queen.

Catching the boy, Nefertiti swung him in a circle. She hugged Tut and laughed at his chattering. Before she could answer one question, he was asking another.

Nefertiti stood Tut on his feet and smiled as he danced with excitement.

"Why can't I have a crocodile? We could build a pool for it."

"We'll talk about it later," Nefertiti said, and she gave the boy a bowl of dates. He didn't want them, so she took his hand and strolled with him beside the pool. Meren found the interruption a nuisance; he had little patience for waiting while the queen was distracted from business far more important than a spoiled prince. He almost sighed aloud when Nefertiti summoned him to walk with her and the child, and was no more enthusiastic when she took refuge in a kiosk in one of the smaller palace gardens.

Tutankhaten found the kiosk a delight. Mounting the stairs to the painted wooden shelter, he said, "Nefer, you be the thieving nomad, and I'll be pharaoh. Try to raid my city, and I'll chase you back into the desert and kill you. This is my city." Tut ran down the steps of the kiosk and pointed to a line of shrubs. "These are my warriors. Remember. You're the miserable sneaking raider."

"Why do I always get to be the miserable raider? Why can't I be pharaoh?"

"You can be pharaoh next time. I'll be the king of the Hittites."

Meren stood beside the kiosk-city while the game proceeded, his arms full of papyri and his patience wearing thin. When Tutankhaten charged him and delivered a blow to his stomach with a stick that served as his scimitar, Meren dropped the correspondence and doubled over. Huffing and wincing, he gasped when a small, round-eyed face appeared upside-down before him. Meren straightened to find the prince had dropped his stick.

"I didn't mean to hurt you."

Surprised by the compassion he saw in the boy's eyes, Meren said, "It's nothing, highness."

They stared at each other, and Meren found his glare turning to a grin. He dropped to his knees and picked up the stick.

"You must hold your weapon thus, highness." He demonstrated the correct grip. "And draw your arm back like this."

Tutankhaten watched him with rapt attention until Meren noticed the queen. He had no idea how long she'd been watching them.

Nefertiti scolded gently. "You should be more careful, little one. Now practice with your scimitar on the bushes."

While the boy tried to reduce the bushes to compost, Nefertiti retreated to the shade of the kiosk to watch. Meren gathered his records and joined her, but the queen failed to resume their discussion. From the corner of his eye he observed the fine lines that had appeared at the corners of her eyes and between her nose and mouth. She was exhausted from grieving over her lost daughters.

Not long ago Ay had confided the secret of Nefertiti's plans for reconciliation with the priests of Amun. Meren thought the idea insane and suicidal. If Akhenaten discovered what they planned, his fury would destroy them all. And Meren would be one of the first to die, for he carried messages between Ay and the priests of Amun hidden in Horizon of the Aten.

Suddenly Nefertiti turned to him. "My talks with Smenkhare are going well."

"He knows, majesty?"

"No, but he sees that Egypt is not well and that something must be done."

The queen gazed out across the garden to the flower beds, blue with cornflowers. "I know you think my course perilous and foolhardy, Meren."

Meren bowed. "It is not for this humble servant to question the will of the great royal wife."

"There's no choice," Nefertiti said. "But I worry. Smenkhare isn't strong, and it's possible that Tut will be pharaoh while he's still a child. Should that happen, there will be a fight for control of him." Nefertiti met Meren's gaze calmly. "I may not be there to protect him, and he needs someone who values his welfare and Egypt's above wealth and power."

Meren turned to watch the boy. The siege of his enemies forgotten, he was standing at the edge of the pool, trying to spear a fish. Meren tried to imagine the double crown of Egypt on that small head but failed.

"My father and I agree," Nefertiti said, interrupting his speculation. "We want you to watch over the boy for us."

Meren's jaw lost its mooring, and his mouth hung open.

"I was watching you just now. You have patience. You're gentle but firm, and Tut likes you. If he's to survive and rule Egypt, he'll need men like you."

Across the garden, the gates opened to reveal a great retinue of priests, Akhenaten in their midst. Nefertiti whirled around and confronted Meren.

"Your answer, quickly. Do you swear to protect him by the power of Amun?"

"I will, majesty."

How long ago that day seemed. Had it been almost ten years? Meren yawned and tried to turn on his side without jarring his wound. After swearing to protect Tutankhaten, he'd left the garden before Akhenaten could see him. He remembered the queen's parting words.

"Sometimes I fear what is to come, Lord Meren, but at least you've given me some peace, for now."

Had Nefertiti suspected what was to happen? Had she known that this drinker of blood was near? Perhaps she had, for but a few years later she was dead, her body embalmed and closed in that tomb in the lonely desert, her work incomplete, and Akhenaten still on the throne.

Meren lifted himself up, cursing at the unfairness of her fate. Gentle, beautiful, and wise, Nefertiti had devoted her life to Egypt; her reward had been an ugly death. And if it cost him his life, he would discover her murderer, this drinker of blood, and cast him into a lake of fire.

Breinigsville, PA USA
17 August 2010
243735BV00003B/1/A